The Reluctant

Gardener

S. C. Rozée

First Published in Great Britain 2023.

This edition first published in 2023.

A CIP catalogue reference for this book is available from the British Library.

Cover design by Very Much So

Paper back ISBN: 978-1-7392424-0-4

eBook ISBN: 978-1-7392424-1-1

Before you embark on a journey of revenge, dig two graves.

Part 1

Part 1

Renowned counterterrorism operative John Brown was sitting outside his boss's office waiting to be fired. He was thinking about the mistake he had made, the unnecessary deaths he had caused.

It all started when Claire handed him the file and told him to bring them down. He accepted the challenge, a chance to prove himself, and threw himself into it. He put it all together, all the working parts of the organisation over the course of six months, and Claire looked on in astonishment. Talk of promotion was thrown around the office. How could he possibly miss this chance to progress in his career?

On the day of the raid, John briefed his team on the details of the operation and what to expect when they burst through the doors in the early hours of the morning. His heart pounded in his chest as they drove to the target.

The block of flats came into view and John sensed success

before he had even kicked the door down.

His team manoeuvred down the corridor to flat 34. It was there on the door, obvious to anyone who cared to look, and soon the sleeping occupants would receive their final wake-up call as free citizens. He took a breath and proceeded as planned.

John charged in, his eyes looking down his rifle's sights. He shouted for nobody to move. He knew they had weapons. So that was why, when he entered the first bedroom and saw the man reach across to the bedside table, he took the shot. An accurate shot to the chest. A member of his team detained the screaming lady lying next to the man, and John moved on.

Someone raced across the hallway. John followed them into the kitchen. They had a knife in their hand and terror in their eyes. John could not have made it clearer that he wanted the knife to be put down. But their shaking hand refused to let go. John pulled the trigger and the knife fell to the floor.

His team had detained, without hindrance, the flat's remaining occupants. They were cuffed and sat outside in the corridor, ready to be driven off to holding cells. It was a success – a resounding success. Until he heard a child's cries.

He hurried out into the corridor. He saw the family lined up like criminals, and sitting with his mother, the women who had been in the bed with one of the men he had killed, was her child.

According to the intelligence, there were never meant to be any children in this flat. The terrorists had girlfriends, but none of them had children. John realised his mistake at that moment, as he stared at the distressed, crying child who held on to his mother like she was the only source of comfort he had left in his life. John saw the stark open eyes that had been witness to violence no child should ever see. Fatherless, innocence destroyed – by his mistake.

John tried to hold himself together, but he could not avert his eyes from the horror he had caused. He could not move. He could not hear what his team member said, so when they raced down the corridor to the correct flat, he did not follow them. John learnt later that it was empty, but by then, it didn't matter to him.

Now he was hunched over, looking at the floor, knowing that the people walking past were looking down on him. He didn't need their pity; it wasn't going to undo what he had done. No one was envious of his position anyway. The end of a six-month-long inquiry, and this was the result. And even though he had been found not guilty – the victim of being outwitted by terrorists; not neglectful, just unlucky – here that failure would not stand. Publicly, he was a free, innocent man; internally, he was a rising star who had fallen on his back from the simplest of tricks – judged to be too hot-headed, given too much responsibility too soon, out of his depth.

His ultimate unemployment, however, was preying on his mind. He didn't know what he was going to do. His skills in this job weren't transferable to the civilian world. He had nothing else going on – this was it as far as he was concerned. Losing this would be like walking into a tunnel with no light at the end. Everything he wanted he had right now. That was the word, however: had.

The door to Claire's office opened. John looked up and saw her secretary wave him in.

Their usual small talk didn't happen. She returned to her desk, letting John find his own way to Claire's office door. He took a deep breath, grabbed the handle, felt the cold brass between his fingers, and entered for the last time.

Claire was at her desk and hadn't noticed John sneaking in. He wondered what was going through her mind; he wondered what she was typing. Did it have anything to do with him? His dishonourable discharge papers, perhaps?

'Sit down,' Claire said without taking her eyes from the screen. John did as he was told and sat on the chair at the end of her desk. Beads of sweat dripped from his armpit down his arm. He shuffled in the chair, never comfortable. He wanted to undo his tie; it would make it easier to breathe, but he didn't want Claire to see him struggle. He wanted to put on a strong, defiant front, to go out with whatever dignity he had left – Claire would respect that at least.

'Well, there really is no easier way of doing this,' Claire said, her words drowning his sinking heart. Soon he would be standing alone outside the building, picking up the pieces of the wreckage, wondering what was next in his life.

Claire paused for a moment.

'I can handle the bad news, Claire. I just want you to say it.'

'You're going to be leaving us, John. There's no two ways about it. It's a shame, really, because you're a good operative who showed great promise. You planned, briefed, and executed this mission to great distinction. It's such a shame it went sideways for you. If it hadn't, then we might have been talking about promotion.'

Why did she have to mention promotion? Why did she have to rub it in? His hands trembled in his lap, and he tensed his body to make them stop. But that only exacerbated the sweating.

'So what? You want me to put this down to experience? That won't help me on the outside. This is where I see myself. It's some fulfilment in my life. It's my duty. Surely all the other operatives have made mistakes before?'

'We've all made mistakes. No one is denying that.'

'Then let me learn from this one.'

'I can't do that, John. I can't do that because no one has made a mistake where two innocent people were killed.'

The room felt like a blizzard was cascading through it. The sweating stopped – John's body had frozen in the chair. It was the first time Claire had spelled it out so bleakly. And John realised in this moment that he hadn't even fully come to terms with it.

'But I won't leave you high and dry,' Claire said, the start of a smile growing on her face. 'I genuinely think you deserve better than that.'

'What are you suggesting?'

'Well, it's not so much a suggestion as an admission of guilt. I put you in charge of this, and the people around me thought I was jumping the gun with you. A guy with only five years of experience under his belt ... they thought I was foolish to put you in this position. So part of this is my fault. You weren't ready.'

'But I am ready.'

'Listen to me, John. This *will* blow over. And you can come back from this. So I won't fire you.'

John looked up at Claire, unsure what she meant.

'I'm going to give you the opportunity to resign. You can at least come back from that.'

Was resigning admitting to his failure? So Claire could pin the blame on him? John remained silent.

This was not the career he had believed he was going to have. To him, this felt like the end of the road. His life was coming to an abrupt stop before it had even begun, no matter what Claire said about this blowing over.

'Trust me, John, resigning is the best way.'

'But I don't want to go. I'm not done here. They're still out there.'

'I know. Trust me, I know. And don't worry about them. I've got another team on it.'

He was being forced out. His assignment had already been handed to someone else. His eyes darted across the room and his breathing was laboured.

What choice did he have?

There was no escape route out of this one. He was cornered, and what really got to him was that part of the reason he was in this mess was himself. His ego had blinded him. He had thought he was on top of the world when Claire had told him he was going to lead this operation, and he had let his confidence overrun his judgement.

And now two innocent people were dead.

He hated that he couldn't bring them back. The child, however ... the crying, fatherless child. He deserved better. But what good was a dream compared to reality? They weren't coming back. But could he come back? Come back and make amends for his mistake? If he was fired, there would be no way of doing that. If he resigned, Claire was right. He could come back. After how long, though? He knew, however, that he had only one option.

'When do you need my resignation letter by?' The words left

a bitter taste on his tongue.

Claire opened her desk drawer, pulled out an envelope, and dropped it on the desk. 'I just need you to sign this one.'

John took the letter. It weighed nothing in the clammy palm of his hand, yet it had the power to delay his career.

He didn't bother reading the letter. What did it matter what it said? It wouldn't make a blind bit of difference to the outcome of this conversation. He took the pen Claire offered him and signed it.

'I know this isn't easy. But you need to trust me on this.'

John looked at his empty hands and shook his head. 'Now what do I do?' he asked the room.

'Get out of the city would be my advice. It's too claustrophobic around here, and you need space to think, to reflect. Go on holiday or something. The next few weeks are going to be the worst. But eventually you'll get through this.'

John didn't reply. His eyes were fixed on the floor.

'You need time to process all this. It's difficult, I understand that. But why not try to live your life for a couple of years and then see how you feel?'

He stood up, shook Claire's outstretched hand, and didn't speak to another person, didn't even look back as he exited the building.

He returned to his flat, sparsely populated with furniture. The walls were still the same off-white colour they had been when he'd bought the place – in a good central location close enough to the building he'd just walked out of.

He packed a bag, emptying what he would need from his half empty wardrobes and drawers. He walked out of his flat. He didn't bother to leave a note. No one else lived there. No one to say goodbye to. He had made sure of that years ago.

2

John stopped driving when he got to his old house. He looked out and saw the place where he had grown up, and memories flooded his mind. But now it was empty. Empty since his mother had died a year ago. He hadn't had time to find a tenant with his job keeping him busy. Had he even found the time to mourn her?

He walked through his childhood home, the stagnant air, the surfaces covered in a film of dust. It was the same house, but the atmosphere was different. It was stale, like water left inside an airless container. This house had once been filled with his mum's warmth. Now it was cold to the touch.

Down the hallway, on the wall was a collage of pictures in a frame – the only thing in the house which gave away that he had once lived there. The pictures of just him and his mum stared back at him. Each photo showed them smiling. Had he failed her? He looked at the pictures. Some of them didn't quite fit their respective frames; they had been cut to remove someone.

He saw his exhausted reflection in the glass. How had he let it come to this? How could he have lost sight of what this had always been about? The tears came, and he touched his mum's face in the picture where he had always thought she looked her happiest.

'I'm sorry,' he said, but the cut edges of the photos still to this day gave him a tightening feeling in his stomach, and the anger that had long been there, simmering inside of him, finally erupted and he hit the wall. His knuckles cracked and started to bleed. But he hadn't hit the wall hard enough to break them; he had told himself a long time ago that he would never let him get to him like that. But the single punch was followed up by his other palm smacking against the wall as he swore at all that had happened during the past six months.

John cleaned his bleeding knuckles in the sink and wrapped them with a bandage from the first aid kit he always kept in his car. The cuts were only minor. They'd heal in a week. Unlike everything he had been doing until now and the family he had destroyed.

A knock on the front door made him jump.

'Andrew! What are you doing here?' he said after opening the door.

'I saw your car outside and thought the exact same thing myself.' Andrew went to shake his hand, but John pulled him in for a hug.

'What have you done to your hand?' Andrew asked.

'Taking my frustrations out on a wall.'

They looked at each other for a moment, then Andrew asked again, 'Seriously, though, what are you doing here?'

'I lost my job – I was forced to resign.' Saying it out loud didn't make him feel any better.

'Really? How come?'

'One big, awful mistake.'

'What did you do?'

The traumatised child flashed across his mind. 'Took out the wrong people.'

There was a moment of silence between them. And John gave Andrew that knowing look that told his friend when he didn't want to talk about something.

'Well, why don't you come around to ours? Harriet would love to see you, and you haven't met Sarah yet.'

He wanted to say no. Being around other people right now wouldn't make him feel comfortable. But neither was the thought of being alone.

'Okay. But first you've got to give me a hand unloading the car,' John said, gesturing towards his bandaged hand.

'You deliberately punched that wall just to make me help you, didn't you?' Andrew joked.

'It's only a few boxes and a suitcase.'

Andrew lifted the suitcase out of the boot for John to wheel in, and he piled up the boxes so he only had to make one trip and they returned to the kitchen.

'How long do you think you're going to be back?'

'I'm not sure. I never wanted to leave in the first place, but there was nothing I could do. They forced me out. I'm stuck here until it's time to go back.'

'When will that be?'

'When enough time has passed. Or some kind of crisis kicks off, I guess.'

'What do you think you're going to do while you're stuck here?'

'I haven't got a clue.'

'I think I might have something in mind that you could do,' Andrew said.

'Look, I'm going to be honest with you. I don't plan on staying here for a long time; a few months, maybe, at most until all this blows over.'

'You think it's going to blow over in a few months?' Even though Andrew didn't know the truth behind his resignation, John knew he was right. How long did it take for two deaths to 'blow over'? Was he ever going to be able to return to his old job – his old life? Was there even anything here for him?

When John walked into Andrew's house, he noticed first the pictures of the three of them on the wall – all smiling, all happy and content with their lives. Where his life had become stale, grey, and cold, theirs was filled with joy, happiness, and love.

He saw himself smiling in the reflection of the pictures. The tension that had built up in his body subsided enough for him to allow himself, at the very least, to drop his shoulders.

'Harriet, look who I've just bumped into,' Andrew called down the hallway.

Harriet appeared out of the kitchen, a tea towel draped over her shoulder and a pot of baby food in her hand.

'John! I haven't seen you since our wedding,' she said,

embracing him. 'And I'll tell you what, my mum is still horrified by your best man's speech.'

The two friends looked at each other, smirked, and John recalled the memories of that day. 'Well, I did my best,' he said.

'What's happened to your hand?' Harriet asked.

'It's nothing,' John said, waving it off.

'Let me take your coat. Then make yourself at home. You still take your coffee black?'

'Yes please.'

John and Andrew sat on the sofa in the lounge.

'I forgot that you two haven't seen each other since our wedding. Which reminds me, it's our two-year anniversary next month.'

Harriet walked into the lounge with a mug of coffee. 'And of course you haven't met Sarah yet either.'

'No, I haven't. How is she doing?'

'She's perfect,' Harriet said. 'Although she's sleeping now after her lunch. I was just tidying up. I'll try to bring her down without waking her.'

'It's okay,' John said. 'If she's sleeping, I'll come back and see her another time.'

'Oh no, it's fine. Don't worry about it. How long are you staying for, anyway? It's not like you to be around for a long time. In fact, it's not like you to be around at all.'

'I don't know,' John said. 'I was forced to resign and now I don't know what I'm going to do.'

'Forced to resign?' Harriet's voice gave away her surprise.

'Afraid so.'

'How come?'

'It's a long story.'

John watched Andrew exchange a glance with his wife and saw the realisation in her eyes when she knew not to push the matter further.

'What are you going to do in the meantime?' Harriet asked.

'I don't know. I was told I'd be able to go back once things blow over. But how long that will be ...' John shrugged and fell back onto the sofa.

'You'll figure something out.' She left the room to get her daughter. John sipped his coffee.

'So how bad was it, then?' Andrew asked.

'I thought you knew better than to ask those sorts of questions.'

'I do. But you've never been like this.'

'Don't worry about it.'

They were silent for a moment. And in the quiet, John wondered what Andrew was thinking. He wondered if his friend would extend his hand in support, but he wasn't interested in anything like that right now – it wouldn't get him his job back.

'Maybe it's time to move on. Perhaps this is a blessing in disguise.'

'If it is, it's not very apparent.' John continued to drink his coffee, unbothered by its hot temperature.

'Why don't you resurrect our old gardening business?' John met Andrew's off-hand suggestion with silence.

Harriet walked into the lounge with a bundle of blankets that concealed her daughter. 'Here she is,' Harriet whispered, placing her into John's arms, and it took strength for him not to flinch.

He looked down at her. She was lying completely still. Peaceful, comfortable, vulnerable. John couldn't help but think that he could crush her in his arms, and he despised himself for thinking such a thing. One day, this small piece of life would have to overcome struggle after struggle, and it wouldn't matter whether she did everything right, because success isn't always guaranteed. Not in this world.

She wriggled around in his gentle hold and stretched her arms above her head. Her eyes opened and looked straight into his like spotlights on an actor in the theatre. What did she think of this stranger? She reached out her hand and John let her grip his finger. She wrapped her fingers around it and giggled. Would she still hold on to him if she knew what he had done – the trauma his actions had caused? The innocence of childhood is as inevitably lost as life is to death, John thought.

'She likes you,' Harriet said. 'And I can tell you like her by the way you're smiling.' This comment snapped him back into the room. How could he dare to smile? 'Maybe you should start a family!'

John handed the baby back to her mother and said, 'No. Not in my line of work. I'm not putting a family through that. It's not fair.'

'You won't be doing this for the rest of your life,' Harriet said. 'What will you do when that time comes?'

John sipped his coffee and said, 'I'll cross that bridge when I come to it. I've got plenty of time left in me.'

'What do you think about restarting our gardening business, then?' Andrew said, changing the subject.

14

Harriet laughed. 'That might not be a bad idea. It'll keep you busy and it's not an office job.'

John thought about the suggestion.

'Unless, of course, you're good for the money?' Andrew said.

John would only be good for the money for a month. After that, he knew he would need to get a job, even if it was to just pay the bills.

'I'll tell you what,' Harriet said. 'We're having a new child start at the school in the new term. They've just moved to the village. They're living in Mr and Mrs Clarke's old house. Did you hear about them?'

John said that he hadn't.

'They've been moved into a care home. It was only a few months ago. Their children had to put the house on the market to pay for their care, and this lady, Olivia, has moved over from Columbia with her son. She asked me, when I showed her around the school, if she knew any decent gardeners and I joked about your old business. Look, I know it was for drinking money to get the two of you through uni, but I can call her and tell her you'll be round tomorrow to look?'

'I don't think it'd be a good idea. I've done nothing like that for ten years.'

'It'll be good for you,' Andrew chipped in. 'It'll help take your mind off things. Plus when the time comes for you to return to London, you can go at the drop of a hat.'

John thought for a moment. 'No. It's too much of a rush. But thanks anyway. And thanks for the coffee.' Suddenly he felt like he wanted to be alone. He said goodbye and left to return to his empty house, where he hoped he would find an ounce of solace.

3

I was eight years old when my father started to abuse my mum. Although I was still young and didn't fully understand how a marriage worked, it didn't take me long to realise that what was happening downstairs while I was trying to sleep was not normal. No boy should ever have to witness what I saw my father do to my mum. No child should ever fear going downstairs.

The part I found the hardest, the question that took me the longest to answer or to even begin to understand, was why. It hadn't always been like that; the first seven years of my life, as I look back on them now, weren't any different from anyone else's at my age. But seeing how my father turned out, I questioned how much of it had been real in those first few years. Did he ever love me? Did he ever love us?

When we started history at school, we looked at ancient Rome first. Learning about disciplined soldiers who could conquer any land they wanted had me hooked. To me, these people were unlike anything I had seen before with their gold-braided armour, huge shields, and deadly tactics. I wanted to be a Roman soldier – a centurion. They were so ahead of their time that I remember being beyond impressed. It was the first time in school that I had actually looked forward to a lesson.

I often dreamed about what it would be like to live in ancient Rome, to be an emperor who conquered distant lands to return a hero. Looking back on it now, I wonder how I would have thought about them if I'd known they killed many people in bloody battles. But we were only seven years old, so we were spared the intricate details.

All the pictures we had been shown of ancient Rome, all the segments of documentaries we had watched, had always bathed Rome in Mediterranean sunlight, and on a rainy school day when we weren't allowed to play outside, I envied Roman school children, who never had to be confined to the classroom because of inclement weather.

Ancient Rome, then, was what I predominately talked about at the dinner table, and my father engaged with me on this. But when I spoke of centurions and emperors, he changed the subject to gladiators.

He told me that if ancient Rome was here today, I would be a gladiator. And when I told my father I would be a centurion instead, he snapped back and told me that I would be a gladiator, just like him – just like everyone else he knew – because gladiators were slaves forced to fight against each other to entertain the richest in society.

I think my face must have dropped when he spoke, because

17

Mum would always come in and say that if I wanted to be a centurion or even an emperor, I could. And she always smiled to reassure me that it was okay to have my own way of thinking. Yet these discussions always ended up with my father trying to lecture me about the world.

'Listen, John,' he'd start, 'you'd be a gladiator. They were slaves, forced to fight against their will for an emperor's entertainment. And emperors were always born into their role. If you're not born into a privileged position, you'll never be able to escape what you really are. And that's a slave to people in positions of power.'

I can't remember if I cried the first time he told me this, the first time he burst out like that. The shock of hearing a polarising view of the world shattered my dreams, and I would soon learn to suppress my tears for my mum's sake – she never liked to see me cry.

But almost, I now think, to make his point clear, my father one day – and this is the last good memory I have of him – took me to a museum. And I remember feeling excited, because for one, although we didn't share the same views, we had one interest in common, and two, I had this ignorant optimism that once I showed him how good it was to be a centurion or an emperor, he would change his mind and want to be one too.

It was just him and me that day. Father and son. I smiled the whole way round, because even though we had been taught this in school, seeing actual artifacts and soldiers' uniforms and emperors' robes that were thousands of years old amazed me beyond anything else in my short life so far. We walked around the exhibits with me leading the way, pointing out the things I liked to my father, and I remember the look on his face, like he was just acknowledging my finds instead of taking any real interest in them.

But of course I wanted him to have the same enthusiasm I had. This was a transactional visit to the museum. I would get to see the exhibits and my father would get something in return. I'm not sure what it was exactly. My guess is that Mum just told him to take me, and during the period in his life when he was still choosing to be a good husband and father, he took me, thinking that that was enough. Any actual engagement with me was not warranted or required. During the walk around, however, I think I just liked the idea that I was spending time with my father. What seven-year-old would feel otherwise?

I never got to the bottom of why he changed. But certain things did happen in his life that might have pushed him over the edge. To treat my mum the way he did, however ... I can conclude now that he was only waiting for an excuse to unleash the evil inside him, to reveal to us who he really was.

When he lost his job out of the blue, forced to take redundancy because it was better than resigning, he spent his redundancy package mainly on beer. Maybe it was the beer that fuelled his rage, because I don't think it was the job loss. He had a new job a month later, although it was nothing like his old one. He never left the house in a suit like he used to, and his hours were longer, and the lines in his forehead soon dug deeper like trenches on a battlefield. His face was littered with fatigue; his body became lethargic, along with his mind. That was, however, until he drank.

While he found comfort in opening a can of beer, the sound of the aluminium cap cracking soon became my cue to run upstairs, and I remember, especially if I was watching my favourite show, that I would wish he would make a start while the credits were rolling. Of course, I wished he would never open one in the first place. But I was only eight years old; how was I meant to stop him?

When I was up in my room, I'd play with my toys until I was tired enough to sleep. Sometimes I read, but that was only if I was struggling to sleep, and when I did read, it was books on ancient Rome – although my interest in them had subsided, along with pretty much everything else I used to like.

It usually went like this: my father would drunkenly talk to my mum. I could never hear what they were saying, but I soon learned to differentiate a slurred word from a sober one. His voice would get louder, he would belittle her about anything he could, then, when his voice bellowed and my mum started to cry, I used to grab my pillow and wrap it around my ears, close my eyes, and pull my knees up to my chest. But with my pillow around my head, I had no free arms to play with my toys, and with the demon downstairs, I was never going to sleep until he stopped.

Sometimes, if I was unlucky, there would be nights when I'd hear his hand strike my mum's face. On those nights I had to fight my hardest not to cry. Sometimes it was a battle I won, sometimes it was one I lost. I soon got used to the fact that over his shouting, my mum would not be able to hear me cry, and I stayed silent and still in my room. I knew that this was what happened when I had my pillow wrapped around my head. I knew I was turning my back on my mum. But I was eight years old – there was nothing I could do.

Some nights a glass would smash. I would hear a thud and try not to think about my mum on the floor while my father shouted and hit her. And while I sat motionless on my bed, I longed for the day when I would overcome my cowardice and be strong enough to fight him off.

But my mum always acted, for the most part, like things were okay. She layered makeup on her face to hide the bruises and would always smile and hug me when she saw me. Sometimes she might sob, but I ignored it – I didn't want to think about not being strong enough to stop this. But I always accepted her embrace, because I think I was the only part of her life that she had left to actually live for.

And then there were the days when I would get back home from school and my bags were packed and so were hers. Her mascara ran down her cheeks and her flooded eyes were desperate for me to go on a 'little trip' with her. But whenever she opened the door, she stopped and made an excuse about why we couldn't go. I always hated that we were just a step away from escaping this. We were so close to a new life, yet we could never do it. Looking back on it now, I realise why we never left: we had nowhere else to go.

4

The first day after being forced to resign. Waking up in your bed and staring at the off-white ceiling trying to work out what you're going to do next. John rolled over, looked at his phone, and saw that it was only a few minutes before his alarm was due to go off – the same alarm that had woken him every day for years. His body was still in the job; his mind, however, was somewhere else, drifting. He dismissed the alarm before it rang and stared at the wall. The sun, low in the sky, bled its light around the edges of the curtain. A new day may have been starting, a new life in front of him, but it wasn't calling out to him – it wasn't even whispering.

He only got out of bed because that was what he would have done anyway if the circumstances had been how he wanted them to be. He couldn't remember the last time he had showered for so long in the morning. He had his routine and didn't stray from it during weekends, following it regardless of whether he was working or not. But now was different. After getting out of the shower, he didn't bother going through the ritual of shaving – who was he going to see today?

Breakfast was made and eaten with the same enthusiasm with which he had gotten out of bed. And when he was done at the kitchen table, he went and sat in the lounge and looked outside, because if he hadn't, he would have had nothing else to do. He turned the television on when he got bored with the view that hadn't changed since he had been here last. The breakfast shows, however, were tedious and he couldn't find it in himself to watch. He turned the TV off and looked at his watch. He would usually have been in the office by now, at his desk starting work for the day. Mornings were never this slow, this serene, this frivolous.

He walked around the house to find something to do and stopped when he got to the desk in the spare room. At work, his desk would have been covered in case files, investigation notes, a to-do list, and an empty mug of coffee. This desk didn't have that. In fact, it had nothing at all except a film of dust that he dragged his finger through.

Nothing to do. No raids to plan, no briefings to deliver, no deadlines to meet. He dropped back into the chair and looked around the empty room. He could see dust particles floating in the air.

His phone vibrated and he pulled it from his pocket. But it wasn't the message he wanted to see, the one that would bring him back into the game. It was an email telling him about a special offer. He didn't bother to see whether it was available to him. What did it matter? He didn't need a special offer. He needed a purpose.

Back in the kitchen, he made himself a coffee, and while the kettle boiled, he looked out at the garden and saw himself there with his mum all those years ago, planting, weeding, smiling. He removed the thought from his mind on instinct like he had done plenty of times before. But it did get him curious about how the garden looked after a year of neglect. There were weeds where there should have been plants and the lawn was overgrown, the grass up to his knees. And he couldn't help but wonder what Mr and Mrs Clarke's old garden would look like after a decade of neglect. He doubted they would have been able to do enough work to keep it tidy. They must have fought a losing battle, and he guessed now that it would look terrible.

The kettle clicked, steam poured out of the spout, and after he had made his coffee, he was surprised that thoughts of Mr and Mrs Clarke's garden were still at the forefront of his mind, like they had gotten stuck, too stubborn to remove themselves.

It would take planning and execution to get it back together. He could wake up tomorrow and at least have a reason to get out of bed. It would be something to focus on – a nostalgia trip, maybe – not that he was looking to relive the past, unless it was the one he had been forced to give up. It was a project, though, an operation, a mission.

He held his phone in his pocket. But what would happen when it rang? He would be self-employed, he told himself. Once the call came through, he could go at a moment's notice. The woman who lived there now would understand. She would find another gardener eventually.

When he looked around his empty house again, he still

couldn't find anything to do. The time on his phone told him that there were still many hours left in the day. Could he spend them all, every day, mindlessly waiting for the call to come?

He pulled his phone from his pocket and called Andrew.

5

The front garden outside Mr and Mrs Clarke's old house was in a worse state than when they had first started working on it nearly a decade of summers ago, an indicator that the back garden was going to be much the same.

He opened the wooden gate and walked down the path to the front door, pushing through the hedges that had grown over it. He looked at the front lawn, or what was left of it. Most of it had died, and the pots, dotted about the place with no obvious pattern or purpose, were filled with nothing but dead plants.

John knocked on the door, unsure what to expect, and wondered how different it would be from when he was there last. There was a slight vein of nervousness trickling through his body. Not enough to make his hands tremble, but enough for him to notice. He dispelled this as nothing important, thinking that it wasn't nerves – but maybe it was excitement. He had always enjoyed being there in the past, but he had been with his best friend then. And now it was just him.

Through the door's frosted glass, he saw her walk towards him. She opened the door with an inviting smile. She had long dark hair tucked behind her ears, deep brown eyes, and scarlet lips.

'Hi – Olivia, isn't it?' he said. 'I'm John. Harriet called you. I've come to look at your garden.'

'Hi, John. Thanks for coming. Yeah, Harriet did call. Hopefully you can put it all back together. Harriet mentioned that you and … Andrew, was it? She said you've worked miracles before.'

John gave a nervous laugh, then said, 'Well, I'm not sure about that. It's been ten years since I was here last.'

'Looking at the garden, I can tell,' she joked. 'Why don't you come through and I can show you around and what I want doing?'

'Yeah, sure.'

She opened the door fully and he walked in and went to go straight through, like he had done many times before, but stopped himself. This was no longer Mr and Mrs Clarke's house.

'Please, go through to the kitchen. I haven't had the chance to change the layout yet.'

John noticed that her English was good, like she had been speaking it her entire life.

The smell of the place reminded him of Mr and Mrs Clarke. The scent of baked cakes and newspapers had seeped into the walls, and the house hadn't changed since he'd been there last. The furniture and the colour of the walls remained the same, along with the faded floral carpet throughout the house. One thing, however, was different. There was a painting of a villa on the side of a

27

mountain hung on the wall. He wondered if it was hers but didn't bother asking. It was only a picture.

'Would you like a cup of tea or anything?' she said.

'I'll have a coffee, please.'

'How do you take it?'

'Just black, thank you.'

John stood awkwardly to the side while she went about making him his coffee, and he took this opportunity to look out of the window at the garden. His face must have dropped for a moment when he saw it, because Olivia seemed to comment out of nowhere, 'Yeah, it's not great, is it?'

'No, it isn't.'

The kettle clicked and while the coffee was being poured, the silence returned for a moment until there was a scampering of footsteps above him. They charged down the stairs and stopped shy of the doorway into the kitchen.

John turned and saw a child's eyes staring at him from behind the door. A sudden wave of discomfort rushed through his body. He fought for breath as the fatherless child's cries echoed through his head.

'Here's your coffee,' Olivia said, handing it to him, and he thanked her as he took it and brought himself back into the room.

Olivia said something in Spanish – the only word he understood was his own name.

'Hello, John,' the child said quietly, still half hidden behind the door.

'Hello, young man. What's your name?' The young boy recoiled further behind the door, and John was worried he had scared him.

Olivia spoke again in Spanish.

'My name's Charlie.'

'It's nice to meet you, Charlie.' John crouched down, hoping to appear less of a threat. Not that he had ever been considered a threat. He was of average height for a man in this country and he was never the most muscular guy on his unit. 'What's that you've got?'

Charlie giggled and cuddled his toy. 'This is my dinosaur.' A smile beamed across his face.

'Can I see?' John asked.

Charlie looked down at his stuffed toy, then back up at the stranger in his kitchen, then back down at his toy. He stepped forward from behind the door, unwrapped it from his arms, and held it out.

'Does it have a name?'

'No.'

John looked at the toy, a smiling dinosaur. 'What do you think you should call him?'

'I don't know.'

John returned the toy and with outstretched arms, Charlie took it from him, then asked, 'Why are you here?'

'I'm here to do some gardening.'

'Why?'

'Because your mum has asked me to fix it all up.'

'Can I help you, John? Please.' Charlie's eyes widened and a smile beamed across his face. 'I love the garden.'

Olivia spoke to him in Spanish and his face dropped.

'I'm sure you can help me one day, Charlie. But I've got to figure out what needs doing and the resources I'm going to need. So I doubt I'll be doing much today.'

'Plus it's too cold out there,' Olivia added. 'Now why don't you go back upstairs, because I need to talk to John.'

'Okay,' Charlie said. 'Bye, John.'

'Bye, Charlie,' John said as he stood up, and the little boy ran off upstairs.

'Sorry about that. He's quite enthusiastic about the garden. He liked the one we had in Columbia. Anyway, shall we have a look outside?'

'Yeah, sure.'

'I'll get my coat.'

As she led him out into the garden, he wondered what had made her move away from Columbia. What had her life been like out there? What had made her move to a different country, a single mother with a child? A single mother and child. He couldn't help but speculate about Charlie's father, but he didn't want to; not everyone had the same kind of father he had. Perhaps she had moved here for a better life, but this didn't stop his curiosity. Her situation, however, did provide him with a spur of motivation to get it right for them, whatever their circumstances were.

The garden was overgrown, neglected, and malnourished. Nature had taken back what John and Andrew had once created. Weeds had replaced the footpaths, eroded by time and neglect. The sheds at the back of the garden had rotted, and the vegetable cages, built to keep the birds and other wildlife away, had been invaded by the overhanging branches of the tree in the centre of the garden.

The hedge that lined the perimeter had overgrown so much that John couldn't see the fence that had once defined the garden's boundary. On the other side, in the orchard, several seasons' worth of apples were decomposing into the ground and the trees themselves all needed pruning back, along with the other trees dotted around the garden. The grass needed cutting as well.

'I picked this place because of the garden – well, for its size over anything. Like I said, Charlie loves the garden, and I'd much prefer him spending time outside than being cooped up indoors. I thought I'd try and put it back together myself, and I probably could, but considering I've got some job interviews lined up and will probably only be able to work on it on weekends, I decided to get a gardener instead.'

John remained silent for a moment, wondering if he was the man to do justice to this garden. It was going to be a lot of work, but he empathised with her situation – but of course when that call came, he would go back. At least in the meantime this would give him something to do.

'Yeah,' he said, breaking the silence. 'So, what do you want me to do?'

Olivia started to walk off down the garden, and John followed her. 'The first thing really would be to get these paths sorted. It would make it easier to get around.' She stumbled slightly on the uneven ground. John put out a hand for her, but she regained her balance. 'See what I mean?' she said.

'Yeah. Do you still want them to be shingle paths?'

'Ideally, yeah.'

'That's fine. As weeds have started to come through, I'll have to pretty much dig them all up, put down new membrane, and then put shingle on top. And I should be able to reuse most of these wooden sleepers. They look in good condition.'

'Sounds good to me,' she said and continued down the garden.

After half an hour, she had explained all that needed to be done. She wanted the sheds to be rebuilt and the vegetable cages restored. She told him that they used to have a vegetable garden back in Columbia but never specified more about who 'they' entailed. She explained which trees needed to be cut back and tamed. She explained what she wanted to be done about the overgrown hedge at the side of the garden and what she wanted doing with the orchard.

'So, do you think you're going to be okay with all that?' she asked.

'Yeah. I should be able to do it all. It's quite a big job, though.'

'I know. We're not in any rush. I mean, it's not exactly warm weather at the moment.'

'No, it's not.' John finished the last of his coffee and Olivia offered to take the empty mug. John handed it to her and said, 'You don't mind if I go around again and have a look? I forgot to make a note of everything I'm going to need. I haven't done this in a while.'

'Yeah, sure. That's fine,' Olivia said. 'How come you guys stopped, anyway?'

'This was only a business Andrew and I set up while we were at university. We did alright, actually.'

'Yeah, Harriet said you were always in demand. Anyway, please do what you need to do. And thank you again.'

32

'It's not a problem.'

Olivia went back inside, and John pulled out his phone and started to write down all the tools and resources he would need. He slowly walked back around the garden again, amazed that this was the same place he used to work in. In the orchard, however, he was interrupted.

'What are you doing, John?' Charlie's voice caught him off guard and he nearly dropped his phone.

'How did you get out here?'

'I snuck out the side door.' Charlie giggled, still holding his dinosaur.

'I don't think your mum will be thrilled if she sees you out here. Plus are you not cold?'

'But I want to help you. I used to help Dad with the gardening.'

'You *used* to help your dad?' John knew he shouldn't have phrased it as a question. What had brought them here was none of his business. But still, his curiosity simmered in his mind.

'Dad didn't move with us. It's just me and Mum.'

'How come your dad didn't come with you?' Why did he have to ask this? It wasn't any of his business. But what harm would it cause, he asked himself.

'I don't know. But can I help you?'

'I'm sure you can one day. But right now, I'm only making a list of what I need, so there isn't much you can help me with. And your mum said you can't be out here.'

Charlie went silent and looked around the neglected garden. He crossed his arms, strangling his dinosaur. His bottom lip trembled. John looked up, hoping Olivia would come out looking for him, but there was no sign of her.

John crouched down and tried to look at Charlie, but his eyes were focused on the ground, avoiding his. He tried to reassure him by saying that one day he would get to help him.

'Are you a bad person, John?' Charlie finally spoke.

The question felt like a bullet piercing his heart, and he said, 'No. I'm not a bad person.'

'Apparently Dad was. Mum doesn't like me saying that.'

John tried not to speculate about what Charlie meant by this, and he knew he shouldn't get involved in whatever had caused them to move. It was none of his business. But when he thought about his own father, he couldn't help but wonder if something similar had happened here. To be a single mother and move halfway around the world took a good deal of courage, and John admired Olivia for that.

'Okay, now let's get you back inside.'

John started walking Charlie to the side door. They almost made it without Olivia noticing, but she saw them out of the kitchen window and swiftly made her way outside. She spoke to Charlie in Spanish and Charlie apologised.

'Sorry about that,' Olivia said.

'It's not a problem.'

Olivia took Charlie back inside, and John went back to the job in hand and continued making his list.

6

During the precious few hours between me coming home from
school and my father coming home from work, Mum and I had the
house to ourselves.

She seldom saw her friends since my father had started to do
what he did, and he refused her permission to get a job. Perhaps he
was worried someone might see the bruises; I think, however, he
worried about her meeting someone new – someone who would
actually treat her with the respect she deserved. I wonder, then, if
this was the case and my father knew that what he was doing was
wrong, if he ever had any regrets about his actions. I never had the
chance to ask him.

These precious hours would have been a great time for me to
play with my toys and read my Roman history books without
worrying about when to put a pillow around my head; I could be a
kid again. I could have watched something I liked on TV without
having to listen out for the crack of a beer can being opened. But

thinking about how my mum sometimes cried when she hugged me, I spent this time with her, doing the things I knew she liked. Even though it wasn't every day I got to do this – some days she just couldn't bring herself to get off the sofa or out of bed – I made sure I put the effort in to convince her that she could. And I think she liked that. She knew someone was looking out for her.

My mum, since she was taught by her mum how to bake, fell in love with it, much like myself with the Romans. She was fascinated by the process that allowed seemingly benign ingredients to be moulded together to make something universally loved by all.

So while my father wasn't home, we used to bake together. And we made it all, from cakes to pastries, cookies to brownies and savoury bakes, breads to pies, sourdough to bagels. The kitchen, during this time, was filled with a sea of smells and flavours. Even today, if I walk past a bakery, I return to those delicate moments that are stored away in my mind like buried treasure, when life seemed to give me hope that everything was going to be alright. None of my friends at school knew that I baked. Not even the teachers knew, and I remember, during food lessons, being ignorant of the process, because those moments were just for my mum and me; they were the only occasions when I wanted more than anything else for us both to be happy and to forget that my father would be home soon.

When we baked, we were efficient, baking and tidying simultaneously, always avoiding a mess or a mistake. Not because we were trying to be champion bakers but because of the time my father saw a dusting of flour on the floor that we had missed, and he didn't even need a drink to start his shouting and berating. He argued that because my mum was home all day, the house should be spotless. Still to this day I maintain a tidy space.

Yet moments like that didn't stop us. They made us take more care, because neither of us was going to give this up. They made up most of the happy memories from my childhood. And, of course, they gave us hope that life would change, that my father would one day move on to something else. But that day, I now know, never really came. And I sometimes wonder if I ever actually believed in this hope or whether I just wanted to believe that there was some sort of hope out there. What does it matter, though? My mum and I at least had some happy memories despite the trauma that watered them down.

The only time I thought about stopping the baking was when, at night, after I had retreated to my room, my father shouted at my mum about the cleanliness of a spoon that we had used. That was the only time I wanted to stop baking, because that day I was on washing-up duty. I should have cleaned that damn spoon better. I should have made sure it was spotless. But I made a mistake. We never used the dishwasher, you see. Because once it was all packed up and the cycle had started, our baking time was done. And as the cleaning up afterwards was part of the ritual of baking, we just washed everything up ourselves, because it took longer. There was never a discussion about it. My mum had us start off this way, and this way we continued.

I heard that spoon collide with something that night. Whether it was the floor or the wall as it shot past my mum's head, I had never felt so guilty in my life. It was my fault – I should have done a better job. It was one of the few times that I cried a torrent of tears that soaked into my pillow, my cries muffled by the fabric.

7

As she exited the terminal, she grabbed her suitcase from the conveyor belt and dragged it along behind her like all the other passengers. She adjusted her sunhat to obscure her face from the cameras looking down on her and scanned around outside for the person she'd been expecting to meet.

Her grip on the suitcase tightened when she couldn't see him. Her flight had been delayed for two hours – perhaps he had already left, but then she saw him with his back to her at the edge of the road, waiting, like a monk in meditation. His baseball cap was pulled down over his face. He turned around, sensing her eyes on the back of his head, and glanced at her before turning back to face the traffic. She walked up to him. They never once looked at each other.

'Where's the car?' she asked, looking at her phone.

'In the car park of the hotel down the road. Keep your distance behind me.'

She looked around before setting off. Was anyone following her? She assessed no one was and followed the man's instructions.

She recognised the black BMW, the scratch on its offside rear bumper giving it away, parked at the far end of the car park. She went to the boot, opened it, and placed her suitcase inside. She got into the passenger seat, taking one last look behind her, the man's nonchalant nature not reassuring her, but there was no one there.

They drove in silence as he negotiated the traffic around the airport. When they were clear of it, he introduced himself.

'I'm Carl. Carl Bedford.'

'Nice to meet you, Carl. I'm Antonia. How long until we get to the factory?'

'About six hours. Did you bring everything we asked for?'

'Yes. Of course I did. Do you have everything ready at your end?'

'Of course we do. That suitcase didn't look too heavy, though.'

'That's the beauty of plastics. They're light and can't be detected with a metal detector.'

'How do you get past X-ray machines?'

'The parts are deconstructed. It's not obvious what they are. But if someone wants to get a closer look and asks what they're for, I just lie.'

'And that works?'

'I wouldn't be here, having done this for so long, if it didn't.'

'Well, it all sounds good to me.'

'It is good. Now, Carl, my journey here hasn't exactly gone to plan. I want to get some sleep before I see Gary.'

'Fine by me. He's very much looking forward to seeing you.'

After six hours, they had made it to the factory. Carl woke Antonia to tell her they had arrived, and he pulled up outside the guard's hut and greeted the guards. They let him through without hindrance.

He drove to the end of the compound, past the main buildings, and stopped outside a derelict, abandoned warehouse, not illuminated by outside lights like the other buildings.

Antonia retrieved the suitcase from the boot and Carl waited for her by the door. He scanned a key card. The lock clicked open. Inside the dark, empty warehouse, the sound of Antonia's suitcase dragging along the ground echoed up to the high ceiling.

They continued through to a back office, as bare as the rest of the building except for a desk at the back. Carl flicked a switch on the desk and it moved to the side. A beam of orange light burst up from the floor, followed by the mechanical sound of machinery.

'Watch your step and your head,' Carl said, leading the way down.

Antonia picked up the suitcase and carried it down the stairs. The underground factory stretched the length of the warehouse, and the men working at the machinery stopped for a moment to look at the woman walking past them. Carl led Antonia to Gary's office.

'Antonia, it's good to see you,' Gary said, shaking her hand.

'It's good to see you too.'

'Show me what you've got.' Gary cleared a space on his desk and Antonia lifted the suitcase onto it and opened it. She pulled out the plastic components from underneath her clothes. Gary took them from her and inspected them.

'Get our parts and we'll put it all together,' Gary said to Carl. Carl did as he was told and returned with a selection of metal parts.

Gary put them all together, creating an assault rifle, and weighed it in his hands. Antonia watched while he looked down its sights with a satisfied look on his face. He cocked the rifle, then fired off the action to the tune of a satisfying click.

'You've done some great work, Antonia. I'm very impressed.'

'Thank you. I do my best.'

'After the success of the first phase of our plan, I'm going to need two more of these. And I'll need them made up and brought over quickly. Will that be okay?'

'I can do that.' She pulled a business card from her coat pocket and placed it on the desk. 'Naturally, I've changed my number since we last spoke. If you want to put in an order, then call this one. But the price, if you require it at short notice, will be a little higher.'

'Don't worry. Money won't be a problem. Hopefully I'll be in contact with you soon.'

8

He had, he believed, got off to a good start the previous day. With everything written down, he had been able to get the supplies he needed and could plan the next steps to fix the garden. It was almost like planning an operation except the end result wasn't to put people in jail. Nevertheless, he had woken that morning with a plan in mind and wanted, by the end of the day, to have dug up the path that meandered around the garden.

The promise of pleasant weather had not been kept, and John saw his breath float away in front of him when he knocked on the door.

'Hey, John, how are you?' Olivia said.

'I'm good, thanks.'

She led him into the kitchen, and he closed the door behind him. 'Still take your coffee black?'

'Yes, please.'

And, like the previous day, John stood awkwardly to the side and looked out of the window at the task that awaited him. It didn't daunt him like it had done the day before; Charlie's declaration that his dad had been a bad person had provided him with an extra dash of motivation. And when he watched Olivia reach up to the cupboard to grab the coffee, he couldn't help but look at her differently. He wondered what her story really was. What had happened to her in Colombia for her son to call his own father a bad man? He was just the gardener, however, and that, he told himself, was how he wanted it to remain, despite the thoughts in his head. He put his hand in his pocket and held his phone, wondering when it would ring.

A scurry of footsteps raced around upstairs and came running down the stairs. Charlie stopped just shy of the doorway, not hiding behind it this time, and said, 'Hello, John.' His dinosaur was still by his side and a smile on his face.

'Hey, Charlie,' John said. 'Have you thought of a name for your dinosaur yet?'

'No, not yet. Are you gardening today?'

'Yes, I am.'

'My dinosaur wants to go gardening with you.' Charlie held out his toy. Olivia, with her back to them, laughed as she poured water into the mug.

John crouched down and took the toy. 'I'll take him out with me, Charlie.'

'Thank you.'

'And John will try not to get him dirty either,' Olivia said as she handed John his coffee.

'I'll do my best,' John said. 'In fact, I'll leave him on the outside table.'

'Okay,' Charlie said. Olivia spoke to him in Spanish, and he ran off upstairs.

'Thanks for the coffee,' John said. Olivia continued to laugh to herself. 'What is it?' John asked.

'You're actually going to take the dinosaur outside with you?'

'It's not going to be a problem, is it?'

Olivia, in between laughing, said, 'It's not a problem, no. It's just funny.'

'Well, if you'll excuse me, the dinosaur and I need to make a start on the paths.'

Olivia continued to laugh, and John made his own way out. He placed the toy on the table and headed for the shed to get a spade to start digging up the old path.

When John next checked the time, it was nearly eleven. He wiped away the perspiration from his forehead and, despite the temperature, took off his jumper and laid it on the table next to his empty mug of coffee and the dinosaur. He looked back at what he had managed to achieve so far and wanted to be impressed by how much he had done in one morning, but he assessed himself to be behind schedule. The clay-like ground made it difficult to dig, and over the last decade, the path had sunk into the ground, which made it harder to dig it all out – and the weeds didn't help. The wooden borders that he had deemed to be in good condition weren't as good as he had originally thought. About half of them had rotted at the bottom and weren't going to be much use when the new shingle was laid down. Yet, as he stopped to look at what he had done, he couldn't help but think back to when he and Andrew had first tended to the paths.

John saw Olivia watching him through the kitchen window, and she disappeared for a moment before coming out of the side door.

'How are you getting on? Is he helping?' She pointed at the dinosaur and smiled.

'I wish,' John said. 'This might take a little bit longer that I originally thought.'

'It always does.'

'The ground isn't great for digging and some of the wooden borders aren't as good as I thought they were. But other than that, it's going fine.'

Olivia looked towards the dug-up paths and nodded slowly. 'Do you want another coffee?'

'Yes, please.'

She took the empty mug from the table, went back inside, and returned a few minutes later. John had taken a seat at the table, his phone in hand: no missed calls.

'Thank you,' he said when she handed him the coffee. 'So how long ago did you move here?'

'We've been here two weeks now. I don't know if you know what it's like moving countries, but it's not exactly a calm process.'

'I can imagine,' John said. 'You speak really good English, though.'

'Thanks. Yeah, it was my dad who taught me. He really wanted me to go to the United States. Told me it was the land of opportunity and not to remain stuck in Colombia.'

'How come you ended up in England, then?'

'When I looked into it, England seemed like the better place. Free health care and no guns. I've seen too many guns in Colombia to want to see another one again in my life.'

'It can't have been easy, though, emigrating as a single mother?' A question, he thought, he might have overstepped in asking; it wasn't his business. But Charlie's comments from the previous day still played in his mind.

'It wasn't easy. But I thought now would be a good time before he starts going to school. The education system here is better than the one back home.'

John couldn't help but think that the school year had started months ago. Why had she chosen to move now? Unless the immigration process had been delayed for whatever reason.

'Would you say you're happier here than back there?' he asked.

'I would, yeah.'

He stopped himself asking any more questions. This wasn't an interrogation, but at least he had heard from her that she was happy here. 'I better get on, then,' he said.

'Yes, absolutely.' And she went back inside, and John returned to digging up the paths.

9

Up until that day, the day it all changed for my mum and me, my father had never laid a finger on me. Maybe it was because until that point I had been too scared to confront him, hidden away in my room at the first sign the mood was inevitably going to turn sour, for him to actually need to hit me or fight me off. He could always have climbed the stairs – I always feared that – and come into my room whenever he felt like it. But he never did. I guess he was too preoccupied with my mum.

By that point, my voice had broken, hair had started to sprout across my body, and my first spot appeared on my face. And despite being at a different school now that I was older and thinking that this would be a new start, a new opportunity to make the friends I had isolated myself from in my previous school, I still spent most of my time alone except for the precious few hours with my mum. While people in my class started to talk to girls, go to parties, and drink underage, I stayed away, worried that someone might find out

*how we lived. My mum never mentioned my lack of friends to me.
I'm not sure she noticed – it can't have been the most prominent
thing on her mind – and even if she did, I think she didn't say
anything because if I started going round to friends' houses, she
would deeply miss our time together. I think it was the only part of
her life she found any sort of enjoyment in.*

*As I got older, we branched out to more than just baking.
Sometimes we would get out of the house and go to the garden
centre, a place I felt comfortable going to with my mum because no
one my age would go to a garden centre. I wondered how my mum
felt going to a public place where she might bump into someone she
knew. I remember the moment when I realised why she wasn't
bothered by this. I was in school, sitting at the back of the
classroom, and realised that I was always surrounded by other
people through no choice of my own five days a week and had been
for years. My mum, thanks to my father, had been imprisoned in the
confines of the house for years, rarely stepping outside and only
doing so if she really had to. She knew no one. And no one knew
her.*

*There was one time, however, when we were looking for
bedding plants, while she was scanning through all the ones on
display, that I was certain I recognised a woman who glared in our
direction across the centre. I was sure she was one of Mum's
friends. But when she caught my eye, she looked away and walked
off.*

*Our garden hadn't been touched in years, so doing it up, to
some extent, turned the fatigued, neglected space into something of
a sanctuary for us. My father rarely went out there, and it felt like*

we had our own special place all to ourselves in this compound. It wasn't just a precious few hours we had. We now had a place of our own to enjoy them in. Because even though we baked in the kitchen, my father used to hurt my mum there too. The garden, then, was sacred to us.

My father accepted, for want of a better word, our renovations. At last, as he said to me while I was in earshot, his 'pathetic waste-of-space wife was actually getting off her fucking useless arse to fucking do something'. It wasn't the positive response we wanted from him, but at least he didn't stop us. Until, of course, the day it all changed.

When the recession hit and he was told, along with the rest of the people he worked with, that they were not going to be getting a pay rise next year, my father was annoyed. When inflation continued to grow and it became apparent to him that his monthly paycheque wouldn't meet the basic cost of living, he was beyond angry.

Going over credit card statements one night, he saw the transactions for baking ingredients and plants, which to this day I will argue didn't add up to much. But my father was not a rational man, so expecting a rational response from him was like waiting for a bank to donate their gold reserves on your doorstep because they didn't want them anymore; impossible.

That night, after I'd retreated to my room after his first can of beer, I put my headphones on and listened to music while I did some homework. I think that was how I managed to justify to myself, as I got older, my absence on those nights. Time after school was spent with my mum – not doing homework that could be done later.

But it was like it was meant to be that night, like someone had decided that we had suffered enough and now was our time of redemption. A song finished, the last one on the album, and as I scrolled through to find another, I heard my father scream at my mum and tell her that she wouldn't be baking her 'stupid fucking cakes anymore'. To reiterate his point, I heard a bowl smash and the plastic container of today's fruit cake was opened and the cake was thrown across the kitchen. He growled at her to get the scales and she did and placed them on the floor like he ordered her to. He put his foot right through them. How dare he take from her one of the only things that made her happy! But still, I did nothing. I was nearly as tall as him by this point. I could, I believed for the first time in my life, be strong enough to deal with him. But still, I sat frozen in my room. Except I didn't choose a different song. If I was going to have the courage to do this, I would need enough anger to fuel it.

I heard the back door open. He mentioned something about the garden – another expense he no longer wanted. From my bedroom I watched but could not hear. He had lowered his voice, but his clenched teeth told me his words were still poison. That was when I saw him kick at the flowers we had only planted a few days ago. That was when I saw him attack our sanctuary. My mum covered her mouth to silence her cries. And when she looked up towards my bedroom window, I saw her flooded eyes. That was when I went downstairs.

When I got into the kitchen, my father had stepped back inside, and for the first time in years, I saw his eyes while hurting my mum was on his mind. They spewed rage like lava spitting out of an erupting volcano. They locked with mine for a moment. He didn't recognise who I was; he just saw me as another target. His entire body was clenched, his face tight with tension.

'Get back upstairs, you little shit!'

My mum walked in – or what was supposed to be my mum. I could hardly recognise her frail frame and reddened, tearful eyes. I hadn't seen her like this before. She covered one side of her face immediately with her hair. She didn't want me to see the bruises. But I didn't need to see them to know what he had done to her.

'No,' I said.

My mum cried, shrieked, tried not to look at me – she didn't want to see her own son being beaten by his father, and she said, 'Please, John, it's all okay. Just go back upstairs.'

'Listen to your mother, boy. Fuck off upstairs.'

'No,' I said again, and this time I took a step forward.

'You're just as pathetic as she is, you little shit.'

He took a step towards me, his shoes cracking on shards of glass, and his frame eclipsed the ceiling light.

'Now go back upstairs!' he bellowed, and I could smell the alcohol on his breath.

'No. Stop hurting Mum.' I stepped forward again, my heart pounding, my limbs shaking with adrenaline, and I found the strength to push him away. All I remember after that was him pushing me back and me falling backwards.

The next thing I remembered was waking up in a hospital bed and the stinging pain behind my eyes as the light poured in. But despite this, I felt my mum's warm hand holding mine and the relief that warmed me inside knowing that she was there – that she was okay. When my eyes had adjusted to the light and I could sit up slowly in bed, I went pale, cold, when I saw my father sitting, disinterested, in the corner. He was only here because he was biologically related to me, because not being here would look strange, out of character for a parent. But he was no parent of mine. Anyone can be a father; it takes real care and effort to be a dad. And although it disgusts me to call him my father, I prefer it to his name, because I say it ironically. It's a title he obtained but failed to earn.

When I looked at my mum, despite the situation, despite all that had happened, I saw the acceptance in her eyes, like she was okay with this happening because it was just a fact of life when living with this demon. It hurt to see that look in her eyes, all hope for a better life gone, prepared to throw away this one because she believed it was all she was destined for. It made me sick. But for the first time in a long time, we were all out of the house in a place with doctors and nurses, people who wanted to take care of you, and take care of me they did. They were excellent, and during their checkups on me, I thought they would work out the entire situation. But what I didn't quite see at first – perhaps the medication made me drowsy or the concussion made me slow – was that my mum had layered makeup on her face. The bruises didn't exist in the eyes of the medical staff. This worried me. But it was when a nurse shared a joke with me about falling down the stairs and being on my phone that I realised I was here on a lie.

I saw the look in my mum's eyes when she felt my restlessness. She wanted me to accept the lie – accept the life I was living. But I looked over at my father, that disgusting human being. He did not deserve to be keeping us prisoner like this. He had broken everything my mum and I held dear and destroyed our sanctuary; he would not get away with it any longer.

What I needed next was for him to leave the room so I could explain to the nurses what had really happened, and then they could talk to the police on our behalf. But he remained in the corner like a soldier on guard because that was why he was there: to guard the family secret, guard his abuse.

Eventually, however, he had to leave. Nature was going to call, and the bastard waited until the nurse had left before he went. He must have thought he was clever, but when he was out of earshot, I told my mum that my head was hurting and to go and get a nurse. She went straight for the emergency cord next to my bed to sound the alarm. An alarm that would alert my father. I couldn't risk that. This might be our only chance. I told her not to pull it and to just get up and fetch a nurse. Thankfully she listened and returned a moment later.

I got straight to it. I didn't know how much time I had, and despite my mum's protests that everything was fine, I told the nurse everything.

It didn't take long before the police arrived to arrest my father. Two officers came into the room, and I watched my father the entire time. I saw the sudden panic on his face when they first walked in, then the anger, directed at us, when they read him his rights and told him he was being arrested. My father jumped out of his seat to try and inflict one last strike of pain on us, but when the police officers grabbed him, he didn't put up any more of a fight. My father was a coward. And the police soon had him in handcuffs. The anger on his face was quickly replaced by fear.

At first, it didn't feel real. Both of us had waited for the day we'd be free of him – the day my mum had come to accept would never arrive. And it was that day when the police took my father away that I knew what I wanted to do with my life. Seeing those police officers walk in and take him away like it was nothing more than their job, like they did it all the time, made me see how much good I could do in the world – protect people, protect those most vulnerable in society. I remember when the final realisation that her evil husband was gone shone on my mum's face, and I thought about how many more times I could make something like that happen for other people's mums and daughters, fathers and sons. I was going to try to free them all from a life like this.

10

The castle in Bamburgh overlooked the entire town. The imposing walls and turrets were now out of place in this small settlement. Centuries ago, they would have protected the occupants from anyone who wished to attack. The castle was the first line of defence against an invasion. Today, however, all it could do was sit back and watch, because the enemy was already embedded into the country, and its once-impressive arsenal was now just a showpiece for the tourists.

Carl was sent alone to this quaint town. For all parties involved, this was more of a practice run to learn how the local authorities would respond to something they would never suspect would happen in this part of the world. From this, they would evaluate the details of the next phase of their plan. Who knows, it might not even be necessary to proceed. They might get everything they needed from this one intervention. The chances of that, however, were slim.

Gary had given him explicit instructions. Get in, do what you need to do, then get out. There was no time for hanging around, no room for mistakes. It may well be a practice, but that did not make it any less illegal.

Carl watched the local townsfolk from the front seat of the black BMW as they went about their lives. He was parked outside a hotel in the centre of the town. People were drinking outside, enjoying the sun and the warmer than usual temperature it brought with it. Cars drove past and people walked by, oblivious of what Carl was about to do and the weapon in the car boot.

Carl's hands trembled – it was over twenty years since he had taken a life, but he was ready to do it again. He looked over at the drinkers outside the pub and picked his targets.

One of them got up and disappeared into the pub. He returned a few minutes later with three new pints and joined his two friends. They looked happy, content. Their guard was down. Carl took a deep breath, closed his eyes, and calmed his chaotic mind. Then he got out of the car. He went to the boot, opened it, and, like a well-rehearsed procedure, pulled out the homemade rifle.

He tried to be discreet. He didn't want someone to witness the power he had in his hands and scream the place down, causing needless panic that would only disrupt the inevitable.

He loaded the rifle. He knew he needed to be quick.

He slammed the boot lid – that got a few people's attention.

Raising the sights of the rifle to his eye, he targeted the three friends. They made eye contact with him. They dropped their pints; glass smashed on the ground and they scrambled to get away. People's heads turned towards the noise; they saw others running and looked to see what they were running from. When they saw the gunman, they couldn't get away quickly enough.

He fired his rifle. It kicked back into his shoulder. He fired again and again, the loud crack echoing against the centuries-old hotel walls.

One by one, the three friends fell to the ground underneath a glittering red mist.

He raced back to the car, threw the rifle onto the passenger seat, and started the ignition. His foot pressed hard on the pedal, the wheels spun against the tarmac, and he flew down the road. It would not be long before he was told to do something similar again.

11

The killings had been front page news for three days; the stain of death, the taking of innocent life had been plastered across the media. But it was only a killing in a small town, and with next to no evidence found at the scene and the police having no leads, by the fifth day the story had fallen down the pecking order – soon to be just a memory.

And every day since the attack, John had kept his phone close to him. But it never rang. Why would it? It was only three guys, and the police were sure it was a murder. This, however, didn't sit right with him, thus his wistful hope of receiving a phone call he knew deep down would never arrive. In a village of that size, everyone knew everyone, or at the very least locals could be easily identified. The killer, however, had specifically targeted three friends and not a single person in the surrounding area, of which there were plenty, could identify him. From reports he had seen online, the guy hadn't bothered to wear a balaclava or anything to hide his face. Unfortunately for the police, the witnesses could not put together a coherent narrative of what he looked like. Did he have brown hair or was it black? What colour were his eyes? What was his build? They didn't know, so distracted by the chaos, the violence, the gun in his hand that no one could identify him. To John, this wasn't murder. Someone had travelled to this village to conduct an attack – terrorist related? He wasn't sure. But his instincts told him that it wasn't just a standard murder. There was more going on. More questions that needed to be answered. Chief among them was why, if it was terrorist related, had they chosen to target a small village and not a major city? Newcastle was just over an hour down the road. Why hadn't they attacked there? It would have been more likely to receive worldwide news coverage.

Five days after the attack, however, it felt like the country had moved on and the chances of him getting a call back to London had gone from slim to negligible.

He stopped staring into the overcast sky, picked up the bag of shingles, slit the top open, and let them fall onto the path. After raking them level, he stopped again; his mind wanted to find its way back to its previous schedule of daydreaming, but his eyes diverted to the window in the kitchen and there he saw Olivia. He smiled at her, she smiled back, and he grabbed the next bag of shingles. While he raked this batch smooth, he heard her walking up behind him.

'It's starting to come together now,' she said.

'It is, yeah. Although I think I'm going to need another bag of shingle – maybe two.'

'That's fine. It's looking good, though, so thank you. How

much have the supplies cost you so far?'

He counted it up in his head to give her a rough estimate, but he had kept the receipts, so when it came to writing his invoice, he reassured her half jokingly that he would refer to them and of course attach the receipts to be totally transparent. He hadn't written an invoice before, he realised – that had been Andrew's department. He didn't let on to Olivia, however, that this was the case. No one liked the idea that their money was being handled with a cavalier attitude. And it was this that got John wondering where she had gotten the money from to pay for this. She didn't seem to be concerned about it, considering she didn't have a job here yet. But it wasn't his business as long as she paid.

'So once this is done, what are you going to start on next?'

'I'm going to have to start on pruning back the trees, especially the orchard. It's going to get warmer soon, and the sooner I cut them back the better, really.'

'Sounds good to me.'

'Do you have any large bags to put the cuttings in so they can be taken to the tip?'

'I have no idea.' Olivia shrugged like it was something that she had never given much consideration.

'Mr and Mrs Clarke used to keep some in the hut out the front.'

'I've not really had much of a look in there.'

'I don't blame you,' John said. 'It was just a dumping ground mainly for all kinds of stuff we couldn't find a home for elsewhere. Anyway, I'll go and have a look.'

He headed towards the front garden and Olivia said, 'I'll come with you.'

'Okay,' John said with a hint of bemusement in his voice which Olivia caught on to.

'Only because I haven't seen inside it.' She wrapped her arms around herself, and John wondered why she didn't just go indoors if she was cold. The hut really wasn't worth being cold to visit, but her stubbornness he found, to his surprise, was a little endearing. If this woman had managed to travel halfway around the world to get away from her husband, she wasn't going to let the cold stop her doing something.

'Are you going to bring the dinosaur?' she said.

'You said I couldn't get him dirty.'

'It's really that bad, is it?'

'You'll see.'

A decade ago, you could have seen that the hut was made of stone. Now the outer façade was covered in ivy.

'It's not exactly the Ritz,' John said before pushing through the overgrown hedge that blocked the entrance. 'I should probably cut this back as well,' he said to himself.

'The Ritz?'

'It's a hotel in London. A very nice hotel, in fact.'

'Never heard of it.'

'Really?'

'Yeah. Should I go?'

John laughed to himself, then said, 'It's expensive. You won't get much change out of a thousand for a room for the night.'

'Only a thousand? I'll go for the entire weekend, then.' Olivia laughed.

John pulled his phone from his pocket and used the torch to

illuminate the mess. Moss had grown on the inside of the walls, wood that had been stored that he had forgotten about had rotted away, and an old spade had rusted to the point that there wasn't much left to identify what tool it had once been. Yet in amongst the old, decaying mess, he saw the large blue tarpaulin bags.

'This really isn't the Ritz,' Olivia said, grimacing at the mess.

'When we first looked in here, Andrew and I found a dead pigeon and its nest.'

'Do they have dead pigeons in the Ritz?'

'Only on the menu,' John quipped.

He grabbed the bags and pulled them out, coughing as the settled dust burst up into the air. 'This reminds me of a little house on a hill in Colombia,' Olivia started. And even though John wanted to get back to work, he didn't want to pass up the chance to hear about her life before she had moved here.

'When we were younger, only school children, my friends and I used to play outside, running around, usually playing tag. I wonder how long it will be before Charlie learns that game when he starts school. He'll probably insist on playing it around the house. And outside with you, no doubt.'

John caught himself off guard when he smiled at the thought.

'So, there was this hut – house thing at the top of a hill. Apparently, the old man who lived in it was a bit of a loner. He didn't have any family or friends; he'd kept to himself his whole life for whatever reason – none of us knew.

'Anyway, we used to try and see how close we could get to his hut, and without fail, every time we got close to his fence, he always appeared from the house and shouted at us, and we ran away scared,

62

then laughed about it when we got to the bottom of the hill. He died a few months after we started this game. From what I heard, no one went to his funeral except the priest. It's not exactly a happy story, it just reminds me of that.'

John headed to the back garden and Olivia followed.

'Is that how you spent most of your childhood, then – teasing old men?'

'Maybe not all of it. But I remember, because we were in a small village, we had acres and acres of beautiful countryside to run around in.'

'It sounds nice.'

'It was. How about your childhood? Did you spend it running around outside teasing old men?'

John went quiet for a moment and thought about whether to answer honestly or not answer at all.

'No, not exactly.'

'What did you do, then?'

'It's a long story.'

'Okay,' she said, and she paused for a moment and watched John's eyes drop. 'I can make you another coffee if you like?'

'Yes please. That would be great.'

She made for the house, then turned and said, 'I almost forgot to mention, when you come next week, Charlie will be starting his first day at school and then I'll be going off for a job interview, so I probably won't be back until midday.'

'Do you want me to come by later, then?' John said, and the question was met with a pause from Olivia.

'You'll be fine, won't you, coming at the usual time?'

'I will be, but only if you're okay with that.'

'Yeah, it'll be fine.'

'Okay.'

'I'll make some coffee and put it in a flask by the back door for you. It should still be warm enough when you get here.'

'Thank you.'

Olivia went back inside, and John went back to the garden.

12

Of course, that wasn't the last I saw of my father. Thankfully, the judge refused him bail. It was understood that to do so would potentially put my mum and me in danger. The hardest thing I've ever had to do in my life was listen to my mum breaking down on the stand as she told the jury, under the watchful gaze of her husband, how she had accumulated all those bruises, how she struggled through years of abuse and still had sleepless nights because of it. I had never thought someone could be so brave – to open up like that for all the world to hear.

We cried together when the jury unanimously agreed that my father was guilty. He was sentenced to eight years in prison. Eight. It was nothing. But to us at least, it was eight years of freedom.

We celebrated by going to the garden centre. We had tea and cake and looked around the flowers. It was there that a woman walked over to us. The same woman who I thought I had recognised that one time. It turned out she did used to be one of my mum's friends, and she cried as she hugged my mum, telling her how sorry she was that she knew nothing about it all. Our case had made the local news, and soon more and more people came out to praise our bravery and pass on their apologies that they didn't see anything, didn't even suspect that this could have been happening right in plain sight. Neither I nor my mum was too bothered. We had each other, and that counted for more than anything in the world.

On the day that I was informed of my father's death, it was break time at school. Since the trial, I was now one of the most popular people in my year. I remember that the new guy, Andrew, had just heard about why I was so popular all of a sudden and he started to talk to me to offer his condolences. He had known of a relative who had an abusive girlfriend, so he could sympathise with our situation. He was inviting me around to his house to play video games when the headteacher asked me to follow her to her office.

On the way, I asked her what all of this was about, but she said that when we got to her office, she'd tell me then. It was the warmth in her voice that told me something was wrong. She was overcompensating for something. I knew I wasn't in trouble, and I knew this wasn't because of some good work that I had done. I wasn't that good academically.

In her office, there was my mum and a police officer. My mum hugged me, and I wasn't sure what she was thinking. It was my mum who told me that the prison had rung. My father had died in his cell. Alone. He had only been there two weeks, killed by a heart attack that took him out almost instantly. He wouldn't have suffered. Nobody said that, but we both knew that was the case. Two weeks inside and then gets the easy way out. It was a shame, really, I think as I look back on it now, that he didn't suffer a little more. Either in prison or during his heart failure. I think he deserved it after all he did to us. But life isn't always fair.

I was allowed to go home, and we were silent during the car journey back. And we were silent when we got home. I didn't know what to think; I was still processing it all. In the back of my mind, I'd always known that I was going to face my father again in eight years, face the fact that he was a free man. But now that possibility no longer existed. When I realised this, a wave of happiness so great I cried flowed through me. I could feel myself breathing and thinking easier for the first time in years. I went downstairs and saw that my mum had been thinking the same thing.

My father hadn't written a will. But like my mum, he had no next of kin, so the small savings he had left and the house went to my mum. We put it up for sale immediately and it sold, thankfully, pretty quickly. We moved to a different village. One which we would call home and the one where Andrew also lived. The new house was a downsize, but it was perfect for us. To be in a place with no bad history, where you didn't have to be scared every time you walked through the front door. It was our final escape. It was the start of our new life.

With the spare money from the house sale, Mum started her own bakery, and her cakes, once only enjoyed by us, were now loved by everyone who came into her shop. And I thought this stream of happiness could last forever, but life always throws something back at you eventually. Only this time it wasn't me on *the receiving end.*

By this point in time, Andrew and I had known each other for two years. It was the summer when we were sixteen; we'd just finished our final exams and were enjoying the extended summer break. It was a warm day, and the two of us, along with the rest of our friendship group, decided to go to the outside pool in the local town. We had a great time. Andrew finally started to talk to the girl he had a crush on, and I was talking to the girl I had kissed at prom. I can't remember what we were half chatting, half giggling at. But I remember seeing Andrew's face drop, like an anchor in the ocean, when he answered his phone.

We got the next bus back to his house, and at the kitchen table, Andrew's dad was crying. I awkwardly stood aside while his dad told him what had happened. Andrew's dad's best friend, the kind of close family friend you called uncle, had been killed earlier that day in a terrorist attack in London. An extremist had driven a stolen car through a crowd of people, and Craig had been one of the victims.

It was the first terrorist attack that I remembered where I could also understand what had actually happened and why. This would not be the last time I would hear about something like this while I was at school. And it was the fact that this wasn't the last time, along with seeing your best friend's dad crying at the kitchen table because his best friend had been killed, that further spurred my motivation to join the police. And it was also the moment that got me interested in counterterrorism. There was plenty of evil in this world. And I wanted to do my part in trying to get rid of it.

13

Carl returned to the underground factory to a hero's welcome after he had taken the precaution of lying low for a week to fall off the face of the Earth. Each worker went up and shook his hand, and when he walked into Gary's office, he reclined back in the chair and felt like putting his feet on the desk. He knew, however, that Gary would saw them off if he did. So, despite his rising self-esteem, he kept them planted on the floor; now was not the time to be guided by ego.

'Everything went to plan, then?' Gary said.

Carl gestured with his hands out to the side and said, 'Well, not everything.'

'No. But the reaction we can't exactly control, and it's not like we were expecting it to go the way we wanted. The police saw it as murder when we wanted it to be terrorism.' Gary reached into his drawer and pulled out a cigar box. He offered one to Carl, who accepted, and took one for himself. 'This was a rehearsal, and with three complete strangers dead, I'd say it's a success except this drawback.' He leant across the desk and lit Carl's cigar.

'Well, when you put it like that, then yes, it's a success. Having not killed anyone for two decades, it felt like stepping into an old pair of shoes, to use a cliché.' Carl puffed on his cigar and the small back office filled with smoke. 'Plus the weapon worked very well. I was impressed. Antonia knows her stuff.'

Gary smirked and said, 'She certainly does.'

'My only genuine regret is that I should've picked out better targets. Going for three people at the same table looked like a targeted attack, and that's probably why they think it's murder. I should've spread the targets out.'

Gary waved his cigar in the air. 'Don't worry about it. What's done is done. It just means I can confirm with the client that we're happy to go to the next phase. The part where the action really ramps up.'

Carl laughed to himself. 'I'll get two more guys lined up for the next attack. Once the target and date are confirmed, I'll let them know.'

'I don't know how you do it, Carl. Do you have a soul inside you?'

'Of course I don't. What use is a soul in this game?'

Gary's phone rang. He answered it and put it on loudspeaker. 'Hello.'

'What's your assessment?' was the question from the voice modulator.

'My assessment is positive.'

There was a brief pause. Neither of the two men smoked their cigars. Their eyes were on the phone.

'I'm happy to move on to the next phase. The location and date haven't changed.'

'Understood.'

The line went dead.

They leaned back in their chairs.

'So, happy with the specifics for the next target?' Gary asked.

'Yeah. We just need two more weapons.'

'I'll call Antonia and put another order in.'

14

The murders in Bamburgh were out of the news two weeks later. The world had moved on and the three lives lost were to be forgotten about. John, from what he had read online, knew that the police were at a dead end. They hadn't delivered a press conference to reveal any good news – they never did if they didn't have any. Which told him that the killer had gone and was unlikely to be caught.

How could someone murder three people in broad daylight and get away with it?

Bemused by the situation, John tried to put it out of his mind. He had to accept there was nothing he could do except be left to question why no one had considered the terrorist aspect.

While he was making dinner for himself and Andrew, he watched what little footage there was of the attack – of the car, a black BMW, driving away. Each time, he paused the video when the registration plate was at its clearest, but the picture was too grainy and the car too far away for him to make it out.

How could you not remember a registration number? How did someone not see it? Of course, for him and his training, it would be second nature. To someone experiencing something like this for the first time, however, a registration plate isn't exactly going to be the first thing on your mind. Keeping yourself alive is.

The only thing that John could make out on the car, the only unique thing about it, was a scratch that ran down the rear of the vehicle.

There was a knock on the door, and John put his phone in his pocket and answered it.

'Evening,' he said. 'Come in. There's beer in the fridge.'

'Sounds good to me,' Andrew said as he headed straight for the fridge. 'Do you want one as well?'

'Please,' John said, getting a bottle opener from the drawer.

'I see you've got all the essentials.'

John opened the beers, and they clinked the bottles together and took a sip in unison.

'So how is the garden?' Andrew asked.

'It's in a right state. Worse than when we found it.'

'And you think you're going to be able to do it all yourself?'

'Given enough time, yeah. Olivia's not too fussed about how long it takes.'

'What is her story, then? Harriet never asked her why she moved over.'

'She's not really said anything, and I've not really asked. Although her son, Charlie, mentioned something about her husband being a bad man.'

73

Andrew thought on this for a moment, then said, 'What do you think of that?'

'I'm not reading anything into it,' John lied. 'It's none of my business. I'm just waiting for the call.'

They sipped their beers and John returned to cooking dinner. 'What are you making?' Andrew asked.

'I used to make this in London for the guys when they came over. It's a Mediterranean pasta bake.'

'Is it any good?'

'What do you mean, is it any good?' John laughed. 'Of course it's good. They all liked it.'

'I just don't ever remember you being much of a cook. A baker, yes, but a cook ...' Andrew sipped his beer.

'Let's just let the food do the talking,' John said.

'If you say so. Anyway, what's she like?'

'What's who like?'

'Olivia.'

'What about her?' John asked, turning away from the cooking to look at his friend.

'Is she nice?'

'Yeah, she's nice.'

'So, what does she do? What did she do in Colombia? What's she like? You know ... the usual things.'

'Is this you asking or Harriet?'

Andrew chuckled and said, 'Okay, it's mainly Harriet. As she's going to be teaching her son next week, she was just wondering.'

'I don't really know, to be honest. And anyway, I'm not

74

exactly going there to get to know her.'

'Are you not?' Andrew said, with a raised eyebrow.

'What do you mean?' John opened Andrew's second beer.

'Well, there's two things. First of all, compared to when you first got here, you seem much more relaxed, which seems a little dubious. Then, second of all, the thing her son said to you … it doesn't make you wonder? Look, I'm not trying to hold it against you, but you must admit to yourself that it does get you wondering.'

John didn't answer at first. He stirred the sauce in the pan, added some seasoning, then said, 'Yeah, of course it makes me wonder. But at the same time, she's moved across the world. She's obviously pretty resourceful.'

'So you're impressed by her.' Andrew said, with a smirk on his face.

'Impressed? And what do you mean, I'm more relaxed? The last time you saw me, I'd just been forced to resign.'

'But I bet you still have your phone on you at all times. And considering what happened up north, I bet you got a bit twitchy, and since it's out of the news, you're probably not exactly happy about that, and the fact that you didn't get a call would only worsen that frustration. Yet you're stood there quite content.'

'Okay, first things first – I'm not content with the situation,' John said, and he paused for a second to think about what Andrew had said. 'Plus it's been a couple of weeks since then. There's still time for a call to come through.'

'But have you thought about it? You know, not going back?'

'What? No. I'm going back. It's just a matter of time.'

Andrew didn't reply immediately. He sipped his beer, and

John finished his and got another from the fridge.

'Right, this is nearly done. Do you want to eat it in here or in the living room?'

'If there's a TV in your living room, then in there.'

'TV? Why? Are Manchester United playing?'

'Yeah. They've just kicked off about five minutes ago.'

'In the living room it is, then.'

They watched the next twenty minutes of football in silence as they ate their food. The only comments came from Andrew either complimenting the food or berating his team's players, who had already conceded twice.

'So, come on, tell me the truth. Are you really not bothered about what happened to her in Colombia?'

'Look, Andrew, when that call comes, I'm going back. It's what I need to do. You know that.'

'Okay, if you say so. It's just …'

'It's just what?'

'I don't know. You just seem content.'

'Content because I know I'll be going back soon.'

The match ended with Manchester United making a dramatic comeback, scoring three goals in the last ten minutes of the game, something that Andrew was ecstatic about. John had once supported a team but eventually lost interest. But he enjoyed watching the players on the pitch scrambling about for the ball, for that last-minute goal that would win them the glory. It was tactics and teamwork, things that reminded him of operations.

When Andrew had left, after all the beer had been drunk and all the food had been eaten and they had laughed together, John couldn't help but return to what he had said earlier. Content. How could he be content? This was not the situation he wanted. In the end, he put it down to him having his childhood best friend over for dinner, something that he had seldom done since he'd joined the police.

15

I properly began training for the police when I was at university, and although I occasionally went to the gym while I was in sixth form, sometimes with Andrew but mainly on my own, I was too focused on my studies to really put in the effort required to make any real progress.

I knew when applying to university that I didn't necessarily need to go in order to join the police. But when speaking to a recruitment adviser, they suggested that I did. It would give me greater chances of career progression and promotion later down the line. For a week after hearing this, I was torn between whether to go or not. University was three more years of study. Three more years in which I would not be out arresting the awful people that plagued so many families.

It was my mum, however, who convinced me to go in the end. All she said was that she regretted not going and she didn't want me to risk feeling the same regret when I was older. This regret of

hers, I could feel, came from the simple fact that ever since my father had gone to prison – or perhaps when he died, I could never really tell – she had replayed something in her mind repeatedly, like a highlight reel, except this wasn't a greatest hits. It was all the times she had been hurt, all the times she had cried. And she replayed those haunting memories back and wondered all the time what she could have done to avoid it. She believed that if she had gone to university, she would never have met my father, or at the very least been in a position to earn more money and therefore escape him sooner. And although I never asked, I hoped that my going to university helped her to be more at peace with her entire situation than if I had just joined the police.

Andrew and I both wanted to go to the same university – partly to stay together, partly because this place was where we individually wanted to study.

I remember the day we collected our A-level results. It felt like judgement day; the rest of our lives hinged on this single moment of opening the envelope and staring down at the paper to see the single letters next to each subject.

While most parents were told to wait in the car, my mum insisted that she would be coming into school with me. I was going to ask her to come with me anyway, but she beat me to it. She held my hand tightly, like she did when I was four because I used to run off. She had a smile on her face, like she already knew I had achieved the grades I needed to get into my desired university and she was looking forward to seeing the smile on my face. Being one of the few people who had brought a parent along with them, I thought I might get some funny looks from my fellow students. But they all knew the story. So that day, we received a lot of sympathetic smiles.

Andrew, who was walking behind us, was doing his best not to laugh. I could hear his laughter, though, subdued by his hand and the occasional cough. Not that he could laugh, because he had a smear of dirt on his face. It was that summer when we had started our gardening business. I can't remember whose garden we were working on that day. It wasn't Mr and Mrs Clarke's, because they would have gotten beer for us, and we wouldn't be completely sober turning up to get our grades. But I only told him about the dirt after we had our results. I told him it was revenge for giggling like a girl, and we both laughed.

Andrew and I walked up to the desk where they handed out the envelopes, and with the envelope in hand, I had never known a piece of paper to weigh so much. I wasn't sure if I was still sweating from the work or because not just my future but, I believed, my mum's peace of mind was in my hands, and I looked up to see her as I walked back. I must have had a worried expression on my face, because her smile only grew and she put her thumbs up. This was permission for me to open the envelope.

I looked at Andrew, Andrew looked at me, and in unison we opened them, pulled out the paper, and saw the grades. We looked back at each other with wide eyes, and smiles stretched across our faces. I ran up to my mum and hugged her, and she failed to hold back tears.

University was a whole different world for me. The most revealing thing was when I learned that my childhood was not unique.

Domestic violence could wear any disguise it wanted to. There was no discretion. Anyone, unfortunately, could be a target. I guess it goes without saying that this motivated me as I went to the gym. My father had gone without much of a fight – he was a coward. But I had heard stories where this was not the case. Being strong, then, was in my mind a necessity to make sure I could take away those who sought to do harm to others.

And whenever a terrorist was successful, even though they were a rarity, it didn't matter where in the country or what city it had happened in, I was always reminded of the day I saw Andrew and his dad at the kitchen table, crying because of their loss. Terrorists didn't care who they hurt. As long as people died, it didn't matter to them.

I still can't decide, not even now, what is worse: a targeted attack on an individual or a targeted attack on strangers.

I did limit how much I drank; I didn't want to do anything stupid under the influence that would affect me getting into the police. When Andrew and I did go out, it was inevitable, really, that without responsibilities and with no parents around, we would try to chat up as many girls as we could. I guess I got it right first time, because the girl I met on my first night out I ended up staying with for a year. Not that our first couple of dates would have suggested that that would be the case.

I don't want to sound ridiculous, but I fear I might. I'm not sure I can really be blamed for my actions to begin with. I always overcompensated when it came to being respectful and nice towards her to the extent that she initially thought I was desperate or had some kind of kink that involved worshipping the ground

81

someone walked on. But I just never wanted her to feel like my mum must have done. I never wanted to upset her or see her cry or make her feel like she wasn't enough. It took me a couple of months to tone down how I acted around her. If anything, with it being my first relationship, it was more like training for the real thing. I made mistakes – we both did. Nothing too serious, but we learned a lot about relationships. And that's why it came to an end. It was like the course was over and we had gotten out of it all we were ever going to get, and we both agreed that was the case. There weren't any tears.

A few months later, when our feelings for each other had dissolved enough, we still saw each other as friends. I remember her being a big supporter of my ambition to join the police force, and for that I will always be grateful. Mainly because university was the last time I had a meaningful relationship. Everything was put to the side when I started my police training. Relationships were pushed off the shelf eventually.

It was my mum, however, as usual, who, when the opportunity came up, suggested I go into counterterrorism after a few years of patrolling the streets. I think she wanted me to distance myself as much as possible from anything that could be linked to my father. I think she just wanted it all to be over with.

It was my first week in counterterrorism. After five years of being on the streets, after making over a thousand arrests, 246 being for domestic abuse, I had applied to the counterterrorism unit.

A team was on a raid in the early morning. Claire, my new

boss, had told me to go along, not to take part but just to observe. Having only been there a week, I hadn't seen much of the planning, but the brief I had seen that morning suggested that this raid shouldn't be a challenge for any highly trained operative.

The only thing I had picked up on was that the team leader on this operation had, two months ago, been gifted with a baby girl. In fact, as he was showing me around the unit on my first day, he spoke at length when we got to his desk about how incredible it was to be a father. He showed picture after picture of her and told me the stories behind each of them, gushing over her while he did. I can still remember her name: Emily.

It's a regret of mine that I didn't raise my immediate concerns with Claire earlier. But I had only been there for a week. I still didn't know everybody's names, and my few years in the police couldn't compete with those who had a mountain of service years to their names. I justified it to myself by thinking that this man would focus once he was on the mission, the same way I did whenever I was out on patrol. Whenever I visited my mum, I acted differently, adapting to different scenarios. I thought this guy would be the same. I thought wrong.

It turned out that it was his first raid since becoming a father. He was on point for the raid, the first man in the door, and when the door was kicked in and he charged in, his eyes looking down his rifle's sights, he peeled into the living room just like they had rehearsed, with the operative behind covering him. The team moved like clockwork, efficient, precise. This was, however, until the new father was met with an enemy carrying a gun.

Instead of taking the shot, the report said, the team leader jumped to the side. The result: the operative covering him took a round to the shoulder, and it took a third person entering the living room to put the enemy down.

I read the team leader's report. It was just six pages of him trying to justify his mistake. In the end, he admitted that he was in the wrong and he wanted to leave the service with immediate effect. His request was granted.

The operative who had been shot made a full recovery. His name is Steve, and he's still on the unit to this day.

What I couldn't help but conclude, and eventually everyone else speculated as well, was that the team leader wouldn't have moved out of the enemy's line of sight if he hadn't been a father to a two-month-old child. If he had been childless, he would have remained in the enemy's firing line to get the shot despite the risk to himself. Except, I guess, thoughts of a fatherless daughter flashed through his mind and he made a selfish decision. It was a miracle nobody was killed. Now, it wasn't the case that no one on the unit had children. I guess some were better at dealing with it than others.

From that single episode, I learned a lesson – never to get close enough to someone to limit your effectiveness on an operation. And although I might have been able to put aside my private relationships when in a professional environment, seeing a man being rushed to hospital after the mistake of someone who couldn't put them aside gave me a wake-up call that life can come to an end thanks to someone else's avoidable mistake. So avoid them I did.

As I look back on what I have done so far in the police and how I have lived my life, I think this might be my biggest regret. I put everything on the line for this job. So, to an extent, I abandoned my mum. I had to know that she could live without me, so I started to visit her less and less until it was only a few times a year. I justified this to myself with the fact that she had made plenty of new friends thanks to her bakery. I never asked her how she felt about my absence. We hardly baked cakes with each other anymore or gardened together. But she never told me to come home and see her, so I went along thinking that it was okay because she knew why I was doing this. She knew I was involved in something bigger than just us; it was a duty I felt I had to fulfil because I had spent years cowering away from my father.

My relationship with my then girlfriend dissolved away. I became distant and she became upset, frustrated, lost. I put her through a lot and I'm not proud of it. But to let her go was difficult. To be alone in a job where stress can be rife ... it was good to know you had someone to talk to, someone who would listen. But I also started to keep her at arm's length. Because this was duty. It was hard on her and even harder on her when she ended it. But what else were we meant to do? She couldn't go on like this, and I could no longer fulfil her emotional needs. And I wouldn't let her come close to mine.

This was bigger than me. This was duty.

85

16

As he made his breakfast, John thought about whether he was content. He didn't have his best friend coming around later for beers and football; it was just a day in which he would make a start on sorting out the overgrown trees and orchard. And he thought about all that still needed to be done, and in this never-ending list he, to his surprise, found himself to be content.

Despite the chill in the air, it was sunny. Perhaps that was why he was looking forward to the day. He wasn't going to be stuck indoors. He would be outside, continuing his operation to restore the garden.

Olivia's car wasn't parked on what was left of the driveway and there were no lights on in the house. She wasn't there and neither was Charlie. It felt strange to be there without them. He wondered why and decided that it was because every time he had come here, there had always been someone there. Was this enough to make it feel strange, he wondered? But he didn't want to think on it too much – he had things to do.

There was a note on the back door and, as promised, a flask waiting for him. He pulled the note from the door and read it.

John,

Like I mentioned, it's Charlie's first day and then I'm going for an interview (wish me luck). I've left some coffee, but Charlie decided that he wanted to take his dinosaur to school today, so you'll have the garden to yourself.

See you later,

Olivia.

He smiled when he finished reading the note and opened the flask. The coffee aroma burst out and the steam danced around his face in the crisp air. He poured himself a cup and took a sip. Then he got started.

It was midday by the time he had finished the coffee, but it had only been an hour before he had realised that he'd underestimated how much work one of the trees needed – the second time he had underestimated something. Yet instead of cursing himself, he laughed and put it down to his decade-long hiatus from the profession.

The tree in the corner of the garden had stretched out its branches into the neighbour's garden and they were now resting on the neighbour's roof. It was a miracle that it hadn't done any damage.

He looked down at the branches all piled up and told himself he would deal with them after he'd had his lunch. They would all need cutting down further before they went into the plastic tarpaulin bags and then off to the tip.

He sat down at the outside table and ate his lunch. While he usually ate lunch at home, he decided he would take advantage of the cloudless sky, even if it was cold. He didn't have an outdoor set of tables and chairs in his garden and had no desire to get one – he wasn't going to be there long enough, he told himself, to enjoy them.

Olivia's car pulled into the drive, tyres crunching the gravel. A few moments later, she appeared out of the side door, smiling.

'Hey, John,' she said. 'Did you find the coffee?'

'I did,' he said, waving the empty flask in the air. 'Thank you.'

'How have you gotten on today?'

John pointed towards the large pile of branches and said, 'It looks like a lot, but there's still more that needs to be done. I can't remember Andrew and I ever trimming these trees, so God knows when they were last done.'

'Do you think it's going to take longer than you thought?'

'This tree, yes, but the others should be alright.'

'You must be trying to con me out of money,' Olivia joked.

'No. It's only because I couldn't see the entire tree from this garden with half of it being on the neighbour's side.'

'Excuses, excuses.' Olivia tutted.

'Anyway, how did your job interview go?'

Her smile grew and she said, 'Really well. They seemed to like me and … well, I think it went well.'

'Congratulations. What exactly is the job?'

'It's just a business administration job. I mean, it's nothing too exciting, but it means that one, I can stay in the country and two, I can work from home, which means I don't have to think about childcare for Charlie.'

'It sounds good. How long until you hear anything?'

'They said two weeks, but I'm still applying to other jobs in case I don't get this one.'

'Well, it seems they like you, so I'm sure you'll do fine.'

'Thanks. Are you eating your lunch out here?'

'I'm just enjoying the sun. I've spent all morning in the tree's shadow.'

'It's a bit cold out here. Why don't you come in and I can make you some more coffee?'

'If that's okay.'

'Yeah, it's fine.'

John picked up his packed lunch, followed Olivia inside, and took a seat at the kitchen table. 'So how did Charlie get on this morning?'

Olivia laughed, then said, 'What a morning. He looked so cute in his little uniform and it was quite funny seeing him walk with his dinosaur in hand. He didn't really know what to make of it at first, suddenly being surrounded by loads of other children. But I was impressed with him. He didn't cry or anything. In fact, it was me who cried afterwards in the car – and I was worried my makeup would run.'

Olivia opened the fridge door and looked inside briefly before closing it again and looking through the cupboards.

'Anyway, yeah, he seemed to be okay, but seeing my little boy all grown up for his first day of school … it's part of the reason I chose to come here. The education system is better than what we have at home, so it felt like all of this was coming together.'

'I'm glad to hear it.'

'I'll be picking him up at half three, so I'll be out of the house again after that – you don't mind, do you?'

'No, of course I don't.'

'Good. Thank you.'

Olivia returned to the fridge after her search through the cupboards had been unsuccessful, but she soon closed it again and turned to look at the kitchen.

'Can't decide what to eat?' John said.

'No, not really. I've not really done much of a big food shop since I've been here, so I don't have much in the cupboards and I've had such a busy morning, so I'm quite hungry. I could eat a bandeja paisa.'

'A what?'

'A bandeja paisa. It's basically a big calorie-dense meal. It was originally meant for workers to give them sufficient energy to work all day. Nowadays it's usually eaten on a special occasion, and today kind of is a special occasion.'

'It certainly is,' John agreed, feeling somewhat guilty that he had eaten the last of his sandwich. 'What's in it?'

'What isn't in it! You've got sausage, beef, rice, beans, a pork rind called chicharron. A slice of avocado is thrown in as well – not sure why. To be healthy, I guess. And it's usually topped with a fried egg.'

'Sounds similar to an English breakfast.'

'I've never had one of those before.'

'You should try it one day. Although if you do it properly, you

90

won't have to eat anything again until tea.'

'What goes into an English breakfast, then?'

'It's an ongoing debate,' John said and laughed to himself. 'But it's usually sausage, bacon, fried egg – but you can have scrambled or poached – baked beans, toast, black pudding, mushroom and tomato, and hash browns.'

'Sounds like you won't need to eat anything for a week! What did you have in your sandwich?'

'It was nothing exciting. Just ham and cheese.'

'You're not much of a cook, then?'

John thought about all the times he had spent baking with his mum after school and a smile appeared on his face. 'I used to bake quite a lot, actually, with my mum after school.'

'What sort of things did you bake?' Olivia asked, leaning against the counter, seemingly forgetting about her appetite.

'All sorts of things – cakes, bread, pastries. I enjoyed it quite a lot, actually.'

'What was your favourite thing to bake?'

'Fruit cake. Well, I say that – it was my favourite thing to eat, which made it my favourite thing to bake.'

'Did the rest of your family like it as well?'

John paused for a moment. The warm thoughts of baking were interrupted by the coldness of his father.

'I was an only child, so it was mainly me and Mum that ate it all.'

'What about your father?' It was inevitable, John knew, that that question would come next.

He took a breath before saying, 'My father wasn't a nice man.

91

He didn't really care about what we baked.'

'I'm sorry to hear that.'

'It's okay. He's dead now. He doesn't bother us anymore.'

'And what about your mother?'

'She died a year ago.' John looked down at the table, struggling to think of anything to say next.

'Have you made fruit cake since?'

'No. I haven't. In fact, I've not baked for a long time. I guess life just got in the way.'

'This might seem like a bit of a stretch, but of course we've moved over here and everything and I've been meaning to start getting Charlie to cook, or at least be involved with it. I think it's a good skill to have, to know how to cook and to bake. And I've never made something like fruit cake before in my life. And you can say no if you want to, but maybe you could show us how to bake a fruit cake sometime? If it's okay with you, of course. I mean, you don't have to if you don't want to. It would just be nice, I guess.'

John was initially taken aback by the offer. It wasn't something that he'd been expecting to be asked that day. Many years ago, however, he had been in a similar situation except for the emigration, when it was just his mum and him. He wondered if perhaps doing this would take him back to those days after school when he had spent the entire afternoon smiling. If her husband had been a bad man like Charlie had said, how could he reject the offer? She was a single mother trying to create a better life for her child. He had seen it before, lived through it, and knew the joy it gave him and his mum.

'It wasn't what I was expecting to be asked today. But yeah,

I'm sure I can.'

'Really? Thank you. I'm not sure when, though, because I doubt I have the ingredients.'

'Do you want me to write them down for you?'

'Yes please. I'll probably go shopping later this week.'

John wrote down the ingredients from memory, impressed with himself that even after all these years, he still remembered them. He gave Olivia the piece of paper and saw her smile reach her eyes.

'So later this week, then?' he said.

'Yeah, later this week.'

John went back outside and continued to prune the tree. The more he cut away, the more the sun shone through. He probably went at least two hours without thinking about the phone in his pocket, but when it vibrated, he almost dropped the tree cutters. He pulled it out and saw that it was just a message from Andrew about the weekend's football match.

17

Antonia walked through the underground factory, black suitcase in tow, following Carl to Gary's office. Carl opened the door for her, and she walked in.

'Well, it's certainly good to see you again, Antonia.' Gary cleared his desk and Antonia dropped her suitcase on it.

'Two lots, just like you asked for.'

'Thank you, Carl,' Gary said, and Carl left the office. 'Please take a seat. This is quite something we've got going on here, don't you think? Would you like a cigarette?'

'Why not?' Antonia took one from the packet offered to her and let Gary light it. She took a seat, blowing smoke out of her nose. 'It certainly is. I'm glad my parts worked successfully. And I'm very glad you rang me again for more.'

'You were always going to be my first choice.'

'But I have to say, your reputation has you working with drug dealers. And the people who were killed a couple weeks ago weren't drug dealers. As I understand it.'

'I just go where the money is. If you don't want your parts to be involved, then let me know. I can always get someone else.'

Antonia took a drag of her cigarette. 'Don't you worry, big boy. I go where the money is as well.'

'How did you know that was us last week?'

'Carl told me on the drive up here. He liked what he used.'

Gary stubbed his cigarette out and stood up. 'Let's get down to business, shall we?' He opened up the black suitcase, pulled out the plastic parts, and admired them in his hands. 'How do you get these so perfect all the time?'

'That's my little secret,' she said.

'I do like a girl with secrets.'

Gary put the weapon together. He weighed it in his hand and aimed it at the side wall. He cocked it, pulled the trigger, and heard the satisfying click.

'Another perfect weapon. Thank you, Antonia. The money will follow shortly.'

She stubbed the cigarette out and took a business card from her pocket. 'As always, my number's changed.' She dropped it onto the desk.

'I'm sure I'll be contacting you soon. Maybe this could be the start of something.'

She walked to the door, locked it, and turned to look back at Gary.

'If this is the start of something,' she said, sauntering towards him, 'then we should just get started.' She grabbed him, pulled him in, and whispered into his ear, 'How do you like your secretive women?'

18

Olivia hadn't mentioned anything about baking since they had agreed to it earlier in the week. Days later, however, after lunch, she told John that she was going to go food shopping and asked him if he was still able to bake with her and Charlie.

He wasn't going to admit it out loud, but the prospect did fill him with a yearning for the familiar, for the memories he had with his mum that didn't involve his father.

'Yeah, that's fine,' he said.

She returned a few hours later with a car full of groceries and a five-year-old child trying to tell her about his day. John went to offer a hand and found that she had managed to unload most of the car already, but he picked up the last bag and closed the boot.

'Hi, John,' Charlie said as John walked through to the kitchen with the bag.

'Hi, Charlie. Did you have a good day?'

'Yeah, well, first of all ...' and John found he couldn't get a word in until Charlie had finished talking, and when he did, John had several questions floating around inside his head and wondered if his school days had been filled with as much chaos as Charlie's. The thought of it made him laugh.

John went to go back outside when Olivia said, 'So when do you want to do this? Ideally I'd like to get it all done and have the kitchen cleaned up before five, when I cook tea.'

John thought for a moment, then said, 'We can start now if you want. Where are the ingredients?'

Olivia looked around at the piles of plastic bags on the counter tops. 'I'm not sure. In fact, I'll pack this all away and call you back when we're good to go.'

'Okay,' John said. 'Are you looking forward to baking, Charlie?'

A smile shot across his face, and he said, 'Yeah!'

She called him back in fifteen minutes later – fifteen minutes where he had to admit to himself that he hadn't done much more to the garden. His heart beat a little faster and a smile crept out, but when he felt his phone in his pocket, he regained control of this sudden injection of happiness and told himself to remember why he was here doing this job and where he was soon, hopefully, going to go.

'What do we do first?' Olivia said.

'John, what can my dinosaur do?' Charlie said, walking up to him, waving the toy in the air.

'I think we'll put him on the side and he can watch for now, okay, Charlie?' Olivia said.

'Okay, Mum.' Charlie put his toy onto the kitchen table and

turned it so it faced the three of them.

'Right, so what do we do first?' Olivia asked again.

'Do you have the recipe?' John asked.

'No,' Olivia said. 'Why would I have the recipe? This is you showing us.'

'Right, okay then.' He had a small team; he had the resources and a deadline to meet. He found it funny how remnants of his job crept into everyday life, even if at times these were dubious comparisons. And with two sets of eyes on him waiting to hear something, he said, mainly to Charlie, 'As we're going to be handling food, it's best we wash our hands first.'

'Yeah, your hands are really dirty,' Charlie pointed out.

'That's because John is working hard in the garden,' Olivia said.

'When can I go out and help?'

Olivia lifted Charlie up to the tap and he washed his hands. 'It's getting warmer next week. But it's up to John, really.' Charlie twisted his head to look at the gardener while his hands remained under the tap.

'You can do if you want, Charlie. If that's okay with you,' he said to Olivia.

Olivia chuckled to herself, then said, 'It's fine, honestly. He'll probably get bored after ten minutes anyway.'

'No, I won't.'

'Well, looks like next week you can help me, then, Charlie,' John said.

'Yay!'

John wondered what he was going to get Charlie to do and

hoped Olivia was right and he would get bored after ten minutes. He wasn't there to entertain a child, but he wasn't there to upset him either. He would find him something to do, he told himself.

'Okay, so now we've washed our hands, we first need to preheat the oven to 170 degrees.'

Olivia set the oven and when she was done, John continued, 'Then we need to get a large mixing bowl and put all the ingredients into the bowl except for the fruit – that comes later.'

Olivia got out a large mixing bowl and a wooden spoon and picked up her son so he could see what was happening on the worktop.

John, under the watchful eye of his audience, weighed out the ingredients in grams and allowed Charlie to pour the sugar onto the scales. He had to get a spoon to scoop the majority of it back into the packet after Charlie misjudged how much he needed to tip the packet. It was a mistake that cost them time, and even though it was only a couple of minutes, John's anxiety hit him on instinct. He had spent years rushing through the process before his father got home. Yet here, he was, the only one who cared about the minuscule mistake. Olivia and Charlie laughed about it, and while John rushed to put the excess sugar back, he could feel their inquisitive eyes looking at him, wondering why he was acting so quickly. He stopped and looked at them. And for the first time in his life, he realised that there was no reason to rush. No one was going to come through the front door and start barking at them like a feral dog. It was just the three of them and it would remain that way. There would be no intruders, no monsters that would scare him upstairs.

'Are you okay, John?' Olivia asked.

The anxiety was swapped suddenly for embarrassment and John said, 'Yeah. My father never really liked us baking. So we always made sure we were quick.'

They were silent for a moment. There was still so much between them that hadn't been said. Their pasts that they hadn't spoken about. But Olivia smiled at him, a reassurance that there was no need to rush.

'Dad's not here, John,' Charlie said.

'Anyway, what else needs to be weighed out?' Olivia said, and the vein of awkwardness that sat in the air dissolved and they returned to the task at hand.

With the rest of the ingredients weighed out and poured into the mixing bowl by Charlie under John's guidance, John helped Charlie stir them together into a smooth paste. When the ingredients had been stirred into a smooth paste, John said, 'Do you want to try some?'

'It's not been cooked yet,' Olivia said.

'That doesn't matter.'

John dipped his finger into the mixture and licked it off, and Charlie did the same. John watched for a reaction and after a few seconds his face lit up, so he stuck his fingers in again and hooked out as much of the mixture as he could with his little hand. Olivia did the same, also impressed by the taste.

'It tastes even better when it's cooked,' John said, and he dipped the tip of his finger into the mixture and rubbed it onto Charlie's nose. Charlie giggled at John and wiped it off with the back of his hand.

'Don't you dare do that to me,' Olivia said, with a smirk on her face.

John looked at Charlie. Charlie looked at the mixture on his hand and went and wiped it across his mum's cheek, bursting into laughter as he did it.

'Thanks for that, Charlie,' she said, putting him back on the floor and reaching for a piece of kitchen roll to wipe her face.

John asked Charlie to pour the dried fruit into the bowl, and he did so without spilling it. Then, with all the ingredients mixed together, John got Olivia to scoop the mixture into the baking tin.

'Right, now it's time to put it in the oven. It's going to take a little over an hour,' John said.

'An hour?' Charlie said. 'Why does it take so long.'

'I'm not sure,' John said as he put the cake into the oven.

'We'll start on your homework and when we're done, the cake will be ready,' Olivia said.

'Okay.'

'Thank you, John,' Olivia said.

'It was my pleasure,' he said. 'I'll have to come back in an hour to try some.'

He returned to the garden, leaving behind a kitchen that had been filled with laughter and smiles. Throughout the entire time he had been in there, he realised as he walked back outside, he hadn't once given a passing thought to the phone in his pocket.

An hour later, Olivia came out and called for him. He checked the time on his phone; it was nearly the time of day when he would have finished and headed home anyway. He looked back at the orchard and was happy with the progress he had made.

The kitchen had the rich aroma of a freshly baked fruit cake, a scent that sent John back to memories that were decades old but still vivid in his mind like they had happened yesterday. He noticed the homework book open on the kitchen table and the pencil resting on top of it.

Olivia had already taken the cake from the oven, taken it out of the baking tin, and let it cool down on a chopping board. 'Do you want to cut it?' she asked, handing him the handle of a knife. He took the knife, saw Charlie smiling next to him, and cut into the cake. He cut three slices and handed out the plates and they all took a bite. The cake was met with immediate praise, and it gave John a warm feeling inside. This wasn't like when he cooked for the people on his unit – that was food to line their stomachs so they didn't get too drunk; it was more for function than for pleasure. This cake, however, didn't need to be made. There was no reason for it to exist other than that Olivia had thought it would be good for Charlie to start being involved in the cooking process. He might only be five years old, three years younger than John when he and his mum had first started to bake, but John envied the little boy to an extent – to have all this time to spend with his mum and never have to worry about her husband coming through the door to carpet the day in violence and hatred. This cake had been made for the sheer pleasure of trying, in Olivia and Charlie's case, something new. And the full house of smiles made John's shoulders drop and he allowed himself to relax. To feel content.

'Thank you, John,' Olivia said. 'I'll have to make some traditional Colombian food for you one day.'

'You don't have to.'

'No, I insist. You like the cake, don't you, Charlie?'

Charlie, with his mouth full, responded by enthusiastically nodding his head.

'It sounds nice, I guess,' John said.

'Of course it will be nice.'

'Well, if it's anything like your coffee, I'm sure it will be. Anyway, I'm done for the day, so I'll see you tomorrow.'

Olivia and Charlie both said goodbye and he exited out of the side door.

19

It was a week later, and the weather had improved. The sun finally brought some warmth, and the final dregs of winter now appeared to have drained away to reveal the beginnings of spring.

Since Charlie had last mentioned helping him out, John had kept an eye on the weather to anticipate which day was likely to be the one when he would have his little helper. Today the temperature would crawl into double figures, the highest so far this year, and while the last two days had been wet, today came with the promise of dry weather. If it was going to be this week, he thought, then it would be today.

He wondered how he felt about it. A hint of joy drove through his body at the thought of Charlie helping him, even if it would only be for the anticipated ten minutes. But the first dry day of the week would also, he thought, provide him with a sense of contentment. It would be nice not to return home soaked through with a thick layer of mud wrapped around his boots.

When he got to Olivia's, she was out taking Charlie to school, and John made a start on the three vegetable patches. The borders needed restoring and the broken cages that kept the birds away required a complete rebuild with new materials; the wood hadn't been treated in a decade and nature had eaten them up.

He started by removing what was left of the cages. While the wood would be thrown away, or at the very least chopped up for firewood, the chicken wire could be reused, so he rolled it up and put it to the side. Then he went about pouring out a mug of coffee from the flask that Olivia had left for him, and he was sitting drinking it when she returned.

She hadn't bothered going into the house and instead had come into the garden through the side gate. 'Do you remember two weeks ago when I said I was going for a job interview?'

John nodded and said that he did.

'They just rang me after I'd dropped Charlie off and they've given me the job.' Her face was a beacon of happiness – a weight lifted off her shoulders as the prospect of remaining in the country was now a certainty.

'Congratulations,' John said. 'When do you start?'

'Monday. Yes. I can't quite believe it.'

'Well, I'm very happy for you.' John smiled at her, and she smiled back.

'How's the coffee?' she asked.

'As always, it's great.'

'Just let me know when you need more.'

'I will, thank you.'

Besides refills of coffee, the next time he spoke to Olivia was when she announced that she was going to school to pick up Charlie. When they returned, John could hear the kid talking about something, the tone of his voice one of great excitement, and he guessed that he had just been granted permission to come out and help him.

Olivia came out of the side door and found her gardener finishing off the second of the cages. 'Is it okay if Charlie comes and gives you a hand? I don't want him getting in the way or anything.'

'No, that's fine,' John said.

'Do you know what you're going to get him to do?'

'There isn't really much he can do, but he can always pass me the nails I need to attach the chicken wire to the pole.'

'That will definitely bore him after a few minutes,' Olivia joked.

'I haven't really got anything else for him to do.'

'It's okay, I'm sure he'll be happy doing that for a few minutes.'

Charlie appeared a few minutes later, wrapped up in a thick coat and scarf that obscured most of his face. John tried not to laugh as he walked over, the thick coat limiting his ability to move. Even though he couldn't see the bottom half of his face, John could tell from his bright eyes how happy he was to be out there, and he had brought his dinosaur along with him.

'Mum says I can help you, John,' he said.

'Well, I'm glad to hear it. Why don't you put your dinosaur on the table next to my mug?'

'Okay.'

When Charlie returned, John asked, 'Have you got a name for him yet?'

'No. I haven't had time to think of one.'

How could a five-year-old not have found the time to name a toy, John wondered? He concluded that he must have heard the saying from his mum and copied it.

'What's funny?'

'Oh, nothing. Anyway, I've got an important job for you today, Charlie. I'm rebuilding the cages and I need to nail the chicken wire to the poles. So could you, when I ask, pass me one of them from the box?' John pointed to the box. Charlie looked from the box back up to John and gave an enthusiastic reply that, on the face of it, made it seem like he would be out there for more than ten minutes.

Charlie passed the first nail and watched John hammer it into the pole and did the same with the second one. After the third, however, he started to wander off slightly, walking around the garden, and John thought he would eventually take himself back inside. But when he called him over, he returned with a little run and handed John another nail before returning to the part of the garden he'd been looking at.

The next time John called him back, he noticed that the tips of Charlie's fingers were covered in mud.

'What have you been doing?' John asked.

'Nothing.'

'How come your fingers are all grubby?'

'Well, at school we started making bug houses, and I'm starting one by the tree.'

'A bug house?' John questioned as much to himself as to Charlie.

'Yeah. I want to show you.'

'Okay. Just let me finish off this last pole. Can you pass me another nail, please?'

Charlie handed him the final nail, a new lease of joy behind his eyes as he paced around waiting for John to hammer it in. When it was done, John asked Charlie to hand him the mallet and he did so, despite John seeing that he was gradually losing patience. John used the mallet to bash the pole into the ground. He checked to make sure it was sturdy enough and assessed that it was. He looked at the remaining poles that needed finishing and told himself that he would only be a few minutes.

The bug house had been built at the base of one of the trees in the orchard. Charlie had dug tunnels under the exposed roots using a stick he had found.

'I need some more sticks and some leaves to build a little hut for them,' Charlie said.

'That's great, Charlie. I'll leave you to do this and I can finish off the cage.'

'No, John, I need you to help me with this. There's still more to do. At school we make them really big.'

John thought about how the two of them could compete with

an entire class of children. He looked back towards the house and didn't see Olivia in the kitchen window. He decided a few more minutes wouldn't hurt. Charlie *would* eventually get bored.

Except Charlie didn't get bored and John foolishly lost track of time. He showed Charlie the large tarpaulin bags that were filled with cuttings that could be used to improve the bug huts in line with the expanded tunnel and roads that Charlie hadn't stopped digging with his stick. He told himself he would finish the cages today, even if it would be getting dark by the time he did.

'I need some bugs to live in it,' Charlie said.

John was placing leaves on top of the small structure he had built and said, 'It's still a bit too cold for them. But I'm sure when it's warmer, they'll come and live here.''

'Are you sure there aren't any in the garden?'

'There will be. It's just too cold for them.'

'We need to go and check,' Charlie said, seemingly ignoring John, who found himself going along with Charlie to look for bugs. Having spent a few weeks in the garden, John had a good idea of where they might find some.

John took him to the back of the garden where, a decade ago, Mr Clarke had wanted them to pile up some of the garden waste – bits of wood and leaves – in the hope that it would decompose and turn into fertile soil for his vegetable patch. Years later, however, not all of it had decomposed, and John knew that if bugs were going to be anywhere, they would be there.

'If I move a few of these old logs back, we should find some.'

Charlie stood at John's side, wide eyed, mouth agape. John

took off a couple of the top logs and on the underside, he found bugs. He placed them down by their feet and Charlie crouched down to inspect what was there.

'There's so many of them,' he said.

'Do you know the names of some of them?' John asked.

Charlie thought about his answer for a moment before admitting that he didn't.

'Well, this one is a woodlouse.' John allowed the insect to crawl onto his hand. 'It's got an exoskeleton, so it's bones are on the outside of its body.' John didn't know if Charlie understood what this meant, but he continued to stare in amazement.

'Do you want to hold it?' John asked. Charlie put out his hand and John encouraged the insect to walk onto the boy's palm.

'It tickles,' was Charlie's initial reaction.

'It almost looks like a dinosaur,' John said.

'No, it doesn't,' Charlie said. 'It doesn't look like my dinosaur.'

'You can get lots of different dinosaurs. They don't all look like your toy. Some of them could even fly.' And Charlie's eyes lit up further.

'We've also got a ground beetle here,' John said, picking one up.

'Wow! Do dinosaurs look like that as well?' Charlie allowed the woodlouse to continue exploring his hand.

'Some probably did, yeah.'

'Can I hold that one as well?'

'Yeah, of course you can.' John placed the beetle in Charlie's

110

hand, and he watched it crawl all over his hand, then looked up at John, smiling from ear to ear.

'What's your favourite dinosaur?' John asked.

'The one like my toy,' Charlie said.

'Do you know what it's called?'

'Is it a T. rex?'

'It is, yeah. Its full name is *Tyrannosaurus rex*.'

Charlie attempted to give the full name of his dinosaur but couldn't quite get around the words, so he stuck to calling it a T. rex.

'You know, there's a museum in town with a big T. rex skeleton in it.'

'Now, this doesn't exactly look like the process of building the vegetable cages,' Olivia said, startling both John and Charlie.

'Mum, look at all these bugs. We've made a bug house like we've done in school.'

'A bug house. Not a vegetable cage, then?'

'Come have a look, Mum.' Charlie took his mum's hand and walked her over to the bug house.

'I'll finish the cages before I go. There isn't much left to do.'

'It's okay, John. I'm just amazed that you managed to keep him out here for this long.'

'So am I, to be honest.'

'John said he's going to take me to a museum to see a tyran ... osa ... tyran ... a T. rex skeleton like my dinosaur.'

'Did he now?' Olivia said, looking back at John.

'That's not what I said. I just mentioned there was a museum in town with a large T. rex skeleton in it. It's a natural history museum. I remember it because it's next to a museum that once had an exhibition on the Roman empire. That's what I was into when I was younger.'

'Oh, really? Then we might have to go. Did you want to go to the museum, Charlie?'

'Yeah,' came the immediate reply. 'And John's coming with us as well.'

Olivia and John exchanged a glance, then Olivia said, 'You can come along if you want … I don't mind if you do.'

John almost stopped walking as he thought about the proposition, then he said, 'It's okay. I can tell you where it is, but I'm not sure about coming along …'

'Please, John. I need you to show me the dinosaur,' Charlie said.

'Yeah, John. You need to show us the dinosaur,' Olivia added, smiling.

Again, John thought about the answer. Was it a step too far? He had already baked with them, but that seemed to be more of an education for Charlie and a chance for Olivia to enjoy something that many other people enjoyed in this country. But to go out with them to a museum? He wasn't sure. But it didn't immediately fill him with a sense of dread or a surge of discomfort. It made him, to his surprise, a little nervous to be asked to go somewhere with the two of them, especially with Olivia almost encouraging him.

'Please, John,' Charlie said again.

'Okay. Okay, yeah, I guess I can come with you.'

Charlie gave out a cheerful yell of celebration. He let go of his mum's hand and ran up to John and hugged his leg.

'That's okay, Charlie.' John looked at Olivia, unsure what to do, but Olivia was laughing to herself, and eventually Charlie let go and returned to his bug house.

'Looks like we can celebrate my job by going to look at a big dinosaur – it better be good,' Olivia said, placing her hand on John's arm.

'It will be good. I'm sure Charlie will enjoy it.'

20

Andrew wanted to repay the favour by cooking dinner for his oldest friend and promised him that his fridge would be filled with beer. John, sensing there was more to it than that, checked the fixtures for his football team and, no surprise, they were playing that night. Strength in numbers, John thought, in terms of having control of what was on the telly, so when he knocked on their door and Andrew answered, the first thing he mentioned once Harriet was in earshot was, 'Have you been watching that new show? It's really good – starts at eight. We should definitely watch it after we've eaten.'

'Piss off, John. We're watching the football.'

'I tried, Harriet,' John said.

'Ten out of ten for trying, John, but one out of ten for execution,' Harriet said.

'What do you mean? I really like the show.'

'What's it called, then?' Andrew said.

'You know … it's called …'

'You haven't got a clue, have you?'

All three of them laughed, and even Sarah, leaning against her mother's shoulder, managed a giggle.

'What's got you in such a good mood?' Harriet asked.

'What do you mean?' John made for the kitchen to check if Andrew had delivered on his promise. He had. John opened a beer and took a sip.

'You just seem more upbeat.'

'Well, I don't know. I guess maybe the more days that go by, the closer I must be to getting a call, right?'

'Sounds logical. How's the gardening?'

John managed an involuntary smile before he answered. 'It's okay. A lot of work, but I'm getting through it.'

'Right. You know if I bump into Olivia in the school playground when she's dropping Charlie off, I speak to her. She says you're a great help. Really appreciates it. Especially when you take Charlie out with you,' Harriet said.

His involuntary smile grew, then he said, 'I mean, it's what she's paying me to do. It's not exactly like I'm going to be around to see it finished. Well, I hope I don't. I've got a duty to return to at some point.'

'When is that point?' Harriet asked.

John paused. 'Soon.'

'It'll be a shame, I think, if you have to go back.'

John forced the involuntary smile away, then asked, 'What do you mean by that?'

'You just seem happier here than when I saw you last.'

115

'Like I said, the more days that pass, the closer I'm getting to receiving a call.'

'If you say so. Also, how are the bug houses coming along? Charlie mentioned them to me.'

John chuckled to himself, then said, 'They're ruining the grass around the base of the trees, but he enjoys making them.'

'He's also looking forward to his trip to the museum as well.'

'Does he tell you everything?' John took another sip of his beer.

'Pretty much.'

'You're taking the kid to a museum?' Andrew said, walking into the kitchen. He made straight for the fridge, making a comment about John starting without him.

'I mentioned about the natural history museum. He likes dinosaurs.'

'Loves dinosaurs,' Harriet chipped in.

'Anyway, I mentioned that there was a huge T. rex skeleton in this museum and he said he wanted to go.'

'As long as you took him,' Harriet added.

'Yeah, basically.'

Andrew and Harriet exchanged looks, then Andrew asked, 'You must have made an impression. Is Olivia allowing you to take him?'

'She was going to take him anyway, I think. But ... but she seemed to want me to come along as well. And I didn't have much else to do, so I thought why not?'

'Why not indeed,' Harriet said to Andrew.

There was a pause in the conversation. They exchanged

glances, and before John could open his mouth to speak again, Andrew said, 'I better start making dinner.'

'Yes, you should. I'm getting hungry,' John said.

Harriet was on her way out of the kitchen when Sarah started stretching out her hands and wriggling in her mum's arms. 'I think she wants a hug from you, John,' Harriet said, handing over her daughter. John didn't get a choice about whether he wanted to hold her or not, but he took her in his arms, and she stopped wriggling and rested her head on his chest. Andrew laughed.

'What is it with you and kids?'

John started to bob up and down like a boat in a harbour and twisted and turned his finger in front of her as she made noises and attempted to grab it with both of her hands. Eventually, John let her take his finger and she held it until, after a few minutes, she stretched out her arms towards her mum and John handed her back.

'I'm going to go and put her down for the night,' Harriet said. Andrew kissed his daughter goodnight, and John waved at her as she left.

'Easily the best thing that's ever happened to me,' Andrew said.

'The beers aren't making you sentimental, are they?'

'I've only had a couple.'

'We should change that.' John went to the fridge and retrieved two more bottles of beer.

'But seriously, when you have kids, you'll see what I mean.'

'I doubt that will be for a long time, mate. In fact, I doubt it at all. I'm not cut out for being a father.'

'That's what I thought, but when it happens, something just

changes. Your priorities change and everything you do in life becomes about this small little bundle.'

'Like a duty, almost?'

'Why does everything you do have to be brought back to counterterrorism?'

'It is a duty, though, isn't it? And I guess it's just how I understand the world.'

Andrew stirred away at the food cooking in the pan. 'Well, yeah, it is a duty. If I don't look after her, she'll be taken from me. And Harriet will of course divorce me. And that's the last thing I want.'

'So marriage is like duty as well, then?'

'Is that a serious question?'

'I don't know. It's more of an observation, really.'

'Not all of life is about kicking in doors and arresting who is on the other side, John. I wouldn't swap this for anything in the world. No amount of money could make me this happy. No amount of going out like we did at uni, chatting up girls, sleeping around, could ever replace a single night with Harriet.'

'To you, maybe. But to me ... what else am I going to do? It's all I know. It's what I'm good at, and you know why I'm doing it.'

'Of course I know why you're doing it, and I get that, really I do. Fighting back against the abusers in this world. But you're in counterterrorism now.'

'That's mainly because my mum wanted me to distance myself from arresting people committing domestic abuse. She didn't want me to be chasing after my father my whole life. She probably thought I'd recover better if I left it in the past.'

118

Andrew continued cooking, remaining quiet for a moment, debating with himself about whether he should say something to his oldest friend that he had held on to for years. He had never mentioned it before for fear of how John would react. It was not his intention to ruin years of friendship over a misunderstanding. He had questioned himself, however, because when was John ever around to have a conversation about this? He took a breath.

'Listen, John, I'm not sure how exactly you're going to take this, but promise me you're not going to take it the wrong way, okay?'

'Take what the wrong way? You're not going to complain about my cooking last week, are you?'

'I'm being serious, John.'

'Fine. I'm all ears.'

'And you won't take it the wrong way?'

'What are you going to say?'

'Listen, I don't think your mum actually wanted you to transfer over to counterterrorism.'

'What do you mean?'

'I think that's something you sought after seeing Craig die all those years ago in the terrorist attack. I think you saw that as another problem to solve. And what I think is that your mum didn't want you to stay in the police forever. I honestly believe that she felt that you would get it out of your system and then go on and live your life. She wanted you to be happy, John.'

John didn't respond at first, and Andrew returned to making dinner. John sipped on his beer and looked towards the window but didn't pay any attention to what was on the other side. He thought about how Andrew had gotten this wrong. His mum had wanted him to go into counterterrorism to distance himself from his previous path. She had said that to him, hadn't she? Craig's death was a tragedy and, like his father's treatment of his mum, something that motivated him to stop further attacks. But what did Andrew mean by her wanting him to be happy? Didn't every mum want that for their child? The police, to him, was a duty and one that he fulfilled with great pride. It was his purpose, wasn't it?

'What do you mean?' he finally said. 'I mean about my mum wanting me to be happy.'

'Your childhood was awful, you know I know that. And until your dad died, the two of you were never really, you know, at peace – you know what I mean, don't you?'

'Yeah, I know what you mean. But she knows I was happy in the police. I'm still happy in the police. I also wouldn't change it for the world.'

'I think she just wanted you to be able to have a family and a marriage that was nothing like hers. She wanted to know that you weren't going to be a reflection of your father – that you weren't going to turn out like him.'

'Where are you getting this from? Did my mum tell you something that you shouldn't have told me?'

'You said you weren't going to take this the wrong way.'

'I'm not. I just think there's something you're not telling me.'

'I'm telling you everything, John. I'm telling you what I think, what I see. This isn't a secret conversation I had with your mum, I promise. Look, I'm telling you this because I actually think you're happy here. Like genuinely happy. And because I seldom see you,

I don't know when I'm going to get the chance to tell you this.'

John remained quiet and finished his beer. He placed the empty bottle on the side and crossed his arms.

'A reflection of my father?' he said eventually.

'Which you haven't done.' But the echoes of the fatherless child crying played in John's head. 'I think she, like us all, wants you to know that there is more to life than being in the police. You can have more than one duty in life. I think she wanted you to completely move away from it at some point. Because you're motivated by all the bad shit that happened to you and your mum when you were a kid. How can you recover if that's all that drives you?'

John thought on this for a moment, then said, 'Look, when that call comes, I'm going back to London. There is nothing else I would rather do with my life. It has a solid purpose and there's been a bump in the road, but I'll be back soon. The more days that pass, the closer I am to going back. Look, I've been back for long enough to know what it's like to be here. If, when I return to London, I don't like it and I do become this "reflection of my father", then I'll come back.'

'I'm not saying you will, or that you were ever like your father. But if you promise me that – that you won't just stay there out of sheer bloody stubbornness – then it'll put my mind at ease.'

'Yeah, whatever, I promise. Now, do you want another beer?'

Andrew said that he did, and he got two out of the fridge. Dinner was served a few minutes later, and Harriet joined the two of them in the lounge as they watched Manchester United win comfortably over the opposition. For someone who didn't want the football on, Harriet seemed happy that it was. And when John left a few hours later, staggering home, he wondered if Harriet had enjoyed the game or enjoyed watching the joy on her husband's face as his team won.

21

It had been talked about last week but only properly arranged with a time and date a few days ago. Now he was walking to their house. It was a Saturday. His nerves were a chronic hum in his body. They had appeared right from the moment he had woken up and remained till now, just as he was about to knock. He kept telling himself that it was just a trip to the museum, a transaction, almost; he was only there because Charlie wanted him to go and to keep him happy. This wasn't for him – he wasn't going to get anything out of it except making sure that this child, whose father wasn't, he assumed, in the picture, would have an enjoyable day. And when he thought that he might be the closest thing Charlie had to a father, he scoffed at the idea, embarrassed by it. How could he be a father figure to a child? He wasn't, he told himself. It was just a nonsense thought.

Olivia answered the door. 'Hi, John. We're nearly ready to go.'

Charlie was putting his shoes on, saw John, decided that the shoelaces could be tied later, and ran up to John to give his leg a hug. John shifted awkwardly on his feet, unsure how to respond to such a warm greeting. He looked to Olivia for some sort of guidance, but she was smiling to herself as she went and picked up Charlie's dinosaur from the sofa.

'You can't forget this, Charlie,' she said, waving his toy at him. At that, he let go of John's leg and clutched the toy in both hands. It was a relief to some extent that he had let go of his leg, mainly because of his ignorance as to what to do in response. He didn't want to embarrass himself. Then he wondered how you could embarrass yourself in front of a five-year-old.

'We're going to see a big dinosaur!' Charlie said.

'Yes, we are. Are you excited?' John said.

'Yeah!'

'Right, you're going to have to direct me a bit, John, as I'm not too sure where we're going,' Olivia said.

'I think I can manage that.'

They got into the car and John immediately told Olivia to take a right turn out of her drive. His instruction, though, was met with a sarcastic reply from Olivia declaring that she knew roughly the way to get to town. It was when they were in the town that her lack of local knowledge would become apparent.

'And what makes you think I'll be any better? I haven't gone there for decades,' John joked.

'What is it, then? How do you say here? The blind leading the blind, or something like that.'

'Yeah, something like that. Anyway, how is the new job?'

124

'It's pretty good, thanks. The people seem nice, manager is okay, but apparently he can sometimes miss out some important bits of information if he's giving you a task. So one of the girls told me that I need to make sure I've asked every question I can think of before he's finished telling me what to do. But I don't mind that. I'm usually thorough when it comes to this sort of thing anyway.'

'So this is what you did in Colombia?'

'Basically. Not much changes in business around the world. They're all in it to make money. Only thing that changes is culture and language. But I know the language.'

'And now thanks to the fruit cake you know the beginnings of the culture.'

'Is that all British culture is? Cake?'

'It's an important part of it.' John laughed. 'The unit was always filled with cake back in London. Shop bought or homemade, we didn't really mind. It's a miracle none of us were fat.'

'So what was it that you did in London, then? The only thing I know, from Harriet, is that you were in the police.'

'I was. I was on the streets for a few years, then I was in counterterrorism for five years.'

'I see. So what happened? I mean, coming back here and everything?'

John looked out of the window at the passing countryside for a moment before saying, 'I made a mistake. I was forced to resign.'

'Being forced to resign is better than being fired, no?'

'It is, yeah. My boss gave me the ultimatum in the end. She basically wrote my resignation letter for me. She admitted that she

125

gave me too much too soon.'

'Your boss is a she? Is she a badass?' Olivia laughed.

'I guess you could say that.'

'But what did you do to be forced to resign?'

'It was a mistake I made.'

'A bad one?'

'I can't really talk about it.'

'It's all secret, then?'

'Pretty much, yeah.'

'Okay,' Olivia said, and she took John's instruction to turn left at the next junction. 'So, when do you think you'll go back?'

John paused, then said, 'I'm not really sure. They'll call me.'

'They'll call you? Why can't you just reapply when a vacancy comes available?'

'The dust just needs to settle a little bit. My boss, this badass, as you call her, she does want me back.'

'But you're not sure when?'

He wanted to tell her that he hoped it would be as soon as possible, but with her and Charlie here with him, he, to his surprise, could not bring himself to say it out loud, even though he believed it to be true.

'It could be next week, next month, next year.'

Olivia paused, then said, 'Well, I hope not.'

John looked at her and she looked back like she had said too much, and he wanted to say something, anything to dispel this uncertainty in the air – the question that hung over both their heads. But he never got the opportunity, for the simple reason that a distraction was handed to them. What did she hope would not be the case? That he would go back? But he was just the gardener. There would be others – others who were better than him, at least. And try as he might to keep this about the gardening, snaps of realisation that it could be something else had burrowed their way into his mind. But with the distraction, he didn't need to pay them any attention. At least not immediately.

'John, what's your favourite dinosaur?' Charlie said, a question that John was sure he had never been asked before, but right now a welcome one. Initially he fumbled for an answer, like he was walking across a frozen lake, struggling for balance.

'Well, I'm not really sure. A velociraptor, maybe, or a stegosaurus.'

'What's a steg-or-rus?'

'Stegosaurus. Well, it's a big dinosaur, walks on four legs, has big spikes on its back.'

'Nice! Is there one of those here too?'

'I think so. Along with lots of other dinosaurs and animals. Do you know what it's called when you study dinosaurs, Charlie?'

'No.'

'It's called palaeontology.'

'What's that?'

'Palaeontology. It's the study of dinosaurs.'

'Okay,' Charlie said, and John knew he hadn't quite understood what he was talking about.

'Which way now?' Olivia asked.

'Right at the lights.'

'How long until we get there?' Charlie asked.

'We're only a couple of minutes away and then it's just a five-minute walk.'

'Five-minute walk?' Olivia said.

'Yeah. There isn't any parking at the museum.'

'You'll have to hold my hand while we walk to the museum, Charlie, okay?'

'Okay,' he said, then after a pause he asked, 'Can John hold my hand as well?'

'That's up to John,' Olivia said.

'Please, John.'

'Yeah, I guess I can if you want, but who is going to hold your dinosaur?'

Charlie thought about this, then said, 'I'll hold him. And I'll hold Mum's hand.'

'Okay,' John said. 'Do you still not have a name for him?'

'No. Not yet. I also need a wee.'

'Are there toilets in this museum?' Olivia asked.

'Yeah, there are. There's a café as well.'

'Are you treating me to a coffee, then?'

'I might do. I might even stretch to a slice of cake as well.'

'Did you hear that, Charlie? John's going to treat you to a slice of cake in the café.'

Charlie smiled from ear to ear and repeated the good news to his toy.

They parked up. Olivia frowned at the cost of parking and then, holding her son's hand, followed John to the museum.

'You see on the grass, Charlie,' John said. 'There are dinosaur footprints.'

Charlie let go of his mum's hand and ran towards the

footprints. He jumped from one to the other until he had made it across the entire patch of grass and then returned to hold his mum's hand.

'Right, are you ready?' John said.

'Yeah!'

John could only wish to be five years old again and see for the first time in his life such a dramatic collection of dinosaur skeletons. But through Charlie, whose neck spent most of the day at a right angle, looking up, and whose mouth spent most of its time open, he got to relive the sense of joy he had got when his father had taken him to the Roman empire exhibition. Except he wasn't doing this because he had been told to by his wife. And he thought about that. If this wasn't the same transactional trip to a museum where he was only there because he had been told to go, then what was he there for? He wondered why he had decided to go with them. Although Charlie had asked him, he had expected his mum to tone down the idea, yet she had encouraged it. He remembered when she had placed her hand on his arm and persuaded him to come with them. He was just the gardener, though. There was no place for him here, there shouldn't have been any place for him, but any awkwardness he had thought he would feel – awkwardness he had been thinking about since the day the date had been set – never surfaced.

Watching Charlie become immersed in something that he found fascinating filled him with a sense of joy about which he didn't know how to feel. Since he had joined the police, his mind had only been on one thing. He hadn't given himself the choice to be or do anything else; he had chosen his duty and stuck with it. Nothing else in life had given him a greater pleasure and yet here he was, watching this child wander around the displays, pointing at them, smiling, ushering his mum and him over to see them, pressing his dinosaur against the glass so even he could get a better look.

And it was when Charlie asked John to read a plaque for him that provided information about the exhibits on display in the cabinet that he noticed, in the reflection in the glass, Olivia, a few steps back, looking not at the display but at the two of them. John read the plaque and Charlie listened to the entire thing; he even asked a question and John did his best to answer. In the end, however, he had to concede that he didn't know everything about this particular subject, so he turned to Olivia to see if she knew the answer. She was looking right at him. Her eyes smiled and a rush of warmth ran down his spine.

'Do you know, Olivia?' John said.

'Know what, sorry?'

'The answer to Charlie's question,' John said with a nervous laugh.

'Oh, I've no idea.'

'Can we go for some cake now?' Charlie asked.

'Yeah, I'm sure we can,' John said, and Charlie walked off in the direction of the café, having seen the sign.

'He seems to be enjoying himself,' John said.

'He is, yeah. Thank you for suggesting we come here, by the way.'

'It's just something that I thought he'd like. In fact, if I hadn't come here when I was a child, I wouldn't know this place existed at all.'

'Well, it's a good job you did. Anyway, you must owe me

coffee after all the ones I've made for you.'

'You think so?' John said.

'Absolutely I do,' she said, and she walked next to him the rest of the way to the café.

They took a seat, the place half full. Olivia took a menu for her and Charlie to read. John skimmed it, having already made his decision.

'Is a cream tea that bun thing with jam?' Olivia asked.

'Sorry? A bun thing with jam?'

'Yeah. I've heard of them when I was looking at English food before we moved over.'

John laughed, then said, 'It's a scone with clotted cream and jam.'

'Are they nice?'

'They're pretty good, yeah.'

'Do you like the sound of that, Charlie?' she asked her son. Charlie consulted his dinosaur briefly before saying that he did like the sound of that.

The waitress came over and took their order.

'What's been your favourite thing that you've seen, Charlie?' John asked.

'The big T. rex like my dinosaur. But I also liked the other dinosaurs and the displays. And I also liked touching the dinosaur bone as well.'

'Did you like seeing the extinct animals?'

'Ex-stinked?'

'Extinct. It means that these animals no longer exist. They've all died out and no longer live in the wild.'

'Are dinosaurs extinct?'

'Yes, they are.'

Charlie thought on this for a moment before saying, 'I liked all of it. It's all been my favourite. Probably my favourite day.'

'Well, I'm glad you've enjoyed it. After this, we're going to go up and see the second floor.'

'There's another floor? What's up there?'

'More of the same stuff, really.'

Charlie gave a little cheer and the waitress returned with their order.

'The big question, Olivia, is whether to put the jam on first or the cream,' John said.

'What do you mean?'

'In some parts of the country, they put the jam on first; in others, they put the cream on first. It's a food debate that the nation has never really answered.'

'We have something similar in Colombia, except it's a debate we have with the Venezuelans. Who makes the better arepa.'

Charlie's eyes lit up when he heard the word and he said, 'They're my favourite.'

'What is an arepa?' John asked.

'It's a staple, really – like the Italians have pasta, we have arepa. The debate comes from the difference in how we serve them. We usually serve them plain with a bit of salt or stuffed with cheese.'

Charlie made noises of satisfaction, like he had been eating arepas all day.

'And the Venezuelans serve them stuffed with all sorts of

ingredients depending on whether it's breakfast, lunch, or dinner.'

'Interesting.'

'I'll have to make you one.'

'Yeah, I think you'll have to.'

'So how do you make your cream tea?'

'I go jam and then cream.'

'Jam then cream it is, then.'

Olivia made up Charlie's cream tea, then made her own. They took a bite at the same time, and from their expressions, John could tell straight away that they liked them. Charlie had managed to get cream on his nose. He laughed, then decided that his dinosaur should also have cream on its nose, so he pressed his toy into the cream – an act that didn't particularly impress Olivia, but she saw the funny side and left thoughts of washing the toy until later.

When they were finished, John led them up to the second floor. Charlie's excitement never once diminished.

'Did you think he was going to get bored after ten minutes?' John asked Olivia.

'You seem to have a way of keeping him preoccupied.'

'It's a skill I never knew I had.'

They watched him for a moment as he moved down to the next display and showed the dinosaur the exhibits, now under Olivia's instructions that he was not allowed to press the clotted-cream-soiled toy against the glass.

'Of course, I still owe you some Colombian food.'

'Do you?' John said, slightly bemused.

'Yeah. I said I would after you made fruit cake for us.'

'Well, I don't really know where you can get Colombian food

around here.'

'No. I'll make you some.'

'Are you going to make arepa?'

'Of course, and ajiaco, sancocho, some rondon, and we can drink lulada.'

'I don't know what any of that is, but it sounds nice. And a little bit more than what I made with the two of you.'

'That's fine. It would be like a tasting menu, where you can try it all. But you don't have to if you don't want to. It's only because, you know, I said I would.'

John thought for a moment, then said, 'Yeah, I'd like that.'

'Okay, good. I'll let you know when.'

'Sounds good.'

When they had finished looking around the second floor two hours later and Olivia had driven John back to his house with Charlie asleep in the back seat, his dinosaur dropped into the footwell, he opened the door to his home and found that it wasn't as empty as it had seemed when he had been forced to resign over a month ago. The furniture might have been the minimum he required and there wasn't much in the way of decorative pieces around the place to give it personality, but when he walked through the door, it didn't feel as cold, didn't feel as lonely, and he sat in his lounge and didn't put on the TV to entertain himself. Instead he sat staring at the blank wall, watching the thoughts in his head with an easy smile on his face.

22

John remembered the last time he had put on three different shirts and decided that he didn't like any of them. It was his first date with his first girlfriend; after months of talking to each other, he had finally mustered up the courage to ask her out – an awkward affair in retrospect that he laughed at now. But this wasn't a first date. It wasn't a date at all, he kept telling himself. She was repaying a favour, doing what she had said she would do. Showing him something from her culture because he had shown her something from his. Yet this didn't change the fact that he was just the gardener. He was still in her employment. So why had he gone to the museum with them? Why had he even bothered to show her how to bake? She and Charlie had asked him to, but why hadn't he just said no? There was no reason to accept. Just restore the paths, prune the trees, rebuild the vegetable cages – that was all he was there to do, so when that call came, he could down tools and go.

The phone, however, was on the kitchen table, and he was

staring at what few clothes he had in his wardrobe. All he had to do was pick one shirt and wear it. He couldn't go shirtless, that would be ridiculous, but was it as ridiculous as his current state of indecision? Making decisions, seeing the process of quick decisions, this wasn't new to him. It had been a part of his life for years. The decisions then, however, had been about an operation, an arrest, any number of things that made this one decision different. This was about him. He was deciding for himself. And it may well be just the colour of a shirt, but he wanted it to go with his trousers. He wanted it to fit well because he wanted to …

No. He took a breath – it was just a shirt. He looked at himself in the mirror. What other options did he have? It was either this or the blue one or the grey one, and this one, he was sure, was the best. Yes. This one would do. It was only repaying a favour. It was just tasting some food.

The vibrations travelled through the walls of the house and the ringtone echoed around the kitchen. Tonight was off. Tonight was off? He went downstairs and as he picked up the phone, he saw that the caller was Andrew.

'Hello,' John said.

'Hey, mate, what are you doing tonight?' Andrew asked. An unexpected call because Andrew would normally send him a message.

'I'm busy.'

'Busy? Busy doing what?'

Was there laughter in the background? Had Olivia mentioned something to Harriet in the playground? He couldn't lie when Andrew already knew the truth.

'Olivia has invited me round. She's cooking some Colombian cuisine.'

'Colombian cuisine, you say? That sounds fancy. In fact, it sounds like a date to me.'

'It's not a date. She just offered and I thought it would be nice.'

'Yes. It reminds me of the time when I offered to take Harriet out for lunch. We eventually got married.'

'Whatever. Now are you done taking the piss? Because I need to leave.'

'I'm done for now. But that's only because I don't want to make you late.'

John cut the call, pocketed his phone, and left for Olivia's.

He knocked on her door and through the frosted glass, he saw her adjust her dress and run a hand through her hair. She opened the door, and he was caught for a moment, stuck in silence.

'Hey,' she said.

'Hey.' He stepped inside, brushing past her. He took off his coat and hung it up. 'Something smells good.'

'I'm glad you think so. Can I get you a drink?'

'What have you got?'

She listed what drinks she had, and John watched her as she went over to the kitchen, admiring her figure in her red dress.

'So, what will it be?'

'Sorry?' he said.

'What did you want to drink?'

'I thought you were going to make – what was it? Lulada?'

'I am later.'

'Did you say you had wine?'

137

'I've only got red.'

'That'll be fine.'

She poured two glasses, handed one to him, then leant back against the worktop, and said, 'So I've basically prepared quite a few different things, so you can choose what you want and try a bit of everything.'

'Like a tasting menu.'

'Almost. Except it's going to be served all in one go rather than over six different courses. I'm not exactly a Michelin-starred chef.'

'That's a shame, because I was hoping for Michelin-starred food. I guess I'll have to go elsewhere.'

'Well, off you go, then. Do they do Michelin-starred food in the Ritz?'

'I'm not sure. But it'd be a shame to leave now after you've gone to all this trouble.'

'Oh no, don't you worry, John. It was no trouble at all. In fact, the hardest part was putting Charlie to bed.'

'How come?'

'Because I told him you were coming round and he told me he was going to wait for you and sort of refused to go to sleep.'

'How did you get him to sleep, then?'

'I promised him that you would only build another bug house with him if he went to sleep.'

'You bribed your own son?'

'No … kind of … yeah, pretty much. So, it seems like you're going to have to get your hands dirty again.'

'How is it that I'm coming off worst in this?'

'I don't know. It's just the way it's worked out, I guess,' Olivia said, shrugging.

'So if I go and wake him up, then what …?' John slowly stepped back out of the kitchen, never dropping eye contact with Olivia, who stepped forward, grabbed his hand, pulled him back into the kitchen, and said, 'Don't you dare. It took me an hour to get him to go to sleep just so we could enjoy this evening together.'

John looked down at her hand holding his. Soft, warm, reassuring. Only his was frozen, rigid, taken by surprise, and he felt his heart beat faster in his chest. They looked into each other's eyes for a brief spell of time before John looked down at their hands again and she noticed, let go, and turned away to finish making the food.

'So how has your weekend been?' John asked.

Olivia, flustered, struggled for an answer at first. Not that John minded; it gave him some room to breathe.

'We've not really done much, I don't think. Saying that, Charlie managed to completely scuff his shoes at school playing tag. So he's finally learnt how to play that, so expect it next time he asks to come out and give you a hand. But anyway, we had to go and get him some new shoes. Then we had a coffee. And then I had to drag around him the supermarket to get stuff for tonight – he's never liked food shopping. Even when we were back in Colombia, he just never liked it. But go to a toy shop or something like that and he's the happiest kid alive.'

John laughed and was about to say something when Olivia turned and pointed with the wooden spoon, a drop of sauce dripping onto the floor. 'I bought some throws for the sofa and chairs as well.

I thought they added a bit of colour to the room until I get the furniture that I'd like.'

'They look nice,' John said, wondering why he hadn't noticed them when he walked in. He sipped his wine, trying not to watch Olivia like an actress on stage while she cooked. He asked, 'So what are your plans, then, for redecorating and stuff?'

Olivia stirred something in the pan, then turned down the heat and put down the wooden spoon. She saw the drop of sauce on the floor, wiped it with a piece of kitchen roll, then said, 'So, I've only got some ideas at the moment. I'm not sure when I'm going to start actually doing anything. I think I need to get a bit more settled into the job first. And the garden was always a priority for Charlie.

'But the walls ... I'm going to get rid of the wallpaper – I've never been a big fan of wallpaper – and probably go with a cream colour, something fairly neutral, because I want the colours to come from cushions and paintings, that kind of thing.

'Carpet is going to need to be changed, and I want to get one of those L-shaped sofas, you know, the big ones, and put it towards the back of the room and move the TV so it's above the fireplace. I want to do the shelves, refit the kitchen ...'

'So just a couple of things, then,' John said.

'Yeah, basically. Do you think it's a good idea? Because I'm open to hearing other ideas.'

'I'm not really one for interior design,' John said. 'I'm far more function than form.'

Olivia returned to the cooking and as she started to plate it up, she said, 'You should have seen the house we had in Colombia. I put a lot of work into it.' She put the plates down in the middle of the kitchen table.

'Was it difficult leaving that behind? The garden must have been good as well?'

They sat down at the table; she topped up their wine.

'To a point it was. There was always going to be things that I would miss. But we came here for a better life. So what was the point of holding on to something for the sake of ... I don't know, the sake of I've always done it this way and shouldn't change? My dad, like I mentioned before, wanted me to go to America. And it wasn't until I was older that I realised moving away would be better for me and moving here would be the best place to go.'

'How come it took you until you were older?'

'I guess I enjoyed growing up there for the most part. We were in the countryside, the community was good, I had plenty of friends, but that was all it was. There was nothing else, really. I moved to a city for a bit, but it was fairly lifeless.'

'How come you didn't move to London? It's where all the jobs are compared to out here.'

'It's better for Charlie out here. Plus I think all cities are lifeless, not just the ones in Colombia. They're all made from blocks of concrete. What's good about that? Maybe I'm just trying to hold on to my childhood.'

'Well, I'm glad you're here.'

'So am I.'

Their gaze lingered, then Olivia told John what was in each of the dishes, giving him a breakdown of the ingredients and what was best to eat with what.

John went for the arepa, took a large bite, and melted cheese stuck to his chin. He scooped it into his mouth, and when he had eaten it, he said, 'Yeah. I think I prefer the Venezuelan version.'

'I knew you were going to say that. I bet you haven't even tried it.'

'You should have cooked both so I could make a decision and finally put this argument to bed.'

'Well, I tell you what, the next time I have a cream tea, I'll put the cream on first, then the jam, then I'll put that argument to bed.'

'You do realise that if you prefer that way, I'll have to stop gardening for you.'

'Fine by me. I'll just get someone else.'

'Fine.'

They sipped on their wine, trying not to laugh but failing to do so.

'Is it nice, though? The food?' she asked.

John finished his mouthful, then said, 'I didn't really know what to expect, but this is definitely some of the most amazing food I've ever had.'

'Now you're just saying that to be nice.'

'No, I'm saying it because it's true.'

'Well, I'm glad you like it.'

They continued to eat. John, at first, didn't notice that they weren't saying anything to each other, and when he did, he found that it didn't bother him. It wasn't an awkward silence where both of them were struggling for something to say. It was simply a pause in the conversation while they ate, and when the moment came, they would be able to start talking to each other again. But the question on John's mind, the one that had been there since Charlie had first mentioned it, was tapping away waiting to be asked. It was all he could think to say next. But why ruin the mood? Why bring up the past like that? What if she asked him about his?

'What's wrong?' she said.

John sat back, placed his knife and fork down, and twirled the final few drops of wine in his glass.

'It's just something Charlie said, that's all.'

'What did he say?' She herself had stopped eating and John noticed her looking intently at him.

'It was back when I first got here.' He paused, questioning whether this was a good idea. He could ask anything. But this had been planted in his mind for too long, and now it had grown to the point where he just wanted to know if she had been hurt. It was all well and good praising her tenacity in moving to a different country to find a better life for herself and her son. He had done something similar many years ago when he had joined the police looking for something better, and he knew that knots to the past can't be untied – after all, you are only an accumulation of all that has happened to you so far in life.

'It really is none of my business,' he continued, 'but Charlie mentioned that his dad was a bad person …' He let the words trail off, because the question didn't need to be asked when Olivia shuffled in her chair, breaking eye contact.

'It wasn't an easy marriage,' she started. She paused, tapped her wedding finger on the table, and continued, 'But I knew I had to escape. It wasn't good for me. He wasn't good for me.' She stopped again and tilted her head to the ceiling, her eyes focused on something in the past.

John leant forward, reached out his hand, and touched her tapping fingers with his. Her head came down and her eyes looked straight at him. 'You don't have to tell me if you don't want to. It's absolutely none of my business. If I've upset you with the question, then I'm sorry, but please don't feel as though you have to answer.'

'It's okay,' she said, lightly holding his hand. 'He was a bad man, like Charlie said. I couldn't trust him – there were always secrets that he kept from me, and whenever I asked, he always shouted at me. Put me in my place. He never hit me. I don't really know why – I'm just grateful that he didn't. He wanted me just for himself, though, to be available on demand like a slave. And to never question him. He didn't want me to participate in the marriage. He just wanted me to always obey him. What sort of life was that for me? He hated that I had gotten a job, and it was only because of my dad that he allowed it. I'm not sure what my dad said to him, but it was enough to make him back off. But that was when I finally understood why my dad wanted me to learn English. There are more opportunities in countries like this. So, behind my husband's back and with the help of my family, we planned my escape.' She stopped talking and they were both quiet for a moment, letting the words sink in.

John said, 'I've met a lot of brave people in the police. People that risk their lives for the job, but we have protective equipment that the criminals don't, so we have mitigations for the risks. But with you, you really were escaping for a better life. Leaving the only place you've known, travelling halfway around the world to start again. Olivia, you're one the bravest people I've met, and you should be proud of yourself.'

She smiled and said, 'I can't believe he said that to you.'

'He actually asked me if *I* was a bad person.'

'Well, you're definitely not. Not by a long way. In fact, I'm surprised you used to be a policeman, really.'

'It was something I felt I had to do. A duty. My father was abusive to my mother, and I thought that the only way to put it right, the only way for me to find some redemption in this world, would be to arrest as many domestic abusers as I could.'

'Did you find what you were looking for?'

John thought for a while, reflecting on all that had happened up until that point. 'I'm not sure,' he said. Then he went quiet and looked away into the distance.

'That's why we have dreams, John. They show us the life we really want. Come on, I want to show you something.'

She got up and took him into the lounge. 'I painted this picture because one day I hope to live in a villa on the side of a mountain in a hot country somewhere. It would be a peaceful, simple life, where I could enjoy all that life and nature can be.'

'Not another soul in sight.'

'Exactly.'

'A bit like the man in the hut on top of that hill.'

She lightly stroked his arm and said, 'No, not like that. I'm not going to shout at kids who get too close. It's my dream to have a peaceful life eventually. No need to rush around doing things I don't want to do.'

'It's a beautiful dream.'

'You like it?'

'I think we're all waiting for the day when we can finally rest.'

He admired the painting for a moment, then said, 'I didn't know you could paint.'

'I did quite a bit in Colombia. Mainly of all the animals and plants we have over there.'

'Did you bring any with you?'

'Do you want to see some?'

'Of course.'

'Okay. Just wait here and I'll go and get them.'

She went upstairs and John went and refilled their wine. When she returned, her portfolio of pictures was two inches thick with papers of all different sizes. She put them down on the coffee table and sat on the sofa. John sat next to her and handed back her glass of wine.

She pulled out picture after picture and told him the stories behind how she had made each one and where she'd got the inspiration from, the parts of Colombia she had visited, the sweet memories of her childhood. The bursts of colour drew John in, and her talent left him lost for words. He wondered why more of these pictures weren't around the house. He didn't want to question something that she hadn't done, however, when the efforts of her work in front of him and the stories that went with them still held his full attention even after an hour and a bottle of wine later.

Eventually, she sat back and watched him looking at her work. And when he got to the final picture, a self-portrait, crafted with delicate strokes of a pencil, he too sat back and looked from the picture to the woman, then back to the picture again. 'You really are beautiful, aren't you?'

'You think so?'

'Of course I do,' he said, taking her hand in his.

'You don't look too bad yourself.' She leant forward and held his cheek in her hand. 'I'm so glad you were recommended to me.'

'So am I,' he said, wondering why he had ever once doubted coming here. He shuffled closer to her, feeling the warmth of her body, seeing the subtle imperfections in her skin and never once doubting that he should continue. She pulled him in a little closer and, with their lips only a breath away, footsteps walked across the landing, then scampered down the stairs.

They caught their breath and moved back and saw a set of eyes poke out around the corner at the bottom of the stairs.

'You should be in bed asleep, young man,' Olivia said.

'I couldn't sleep,' he said, rubbing his eyes.

'Well, you need to try, Charlie.' Olivia got off the sofa and went to her son.

'Hi, John.' He waved.

John waved back and said, 'Hi, Charlie.'

'Now come on, back up the stairs. You need to go to bed.'

'I won't be able to go back to sleep again if you don't read me a story.'

John checked his watch, stood up, and said, 'Look, I better get going anyway. It's getting late and you, mister, look like a tired boy.'

'I'm only a little bit tired.'

'I'll see you next week, Charlie,' John said, and he waved goodbye. Charlie waved back. 'And thank you for this evening. It was really good.'

'I'm glad you enjoyed it,' Olivia said.

'I'll see you next week.'

'See you next week.'

And when he left and walked back to his house, he smiled in a way he hadn't done for years.

23

When he'd signed that resignation letter. When he'd left the city, retreating to here, he had thought his stay would only be temporary. When he had woken up that first morning to an empty house, an empty life, today's feelings were something he'd never thought he'd feel while he was here. Feelings like these were something he'd thought he would avoid forever while he had his own idea of what his duty was firmly locked in his mind. Yet this morning he didn't just have a half-hearted doubt that he might have framed things incorrectly up until now. He had a genuine concern that he might need to make up for lost time – that life had slipped away while his perspective had been skewed into believing that arresting the bad guys was a way to atone for his father's actions – that taking them out of society was the only way to avoid being a reflection of what he had grown up despising. Taking revenge against those who think themselves above kindness and respect, those who think they can manipulate and control, those who do not care who they hurt as long as they gain something from it.

Eating breakfast, it felt to him that waiting for a phone call was a waste of time. Could it be that there was more than one way to heal from his childhood? Was it possible that the spark he knew was there between Olivia and him might light the flame to burn away the ideas that had been holding him back? A sense of clarity had cleared away the fog, and behind the mist he saw what a different future for himself could be: not to do to others what his father had done to him, to his mum; instead of looking to lock people up, inspired by a desire centred around a simmering hate, to display kindness, warmth, even love to those in his life. And not just to display it but to live by it.

As was routine, Olivia was taking Charlie to school, then going off to work. The flask of coffee was by the back door, this time with a note:

John,

I hope you enjoy the coffee. You'll need it, because you'll probably be building bug houses later.

Olivia x

He smiled to himself as he thought about that night when the two of them had laughed together, the delicious food she'd cooked, the ideas she'd expressed for the house, her portfolio of pictures, and of course the moment when she had almost kissed him.

But Charlie had woken up, he remembered. Would he be out here building bug houses with him later?

He poured himself some coffee, the aroma a little more vibrant today, and with the warmth of the sun on his back, he took off his coat, placed it onto the table, and looked at the garden – at the changes he had made, the parts he had restored, how much progress had been made since he'd seen the challenge in front of him and decided to attempt to put it right. There was still more to do, and even though you could tell it was the same garden, it no longer lacked the care and attention that had been missing all this time.

The leylandii hedge that stretched along the perimeter of the garden hadn't been cut back, John could tell by the exuberant growth, since he and Andrew had last been there. Hedge cutters wouldn't be enough to bring it back to where it needed to be: a line of hedge only thick enough to cover the neighbour's wooden fence. Mrs Clarke had always preferred a natural boundary to a man-made one, and Olivia agreed. But with it having overgrown by metres and being the length of the garden, there was no doubt in his mind that this task, out of all the others, would take the longest. And the waste created would require multiple trips to the tip.

John decided that the best way to trim it back would be to cut off the hedge's major branches, removing large chunks at a time instead of cutting away small amounts. The branches would then need to be cut into smaller pieces, but that would be more manageable than cutting the hedge into fine strands with a hedge trimmer. He got a pair of secateurs, garden shears, and a saw. With the larger branches buried a couple of metres into the hedge, however, he was first going to have to cut his way in.

Hours went by, and his progress was slow but methodical. And each time he stepped back, he saw how much was still to be done, despite the sizeable dent he had already made.

John heard Olivia pull into the drive, then heard Charlie's voice, his tone ecstatic, and he guessed that Olivia had given him permission to come out and help him – although what he was going to do would be a different matter. He doubted she would let him hold a pair of secateurs, and neither would he, for that matter.

That thought, however, was soon replaced by a more prevalent one: how would they react when they saw each other for the first since they had almost kissed? What were they now? He was still the gardener. But what was he to her? She to him?

When he saw her looking at him through the kitchen window, she smiled and gave a little wave, and he smiled back. Any tension, any awkwardness he had thought would be there never surfaced. When she disappeared, the anticipation of seeing her again, being close to her, sent a shock of nerves and excitement through his body.

'Did you drink all the coffee?' she said.

'I did. But I definitely remember you saying that he was only allowed out again if he didn't wake up.'

'Is that what I said? I can't quite remember. I must have got a little bit distracted by something.'

'Oh really?' he said, stepping towards her, closing the gap between them. 'And what were you distracted by?'

Her eyes flicked between his eyes and his lips and she said, 'Just this guy.'

'Yeah? What's he like?'

'You know, he called me beautiful.'

'Did he now? Well, he's not wrong.'

'So, you see, if he hadn't done that, then maybe I might have remembered what it was that I was meant to remember. But if it's any consolation, he was a very handsome man.'

'Good for him.'

'You know,' she said, placing a finger on his chest, 'if you want to remind Charlie of whatever it was that I forgot, you're more than welcome to.'

It was like she had set it up this way, to say this and for her son to come running – or attempting to run, at least, with his thick coat on, without the scarf this time – out of the side door, a beaming smile on his face, dinosaur in hand. He ran up to John, wrapped his arms around his leg, and John saw that the boy was looking at him with affectionate eyes.

'Hello, John,' he said.

'Hello, Charlie. Are you coming out to help me?'

'Yeah.'

'You're going to make a bug house, aren't you, Charlie?'

'Are we?'

'Apparently, yeah. But first we need to do a bit of gardening, okay?'

'Okay.'

'I'll leave you to it,' Olivia said, walking back to the house.

'What are we going to do?' Charlie asked.

'Okay, so it's a pretty big job. But can you see where I've cut the hedge back?' Charlie nodded and made sure his dinosaur got a good look as well. 'So, all the branches need to be cut up and the cuttings need to be put into the big bags.'

'Am I doing the cutting?'

'You're a bit too young to be holding the secateurs, so I need you to put the cuttings into the bag. Is that okay?' John knew it wasn't the most exciting of jobs, but there wasn't much else he could get him to do. He anticipated that this time, Charlie would lose interest after ten minutes.

'When are we going to go to the museum again?' Charlie asked.

'I'm not sure. Maybe we could go again at some point. Did you have a good day at school?'

'Yeah. We did some letters this morning – I can do the whole alphabet now,' and Charlie proceed to go through the entire phonics of the alphabet. 'Followed by numbers. I can count really high.'

'That's great, Charlie. How high can you count?'

Charlie thought for a moment, then said, 'I'm not sure. But really high.' He decided to start counting, and when he got to thirty, he got bored.

'That's pretty good, Charlie. So do you like going to school, then?'

'Yeah, it's okay. But it's not as fun as being here with you.'

'Oh no,' John said. 'Nothing is as fun as being out here with you.'

Charlie giggled. 'How long are you going to be our gardener for?'

'I think I'll be around for some time. Well, I hope so.'

John handed him a cutting to go into the bag and, with the help of his dinosaur, Charlie put it in, a system that remained in place until the first bag was filled and the dinosaur was covered in small bits of leaves.

'Has he been helping?' John gestured to the toy.

'Yeah. But he's gotten a bit messy.'

'Your mum will probably put him through the wash tonight.'

'He's not that muddy.' And Charlie brushed away the leaves that were loose enough to come off as best he could. 'Are you staying tonight like you did at the weekend?'

'I'm not, no.'

'Oh. Okay.'

'Why do you ask?'

'I drew a picture in school, and I wanted to show you.'

'You can show me now if you like.'

'Can I?'

'Of course you can.'

Charlie raced back to the house and John followed him to the side door. He heard Olivia call out for her son to take his shoes off – an instruction he ignored, because he was quick to return with his shoes still on, holding a picture in the air so it didn't drag along the ground.

The moment he stepped back outside, he handed it to John. There was a house, a patch of sky, and a sun in the corner. Three characters were in what looked like a garden, and each character had a name painted next to them. John couldn't quite make out the crude handwriting, but he knew who they were.

'So, this is the house.' Charlie pointed. 'And this is the garden and that's Mum, and that's me and that's you, John, look. Do you like it?'

'It's brilliant, Charlie.'

'I painted it for you, so you can keep it. Look, it's all of us.'

'I can see that, Charlie. I'm very impressed. You should be proud of yourself.'

'Hopefully you have a frame big enough for it,' Olivia said.

155

John shook his head and said, 'I doubt it. But I'll buy one, Charlie, don't you worry. And then I'm going to hang it up on the wall in my living room so I can see it every day.'

'But you need to keep it here for now, because we haven't finished gardening yet,' Charlie said, walking back to the pile of branches that still needed to be cut.

'Yes, sir,' John said, and he handed the picture to Olivia and returned to the job at hand. He placed the secateurs on the table and grabbed the full bag of cuttings. He told Charlie he was going to drag it out front and then, when he got back, they would make a start on filling the second one.

When John returned, he couldn't see Charlie. He wondered if he'd gone back inside. But he heard laughter behind him. Charlie tapped his leg, declaring that John had now been tagged, and made off down the garden, looking over his shoulder to see if John was chasing him. John went after him and Charlie's laughter grew louder. The boy ran as quickly as he could, but John soon caught up with him and tagged him back. John changed direction but deliberately didn't run off quickly enough, so Charlie soon caught him again and tagged him.

Charlie ran to the orchard, running between the trees until he stopped behind one and, with John on the other side, he went around one way, John went the other and they chased each other around the tree until Charlie made off down the path. John caught him up and they ran back down the path out onto the grass. But it wasn't enough; Charlie caught up, tagged John, and laughed hysterically as he ran away.

From the kitchen window, Olivia watched the two of them

chase each other around the garden and smiled.

Eventually, bemused by the almost infinite energy available in Charlie's little legs, John decided to have a rest and sat at the table.

'Come on, John, you need to chase me. I tagged you.'

'I think I've done enough running around. I need a rest.'

'Okay,' Charlie said, and he walked over to John and climbed up onto the chair and sat in his lap, something that took John by surprise. But he didn't put him down. Charlie started talking to him, telling him a story of something he had learned in school, and John caught sight of Olivia watching them from the kitchen window. They gazed into each other's eyes and smiled.

'Anyway,' John said, after Charlie had finished his story, 'we'd better get on with more cutting.'

Charlie climbed down, stood next to the empty bag, and waited for John to hand him a cutting.

With the second bag filled half an hour later, John placed the secateurs on the table, then dragged it out front and placed it next to the first one. And for a moment, he reflected on the day, on the time he had spent here in this peaceful chapter of his life.

A high-pitched scream pierced the air and punched his ears. He raced back and found Charlie holding his hand, blood seeping through his fingers, tears streaming down his reddened cheeks. Bloodied secateurs lay in the grass.

John tried to get a better look at the wound, but Charlie's fingers wouldn't move; he had clenched them shut.

'What's happened?' Olivia said, slightly out of breath, a small first aid kit in her hand.

Charlie didn't answer; he continued to cry, and John said he'd cut himself on the secateurs. Olivia shot him a disgruntled look, but that was a conversation for later. She opened the first aid kit on the table and John continued to encourage Charlie to open his hand, but to no avail.

Olivia spoke to him in Spanish and slowly, he opened it. She continued to talk to him in Spanish while she found the antiseptic wipes and bandages.

'He's going to need stitches,' John said.

'You really think so?'

'It looks like a deep cut. We're going to have to take him to A&E after we've cleaned and bandaged the wound.'

'I can do that. Get my car keys – they're in my bag by the door.'

John shot back inside and rummaged through her bag until he found her keys. When he returned to the garden, Olivia was bandaging up her son's hand.

'You're a big brave boy, okay, Charlie,' John said. Charlie attempted to stop crying, but the tears kept coming.

'How far away is the hospital?' Olivia said.

'It's about fifteen minutes.'

'Won't it be quicker to call an ambulance?'

'Out here they'll take longer than fifteen minutes to get to us. How are you getting on?'

'Is it tight enough?' she asked.

'Let me have a look.'

Olivia moved to the side. John told Charlie that this might hurt a bit, but it needed to happen to stop the bleeding. He pulled harder on the bandage, and the boy cried out. Olivia spoke to him in Spanish and he tried to stop crying.

With the bandage tied up, Olivia carried him to the car and sat with him in the back seat as John drove them to the hospital.

John pulled up outside the hospital in the drop-off zone. 'I'll drop you off here and come and find you, okay?'

'Okay,' Olivia said, and she got out of the car, her son in her arms, and headed into the hospital.

Ten minutes later, John found a parking space and sat in the car for a moment, angry at himself. How could he have left the secateurs lying around? Wasn't it inevitable? But Charlie knew not to touch them. Or did he want to cut a branch like he had done? He hoped that Charlie would not think less of him, blame him too harshly for not supervising him properly. And what would Olivia say to him? Would this be the last time she let her son out with him? Would he even be their gardener after this? His thoughts ran away with him, and he considered not going in and remaining in the car. Eventually, however, he was going to have to face both of them and hope that nothing would be lost between them. And what sort of person would he be to just sit here and wait while Charlie was having stitches and all his mum could do was watch? He had to go in. If his time with them had taught him anything, he knew he had to go in, regardless of whatever Olivia might say to him for his carelessness. To sit and wait out here would surely undo everything.

The receptionist pointed him in the direction of the paediatric ward and he jogged down the long corridor until he got to the chaos, to the nurses dashing around, and managed to wade through to the ward's reception. They said that Charlie was currently having stitches. He and his mum were with the doctor, and he could take a seat in the waiting area.

He sat down, released the air in his lungs, and rested his arms on his legs. All he could do now was wait.

From his watch, he saw that only ten minutes had passed. But as patients came and went, the seconds dripped by like they didn't want to let go and pass on.

As he sat there, his thoughts ran off again; maybe it would be best if he returned to London, even though he was sure Charlie would be okay, that his hand would recover and all that would be left was a scar. But that was it. The mark he had left on this boy's life. How could Olivia forgive him for not supervising him properly? He had been allowed out because for some reason, John thought, she'd trusted him, and that trust had landed them here.

He wasn't sure which thought hurt worse: Olivia not trusting him again or Charlie not wanting to garden with him.

These were just thoughts, however. They might not be true. But any reassurances meant nothing until he knew for sure that Charlie *was* going to be okay, and then he would have to deal with the aftermath. And despite thinking about returning to London, whether he had a life there or not, the idea didn't fill him with the same comfort that it had done when he had been made to resign. He wanted to make amends and put this right, and when they appeared at the door of the doctor's office, his heart rate accelerated and he stood up, unable to find a comfortable place to put his hands.

Olivia thanked the doctor and walked over, carrying Charlie, his face snuggled into her neck.

'Olivia, I'm so, so sorry. I was so stupid leaving those things out – it shouldn't—'

She cut him off and said, 'It's okay, John. He's going to be fine – just a few stitches, that's all. We have to come back in a week to see how it's healed.'

'Look, this is all my fault. I should have supervised him better. This could have been so much worse.'

She rubbed his arm and said, 'But it wasn't. And I'm sure you must have told him not to touch them. This isn't the first time he's had a little accident in the garden. Is it, Charlie?'

The boy nodded his head *no*.

'But this is the first time someone has actually cared for his wellbeing. So thank you, John.'

He didn't know what to say. It was like the boot pressing down on his chest had stepped off and instead a hand had been offered to him. So instead of saying anything, he hugged the two of them, and Olivia's free arm rubbed his back.

'I'm sorry, John,' Charlie said, his voice tired.

'It's okay, Charlie. I'm just glad you're going to be fine.'

'The doctor said I'll have a scar on my hand.'

'That's okay. Scars show the world that you're stronger than the thing that tried to hurt you. I've got a few myself.'

Charlie went quiet for a moment. John thought he hadn't quite understood what he'd just said, then Charlie asked, 'Will I still be allowed out in the garden with you?'

'Of course you will be, Charlie. Of course you will be.'

Charlie gave a little smile.

24

Charlie had fallen asleep in the back seat of the car by the time John had driven them home. Olivia carried him in and put him to bed. John sat on the sofa and waited for her to return.

The relief of hearing her tell him everything was okay while rubbing his arm still hadn't worn off, and to an extent, he didn't want it to. This wasn't like the previous times when he had felt relief, when the judge or jury had declared a suspected criminal guilty and handed them a prison sentence. That had been procedural, a professional victory; this was about his relationship with two people he had grown to want to be around. Be around more than might wanted to return to a duty he had convinced himself he needed to fulfil? Was this a sign, in his mind, that his life was changing? As he waited for Olivia to return, he thought about his mum and hoped she would be proud of him.

'He wants you to read him a story,' Olivia said.

'I thought he was asleep?'

'He was, but he woke up and asked if you could.'

'I can read him a story,' John said.

'You might have to read it to him a couple of times, though.'

'How come?'

Olivia laughed, then said, 'It's just the way it works with kids. But when you're done, I'll have a glass of wine waiting for you down here.'

'Okay,' John said, and he went to walk upstairs before he realised that he didn't know where Charlie's bedroom was. Olivia told him it was the second on the left.

Charlie, tucked into bed, had the book open, already a few pages through.

'Do you want me to read you a story?'

'Yeah! This one, please. It's my favourite. And can you start from the beginning, please?'

John sat on the edge of his bed, unsurprised by the dinosaur-themed bedding, and turned the book to the first page. Charlie smiled, cuddled his dinosaur, and remained quiet until John got to the first passage of speech, where he made the crucial error of not doing the voices. And when he put on a voice, it wasn't quite right, so Charlie guided him through it.

The second attempt, Charlie decided, was much better, but he would definitely need to hear it a third time to be absolutely sure it was right.

Halfway through the fifth reading, however, Charlie finally started to drift off to sleep. 'Night, night, Charlie,' John said, and he pulled the duvet up.

He reached over to turn off the bedside light, but Charlie, only half awake, said, 'I've thought of a name for my dinosaur.'

'What are you going to call him?'

'I'm going to call him John, like you.'

'I think that's a great idea, Charlie. Now goodnight. Sleep tight.'

'Goodnight.'

John turned off the bedside light and quietly left the room, closing the door on his way out.

'You took your time,' Olivia said, handing him, as promised, a glass of wine.

'Five times I had to read it before he fell asleep.'

'You see, I only ever read it to him three times before I tell him he needs to go to sleep.'

'I'll have to take a leaf out of your book next time.'

'Was the pun intended?'

'Was it a funny pun?'

'It was okay.'

John paused briefly, then said, 'Then yes, it was intended. He's also naming his dinosaur John.'

'He named it after you?'

'He did, yeah.'

They sat down on the sofa, clinked their glasses together, and took a sip.

'Does he make you do the voices when you're reading to him?' John said, and Olivia nearly spat out a mouthful of wine.

'That's what you're thinking about?'

'He mentored me through it the first time; my voice is either not deep enough or not high enough to fit some of the characters.'

'Well, at least you know now.'

'I do, yeah, because I went through it nearly five times. I'm practically an expert.'

'An expert? After five times? I've been doing the voices for years, John. You've got nothing on me.'

'Well, if you want to teach me, I'll be happy to learn.'

They laughed together and looked at each other, their eyes lingering, their pupils dilating.

'Any news on when you're going to back to London?' Olivia said.

'No ... not yet ... maybe it won't happen.'

'What do you mean?'

'I mean ... I don't know if I would go back.'

'But wasn't that what you wanted? You know, waiting for that call?'

'It was. But I'm not sure anymore. A part of me wants to remain here. I'm happy here. It's a different life, completely different. Maybe it is the one I want.'

She put her hand on his cheek and said, 'I'd like it if you stayed.'

He shuffled closer to her and said, 'You know, I put off a lot of things in my life when I was in the police, thinking I was doing it for a higher duty, believing that I was atoning for all the times my father abused my mother. But all I got from it was being alone.

'I never thought I'd meet someone like you. I never thought I'd be thrown into a situation like this, and I never would've guessed that I'd ever have the opportunity to choose what I want in life. But now there's a part of me that I didn't even know I had in me that wants to choose you.'

Their eyes gazed into each other for a moment.

'I still owe you a kiss,' Olivia said.

'You'd better kiss me, then,' John said, and with his hand behind her neck, he pulled her in and kissed her.

25

As they were getting out of the car in the hospital car park, John watched Charlie glance between his dinosaur and his stitched-up hand, and he realised the boy's dilemma. He either held his dinosaur or John's hand; he hadn't held anything with his stitched-up hand for a week and John sensed he wasn't going to break that streak now.

He settled for the fact that Charlie would hold his namesake dinosaur, but as they walked up to the hospital entrance, Charlie handed his toy to his mum and grabbed John's hand. John led them through to the paediatric ward, where, after talking to the receptionist, they took a seat in the waiting room, and John noticed how different he felt this time around. The ward was still chaotic, but his mind was rested. He had even taken to putting his phone on silent.

The wait had been anticipated, and Olivia had packed for the occasion, bringing with her three of Charlie's favourite books, which were read to him by both of them. Charlie had allocated each of them characters in the story that they were to read. In the appropriate voices, of course.

They had nearly finished the second book when Dr Green, who had stitched him up a week ago, called for them to come into her office. 'Hey, Charlie,' she said, upbeat. 'How have you been feeling the past week?'

'Not too bad. I think my hand is getting better.'

'Well, I certainly hope so. Shall we take a look?'

Charlie nodded and took the offered seat next to the doctor's desk. She examined his hand briefly and decided that the stitches had done their job.

'I'm going to remove your stitches, okay, Charlie? Then I'm going to put some medical tape on them. They're just small strips of tape that will go across the cut. And just to be on the safe side, I'm going to wrap it in a bandage. After a week, it can come off.'

'Okay.'

Dr Green looked at Olivia to make sure she understood what was going to happen. Olivia said that was fine.

The doctor did as she said she would, and it wasn't even half an hour later before they were leaving the hospital. Olivia started to walk in the direction of the car, but John called out to her and said he was going to take them somewhere to celebrate Charlie's stitches being removed.

'Where are we going, John?' Charlie said.

'It's a surprise. But I think you're going to like it.'

Olivia came up behind John and whispered in his ear, 'Yeah, where are you taking us?'

'You'll see.'

In John's mind, it was only going to be a short walk to their destination, but the still air and warm sun encouraged them to enjoy the good weather and take a slow walk. John led them through a park where people lay on picnic blankets, joggers passed them, and there were groups of people playing games.

Charlie eventually let go of John's hand, retrieved his dinosaur from his mum, and took off in front of them, but he always made sure he didn't go too far. Olivia took John's hand, but he wrapped his arm around her shoulders instead, and they walked together slowly.

'We don't need to get to this place quickly, do we?' Olivia asked.

'No. We've got plenty of time. Plus it's not too far away.'

'And you're definitely not going to tell me where we're going?'

'It's more for Charlie, so if you want, I can tell you.'

Olivia thought for a moment, then said, 'Actually, I'd prefer to be surprised.'

'Okay,' John said. 'But it's nothing too over the top or outrageous, so don't get your hopes up.'

'As it's you who picked it, my hopes are definitely up.'

Charlie had run himself out of breath and taken a seat on a bench shaded by trees. 'How long until we get there?' he asked.

'Not long. Once we're out of the park, we'll be there.'

'Can I rest here for a bit?'

'Of course you can.'

John and Olivia sat on either side of him, and it was there that

Olivia decided to get her phone out and take a picture of the three of them, all smiling. And together, for a few moments, until Charlie declared that it was time to carry on, they watched the world go by, in their own little section of time reserved for the three of them. The park could have been filled with people, but it wouldn't have changed anything; they would still have been within the comfortable confines of their own world.

Charlie recognised the building immediately and went to run in, but first he took a sharp turn and ran over the dinosaur's footprints. Inside, his face displayed the same amazement it had done when they had first come here, and again he led them around the exhibits while John and Olivia watched, arms wrapped around one another.

At the insistence of Charlie, they went to the café for coffee and, at his heavy insistence, a cream tea, which once again ended up being shared with the dinosaur, despite Olivia telling him not to do it. And he laughed when his toy got a blob of cream on its nose. John tried not to laugh, but eventually he had to give in, which only exacerbated Charlie's laughter and the boy's perception that this was something he should do regularly if it made John laugh as well. Eventually Olivia saw the funny side and hoped that Charlie would accept that it would need to be washed again.

They returned home with the sky bursting with a deep red that threaded itself through the clouds. John cooked that night. Nothing special – not that he would have been led to believe so by the positive reviews he received from Charlie, who noted that if John the dinosaur weren't in the wash, he would also have enjoyed it as much as he had.

After dinner, Olivia put Charlie to bed, with Charlie insisting that John read him a story, a request he accepted. This time he took Olivia's advice and would have stopped after the third read-through. But Charlie didn't make it through the second reading before he fell asleep.

Olivia couldn't believe that John had returned so quickly. 'Maybe taking him to the museum is the secret,' John said.

'It probably is.' She handed him a glass of wine.

They sat on the sofa, her legs resting on his, his arm wrapped around her, and a blanket draped over them. They watched a movie and nearly made it to the halfway point before she pulled him in for a kiss, and like that they remained until the credits rolled.

When he went home that night, the night didn't seem so dark, his house felt like it had never been empty, and, falling into bed to sleep after spending the day with them, he too found himself drifting off quickly.

26

It was the first morning he had woken up in her bed. She was lying on his chest, her head rising and falling with each breath, and when the alarm rang, he switched it off.

'Hey,' she said, looking up at him.

'Hey,' he said before kissing her.

Charlie didn't know that John had stayed the night. It was something they wanted to surprise him with, and by the reaction he had, open mouthed, wide eyed, followed by a running charge at John to grab his legs and say good morning, it was a welcomed one.

With the bandage and medical tape having been removed the previous day, Charlie was keen to show off his scar in school and tell the story of how he got it. John teased him and told him that girls like guys with scars, but Charlie was adamant that they didn't.

Olivia took him to school and John promised he would be there later to pick him up – a promise that was met with a surge of happiness.

The garden was almost finished. All it needed now was a few finishing touches, so when he was finished with his task that day, he took a moment to look back on all that been restored, the transformation that had taken place at his hands and a smaller pair of hands usually preoccupied with something else and, of course, fuelled by coffee.

He was going to have to get other clients, new challenges – a prospect he liked the sound of. Thanks to Andrew and Harriet, word got out, and phone calls soon came his way.

Parents filled the playground, waiting for their children, and John and Olivia made conversation with the parents she knew. When the classroom door opened, a sea of children charged out. John and Olivia searched for Charlie and he came running towards them, a beaming smile on his face, and he didn't stop running until he was hugging both John and Olivia.

While they walked back home, Charlie wanted John to hold his hand, and he spoke at length about his day, about the people who had seen his scar.

Olivia slowed and fell behind them when her phone vibrated in her pocket. It was a work call, so she took it. It was a brief conversation, and when she was done, she went to put her phone back in her pocket, but the device slipped out of her hand and landed on the pavement.

John heard the crack and looked back to see what was going on. She picked up her phone. The entire screen had shattered.

'I know a screen repair shop we can go to,' John said.

'Are they open now?' Olivia asked.

'They should be.'

'Can we go when we get back?'

'Of course we can.'

It was a mid-week afternoon, so the car park was sparsely populated and so was the town.

It was parked inconspicuously down a side street, out of the way, ignored by all who walked past it. But it was there. A black BMW. A black BMW John thought he recognised. The instincts of his previous life kicked in. Should he listen to them? This wasn't an assignment; he wasn't kicking in the door to a suspected terrorist's house. This was a local town that didn't need a constant police presence. But where had he seen that car before?

'John,' Olivia called after him.

John turned to look at her. There was a bemused expression on her face. What was he doing? That was his old life. He couldn't allow it to impede on what he had now, so he ignored his instincts and moved on.

They walked down the small pedestrianised street where the phone repair shop was. Occasionally they glanced into the windows of the other shops, taking their time; no deadline to adhere to, nothing to rush for, together like any other family on any other day.

A toy shop sat opposite the phone repair shop. Its window display mesmerised Charlie and Olivia had to pull him away, promising him they would go inside afterwards.

John and Olivia, in conversation with the young assistant at the counter, weighing up the cost and time to repair against the idea of getting a new, cheaper phone that would cost less than repairing the cracked one, let Charlie out of their sight long enough for him to sneak out of the shop and walk across the path to the toy shop.

He had never seen this toy shop before, and its dinosaur-themed display was a haven in his eyes. He had to crane his little neck to see it all, and he didn't notice the man with the rifle charging towards him and the rest of the shoppers. He didn't hear him cock the weapon either. But he heard the distressed screams and looked around to see what was happening.

John knew he had let Charlie out of his sight for too long, been too caught up in the conversation, and searched the shop for him – he couldn't see him between the stands that divided the aisles. He opened his mouth to call out for him but dropped to the floor instead, taking Olivia with him, when the shooting started.

'Charlie!' he shouted above the thunder that had erupted. He kept a tight hold of Olivia's hand, but when the gunfire stopped, he leapt to his feet. He ran out of the shop to see spatters of blood and bodies. He couldn't see Charlie.

He made for the main street. The gunfire and screams grew louder as he got closer. But once he was there, the shooting had stopped, and the only evidence that shots had been fired were the sprawled bodies on the ground. All he could hear over his heavy breathing was silence.

He shouted for Charlie. No response came.

He sprinted down the pavement to the side street. But the black BMW wasn't there.

Now was not the time to panic. Charlie might still be in the shop. He made his return, guided by this last ditch of hope, only for it to be shattered when he saw Olivia outside the toy shop picking up Charlie's dinosaur.

She turned to look at him. John expected her to break down in tears, but shock prevented that.

For John, however, there was nothing to deny. Charlie's body was not among the dead, and he didn't go anywhere without his dinosaur.

He was gone.

John retreated to the main street and leaned against a wall to stop himself from falling. He looked back at the massacre and the place where Charlie should have been. Why hadn't he listened to his instincts? He knew he had seen that car before.

He began the walk of shame back to Olivia. She hadn't moved. Her hands clung to the dinosaur; her eyes couldn't look away from the only thing she had left of her son.

When John embraced her, he told her he was sorry. And then she cried. There was nothing left to deny. Charlie was gone. And not even the hope that he might have been kidnapped and was still alive was enough to sway the ocean of sadness that was drowning them.

27

The situation had been declared a terrorist incident. It had made international news, leaving an entire country wondering why the terrorists had struck a local town and not a major city. They only targeted major cities. This wasn't part of the script; it had never occurred to anyone that this could happen. And now the politicians and senior officers in the police and armed forces were left scratching their heads. Was this a new threat? Had Islamic terrorism changed tactics? Was the IRA back? No one had the answers.

Olivia was numb. She had hardly spoken, hardly eaten or drunk anything, leaving John to wonder how she hadn't collapsed. And he wondered how many times the moment her phone had hit the pavement had replayed in her mind. If only she'd just held it tighter ...

When it was John's turn to write his witness statement, he spent the first few moments staring at the blank piece of paper. The journey to the police station had been wrapped in silence – neither he nor Olivia had spoken, and the engine running was just white noise. He wanted to know what was going through her mind so he could say the right thing to her, but she didn't need words of comfort right now. They might have eased the pain, but they wouldn't heal it. Getting her son back was the only thing that would do that.

After a few moments of staring at the page, wondering where to start, he got to it, putting into words, like in the many reports he had written in the past, what had happened. And although he knew he would have to take the blame for not trusting his instincts, he wasn't going to let his personal pride get in the way of the sense of professional duty he had once had.

Writing the statement, he found, wasn't just admitting to his mistakes. It was immortalising his regrets. Regrets he knew he was going to struggle to deal with. Why had he let Charlie out of his sight? Why hadn't he trusted his instincts? Why did he have to get so distracted by the man in the shop?

After a raid, they would have gone through the lessons that had been identified. But that was a team effort, and as a team, they would work on rectifying the mistakes. Here, he was on his own, reeling from what had happened. Despite how aggravating it was to write it all down, he knew it needed to be done in order to help get Charlie back. He wondered how Olivia must feel, sitting in the next room, staring at the same piece of paper, reliving the same event in her mind. Although Charlie had grown to be an important part of his life, losing him was nothing compared to losing your own son. And in this room, he hated the fact that he couldn't hold her hand, put an arm around her shoulders while she wrote about the details of what was probably the worst day of her life.

Why couldn't they have had more time to enjoy themselves, to live their new life? Why did this have to happen?

When he was done, he handed the statement to the sergeant, returned to the reception area, took a seat on one of the cheap plastic chairs, and waited for Olivia.

She appeared only ten minutes later, or what was left of her. John got up and hugged her, and she wrapped her arms around him without any real enthusiasm.

'I want to go home,' she said, her voice quiet, her body shivering.

'Let's go,' John said, and he undid his coat and put it around her shoulders.

They were making for the door when the sergeant called out to John.

'What's wrong?' John said.

'I just need to talk to you quickly about your statement, Mr Brown. I have a few questions – it won't take a minute. I know this is hard for you both, but it is important.'

John looked at Olivia and she nodded, giving him the permission he was seeking.

'I won't be long,' he whispered in her ear and kissed her forehead. She sat down and he followed the sergeant into his office.

'I'm going to get right to it, because I know you don't want to be hanging around here any longer than you need to be,' the sergeant started. 'Look, John – can I call you John?'

John nodded *yes*.

'John, I scanned through your statement, and I have to say that

I think you're jumping to conclusions.'

'Sorry?'

'You're the only one to mention a car parked down a side street, and what's more, a black BMW that was also used for the Bamburgh murders.'

'What's your point?' John's body had tensed up slightly.

'My point is that this is total nonsense.'

'Nonsense?' John spat.

'Listen to me, John. This doesn't make any sense to me. What happened up north was a triple murder by one man. And you think this one man has turned into three terrorists and driven all the way down the length of the country to commit a terrorist attack?'

'How dare you question me. And yes, I bloody well do. You can check ...' But John trailed off. Check what? There were no photos or video footage – not even CCTV that showed that this car had been there.

'I looked you up before you came today. Former counterterrorism operative suspended from your unit for six months to then resign. I think you're making this up to try to solve a case to get you back in the game. Because we both know that you were forced to resign to avoid being fired. And you accepted because you didn't want to lose your pension.'

John's body tensed up completely. His breathing deepened and he wanted to hit the sergeant hard enough to knock him unconscious.

'That's not even close to being true.' John slammed his palm down on the desk and shot to his feet. 'Now listen to me, Sergeant. That car was there. I damn well saw it, so don't you ever accuse me of lying. It was there, and after the attack when I went to look for it, it was gone. It was their getaway vehicle, for Christ's sake. Check the reg I gave you.'

'It was the first thing I did. It doesn't exist.'

'So they're using fake plates. Did you check what plates they used up north?'

'No one knows what the plates were up north. We don't have that information despite the videos. Now you're just digging yourself a hole, John. So I suggest you stop digging.'

'You're failing at your job, Sergeant.'

'Just like you did.'

John smacked his palm against the desk again and said, 'You don't know anything about me.'

'I know enough. Plus your girlfriend never mentioned a car. So listen to me, John. I need you to delete this part of your statement or else no one is going to take you seriously. Do you want Charlie back or not?'

How had Olivia not seen the car? John replayed the day again in his mind and realised that she hadn't. It had only been him – only he knew the truth, and if it was only he who knew, then this lead would disappear and getting Charlie back would go from difficult to impossible.

'And what if I don't? What if a competent police officer reads this? They'll believe me.'

'I'll just tell them what I think is really going on here with you and then who do you think they'll believe?'

John knew the sergeant was right. It didn't matter what the truth was, it was always what could be proved, and right now, the narrative at the end of his career in counterterrorism didn't cover him in glory.

How would they find Charlie, then, if they didn't know the truth? Would forensics pick something up? Tyre marks when they drove off that would prove he was right? He wanted to mention this, but this sergeant had decided not to listen to him. His mind was made up, and John knew that anything else he said would only reinforce this man's idea that he was telling lies to try to recoup some former glory. He would wait until the detective came to interview them and hope that they would be more open-minded. He would get the truth out; it just might take a little bit longer.

John stared at the sergeant as he was handed his witness statement back. John snatched it from his hand and put a line through the truth. 'You're going to regret this,' he said, handing back the edited statement.

'I'm focused on getting your boy back and bringing these terrorists to justice. Why don't you focus on supporting your girlfriend and leave this to the professionals?'

It took all the willpower he had not to punch the sergeant. Because what good would punching a police officer do? He would only end up in trouble, and Olivia had too much on her mind already. The sergeant was right about one thing; he did need to continue to support her through this. When he left the office, he forced a smile, hoping that she wouldn't ask too many questions – he couldn't bear to tell her what had really happened. He put an arm around her shoulder and took her home.

A few days later, there was nothing. No arrests had been made;

reports came out that the police had no leads. Not even a ransom letter had arrived.

The detective on the case of Charlie's kidnapping visited to provide them with an update. On what, however, was not specified, leaving John to wonder if this was going to be another waste of time. He knew that when the top people in government and security came on TV to assure the people that everything was in hand, it was superficial nonsense meant to hide the fact that they had nothing. He'd been in those situations before. Olivia ate it up, to John's dismay, but he couldn't bear to take away her last bit of hope.

'Have you found him yet?' Olivia asked on opening the door to DSI Gibson.

'Not yet, Ms Santiago. We're still working tirelessly on the case.'

John noted DSI Gibson's fatigued eyes. But they were no more fatigued than when he had originally told them he would get Charlie back.

'Would you like a tea or a coffee?' Olivia asked.

'I'm okay, thank you, Ms Santiago. Can I come in?'

Olivia said he could and gestured towards the lounge. DSI Gibson sat in the chair. Olivia sat on the sofa and John joined her.

'Have you had a ransom note yet?' John asked. He didn't want to mention the car right away. He didn't want to sound desperate.

'No. Not yet. We'd usually have got one by now. But I don't think this was a kidnapping.'

'What do you mean?' Olivia said.

'We're still looking into his disappearance. But to us, considering nineteen other people were killed, we're struggling to understand the motive for kidnapping Charlie. Or if it was a kidnapping, why kill nineteen people and then not demand a ransom?'

Olivia's eyes welled up. Tears ran down her cheeks and John put his arm around her.

'What are you saying?' John asked. He wanted someone to admit to a mistake; at least then he would have someone to point a finger at and would no longer have only himself to blame.

'They expected adults and saw a child standing there and couldn't bring themselves to shoot him. It's hard for us to believe. Terrorists rarely care who they kill. They could have taken him as a bargaining tool for later – I hate to talk about your son in this way. Or one terrorist made a mistake in taking him.'

'So why did they do it, then?'

'It's a tough one, with this being a terrorist attack. It's hard to conclude why they would take your child – especially as there's been no ransom note or anything like that. But we are doing everything we can to find him.'

'But if taking him was a mistake, what will they do with him? Do you think they're keeping him alive?'

'We don't know if they've taken him as leeway for the future or not.'

'And if that happens? If it's one child's life versus capturing the terrorists, then who's going to be picked?' Olivia held John's arm tightly. The tears still fell down her cheeks.

'We'll never let harm come to him, Mr Brown. If we can bring him home, then we'll bring him home.'

'If?' John's sudden outburst made Olivia jolt in his arms. He took a breath and made a mental note not to raise his voice again, despite how aggravated he felt.

'This entire investigation, including Charlie's kidnapping, is now being moved over to counterterrorism. To get your child back, we've decided the best way is to go after the terrorists that took him. It's the same unit you used to work for, Mr Brown, that's taking this case.'

John's eyes lit up. Tension left his body. Not because he had faith in his old team, but because a plan had formed in his mind. But looking at Olivia, her fragile frame and grief-ridden mind told him he was needed here.

'That's the update that I've come here to tell you. And I think it's good news. It makes sense to me, and, as you know, Mr Brown, they're the best people for this job. Do you have any questions?'

'No.'

DSI Gibson got up to leave, and John led him out. He went outside and closed the door behind him.

'What terrorists take a kid?'

'Sorry?'

'They made a mistake. That's what you really think. One of them made a mistake. And his mistake has cost Charlie his life.'

'Mr Brown ...'

'If you really thought he was alive, then this would still be with you. Kidnapping is a completely different investigation to terrorism.'

'That's not what I think, Mr Brown. I agree the terrorist made a mistake in taking Charlie. But I think they're clever enough to know that treating him as expendable is a foolish thing to do. I let your old guys take this because if we can get to the terrorists, then we can get to Charlie.'

'Do you think he's alive?' John asked.

'I hope he is. But the longer this goes on – I'll be honest with you, one professional to another – the less likely the chance that he will turn up alive.' The detective had nothing left to say and left.

John didn't know what to think. His old unit had the case, and he couldn't help but wonder what he would do if he were there now. Looking through the door's frosted glass, however, he saw Olivia on the sofa, and he walked back inside and sat down beside her.

'What was that all about?' she asked.

'It was nothing.'

'I know it's not nothing. When he mentioned your old unit, you don't think I noticed how your entire body just changed?'

'What do you mean?'

'I mean for you. The thought of going back there. It filled you with a kind of … I don't know, but it's … it's something you can't get here, waiting around while some else is finding him.'

'I've got more joy, more warmth, more of everything in life being here than I ever did there.'

'And now you only have half of that.'

'I'm not going anywhere. You're the only half I have left, and I'm not leaving you.'

28

The idea of going back, the plan he had thought of after speaking to DSI Gibson, hadn't left his mind, despite telling Olivia he was going to stay. But that was the problem. She was there and Charlie wasn't. If he went back, however, there was a chance he could get him back, and he knew she would wait for him. There was also a chance the terrorists had a bullet inscribed with his name, and he couldn't bear the thought of leaving her with nothing.

Andrew and Harriet came by daily. They cooked for them and took on some of their domestic tasks. They tried to provide the two of them with a distraction. Is there anything, however, that can distract you from your own son's kidnapping? Their help meant that neither John nor Olivia had left the house for days. Even the garden, once a paradise for Charlie, was off limits. The happy memories were a reminder of what they no longer had, and John felt claustrophobic. The walls were closing in, and he wondered how much longer he could remain inside before he lost his mind.

He didn't want to find out, so he got in the car and drove without a destination in mind. He ended up returning to the last place on Earth he had thought he would go.

He parked in the same car park. Took the same walk and even stopped to look at the side street, the truth he was holding on to a permanent scar on his life.

He continued as far as he could down the street – it was cordoned off as forensics continued their work. From what he had secretly read and watched on the news, out of Olivia's earshot, he knew that their efforts had so far turned up nothing. No arrests had been made, and there still wasn't so much as a comment about whether anyone was pursuing any leads. No good news to lift the spirits of this heartbroken community, of this devastated country.

Flowers had piled up next to the scene – flowers from family, friends, and strangers who had nothing else to offer except their support. The town had come together to mourn their loss. And he fought back tears. This wasn't just their loss. Here, everybody felt like they had lost something, and everyone looked at those who could protect them, and John wondered how many struggled to sleep at night, stricken with sadness and fear. How do parents explain to their children what has happened? How do they explain that the people responsible are still out there?

A young couple added a bouquet of flowers to the collection. She placed a hand on her stomach as they stood back and took a moment of silence. She tried to ease the tears, but it wasn't enough. Not even her man's reassuring embrace could stop her emotions coming through.

The place felt cold, like its heart had been ripped away, taking the community's innocence with it.

John returned to his car. He went to put his key in the ignition, but it wouldn't go in no matter how much he fumbled around with it. He threw it into the footwell and smacked the steering wheel.

He sunk into the seat. He closed his eyes and tried to think of a way to make all this right. There was only ever going to be one thing he knew he could do, no matter how hard it would be on Olivia. He took his phone from his pocket and dialled the only person who he knew could help.

'John, what the hell are you ringing me for? You must know I'm busy!' Claire said over the background noise.

'Then why answer the call?'

She paused, took a breath, then said, 'Because I guess I needed to know if you're okay.'

'Well, I'm sure you can take a good guess and know that I'm not exactly on top of the world right now.'

'I can only imagine what you're going through, John. Reading your witness statement and knowing it's you that's been through this shit – it's heartbreaking, it really is. But we have a job to do here.'

'And you haven't detained anyone yet. You've got no leads.'

'We're working tirelessly—' She stopped herself. John knew the lines.

'Spare me the bullshit, Claire. I just want the truth.'

She paused, thinking the request over. 'We're not doing too well at the moment. We're hoping forensics might come back with something.'

'Are you confident they will?'

'Reading the statements, it doesn't seem like they stuck around long enough to leave anything behind. Except bullet casings.'

'So when that comes back and tells you nothing, then what? You're out of ideas?'

'I don't know, John.'

There was silence. Then she said, 'Are you hiding something from me?'

'I want back in, Claire.'

'You know that can't happen.'

'Yes, it can. I resigned, remember. I can come back from that.'

'I meant in terms of years, not months.'

'You didn't expect an attack like this to happen. No one did.'

Claire thought this over. 'I'm sorry, John, I just don't know how I can swing it with the higher echelons. If it was up to me, I'd take you back.'

'Just answer me this. What car were they driving?'

'What's that got to do with anything?'

'Do you know?'

'I don't.'

'Well, I do. I know what they were driving. I saw the car.'

'Then why the fuck didn't you put that in the witness statement?'

'I did. But I was forced to take it out. This bloody sergeant questioned my own validity because I'd been suspended, then forced to resign.'

A silence dragged on between them. John wished he could hear her thoughts – he'd know what to say to convince her. Whatever she said, however, wouldn't distract him from believing that he was doing the right thing. For the first time since Charlie had been taken, he finally felt like he had some control.

'How quickly can you get to London?' Claire said, breaking the silence.

'I can be there in under two hours.'

'I need to have some conversations. But we've got nothing. And if you're right, if you actually have something, then I'll get you back in. But I want some assurances before I even start those conversations.'

'What do you need?'

'I need to know you won't lose it. This is personal to you, which on the one hand means you're better motivated than anyone else. But it can also blind you, get the better of you. I don't want you to see this as a revenge mission. I want you to be dispassionate. Maintain the high professional standards you always have done in the past. I need to know that you won't get in over your head.'

'I won't get in over my head,' he said, like he was reading from a script.

It was all he needed to say. His reputation preceded him.

'Get to London. And meet me outside first thing tomorrow morning.'

29

When he returned home, Olivia was waiting for him. She took one look at him and knew something had changed.

'You're going back, aren't you?'

John stepped forward. Saying goodbye to her was going to be nearly impossible. But he'd chosen to answer the higher call. 'Look, Olivia, I'm sorry …'

'It's okay. I can manage here knowing that you're out there. Knowing that you're going to bring him home.'

'If I could think of a better way … I can't bear to leave you here. But I can't sit here and not try to get him back.'

'It's okay. You're doing the right thing. I know you are. I'll be waiting for you when you come back. No matter how long this takes, I'll be waiting for you.'

'I'll bring him back to us.'

He went upstairs and packed his bags. When he went to leave, Olivia stopped him and said, 'There's one thing you're forgetting.' She was holding something behind her back.

'What's that?'

She held out John the dinosaur to him and said, 'He'd want you to have it.'

John took the toy from her. It hadn't stopped smiling, just like Charlie had never stopped smiling.

They held each other tightly. John wiped the tears from her cheeks and kissed her hard, because he wasn't sure when he was going to get the chance again.

'One day, when this is all done with, the three of us can take off to a villa on the side of a mountain and it can just be us,' he said.

'I hope so,' she said. 'I look forward to it.'

Part 2

Part 2

30

Gary lit Carl's cigar before lighting his own. He puffed on it twice, two long drags, and blew the wood-scented smoke up to the ceiling. He wondered if it would be a good idea to get a proper ventilation system in his office.

'It's such a shame we can't go out and celebrate this properly,' Gary said. 'The client rang me an hour ago to congratulate us.'

'I'm glad the client likes our work.'

'How are the other two?'

'They're still lying low, like I told them to. They won't cause us any trouble; they're just waiting for the next attack.'

Gary reached into his drawer, smirked when he saw Antonia's number, then picked out the picture and handed it to Carl. 'The client sent this through. It's a small village in Cornwall; nice place. They want the government to know that we can hit anywhere in the UK. They really want to ramp things up after this success.'

Carl took the picture, gave it a once-over, then asked, 'Are we going to admit to the Bamburgh murders?'

'I don't think we are. What's the point? Everybody's eyes are focused on what we've just done. Bamburgh is nothing in comparison. The client wants you to go for the entire street – ideally no survivors.'

'I'm going to need more men.'

'You better find them, then. And more men means more weapons, right?' Gary suggested.

'Well, yeah, it will do.'

'I'll get in contact with Antonia. I'm sure she'll be able to get them over here quickly.' Gary held her card between his fingers, smiling to himself.

'Why will they need to be quick?' Carl asked.

'Because you'll be hitting that place in five days' time.'

'Five days? That is quick. But I can work with that. This country won't know what's hit it.'

31

'So, what's my role in this going to be?' John asked Claire as they shook hands. Claire led him to the guard's office and got him sorted with a building pass and an ID card.

'You're going to be an adviser if what you've got gets us a lead.'

'And if it doesn't?'

'Then you're out. The powers that be said I couldn't reinstate you as an operative – it's too soon, apparently. But they never spelled out the description of what you, as an adviser, can or cannot do, if you know what I mean. I honestly don't think they care too much. They just want something they can hold up on the news to say they've achieved something.'

'Well, I have something.'

Claire led John through the entrance. Eyes diverted towards them, unsure if what they were seeing was true. The walk through the dull corridors did not suggest that the country had been attacked. But when Claire opened the door to the operations room, any last grasp on serenity had gone. People rushed around, phones rang off the hook, conversations were loud, desperate.

They walked through the chaos, and the noise turned to a hum when Claire shut her office door.

'John, it's good to see you,' Connor said.

'It's good to see you too.' They shook hands, then took seats at Claire's desk.

'Connor's my deputy on this one. I felt I had to take the lead, considering the nature of the attack. And it helped me with bargaining for your return.'

'If I was in your position,' Connor started, 'I'd want to hunt these bastards down as well. Anyway, how are you holding up?'

'Like shit. As you can both imagine.'

'What do you have for us?' Claire asked.

'At the Bamburgh murders, there were witness reports and footage of a black BMW fleeing the scene. I saw that same car parked down a side street in the town. It had the same scratch on its offside rear bumper. And when I chased the terrorists down, the car was gone.'

Connor and John looked at each other, expecting Claire to say something. Instead, she typed on her keyboard.

'What are you looking for?' Connor asked.

'An initial forensics report came through first thing. It stated that 4.2 mm bullets were used. If it's the same with the Bamburgh murders, then there's no doubt in my mind they're linked.'

After a few minutes of silence and Claire scanning her monitor, her eyes lit up. '4.2mm.'

'So they're linked,' Connor said. 'It's quite a change of scene and body count, though.'

'What's significant about 4.2?' John asked.

'You can't buy a 4.2 mm bullet,' Claire said. 'Which means you can't buy a 4.2 mm weapon. They're all workshop jobs. Impossible to trace.'

'They probably used Bamburgh to test their weapons. It would explain the difference in body counts,' John said. 'This might suggest that they originate from around there. But why come all the way down the length of the country?'

'We don't know yet. But give Connor the number plate of the vehicle and we'll see if anything comes up.'

'I bet you nothing will.'

John wrote the number plate down and handed it to Connor, who left the office. When he returned a couple of minutes later, his expression filled neither of them with hope.

'Nothing. It's a fake plate.'

'Any suggestions?' Claire said.

'Let's say they are based in Northumberland,' John started, 'and travelled down the country. They had the foresight to use workshop weapons and bullets. Surely they wouldn't travel on fake plates. The risk of being picked up on ANPR is too high.'

'What are you suggesting?' Claire said.

'They would've used real plates for most of the journey, then swapped them out for fakes closer to their destination. There isn't a big police presence in rural areas – it would be easier to drive around with fake plates.'

'Check the traffic cameras on the A1, all of them, for a black BMW three series, fifth generation,' Claire said to Connor.

'Also,' John intervened, 'I believe I saw three people in that car. It might narrow down the search.'

32

The prime minister made a speech outside No. 10. He condemned the attacks and informed the British public that his thoughts and prayers were with the families who had lost loved ones. It was a standard post-tragedy speech. After the routine words, the prime minister announced that towns close to the one attacked were going to have an influx of police patrols. He did not, however, elaborate further on this plan or offer any more details. Instead, when he had said all he had planned to say, he ignored the media's questions and headed straight back inside, pleased they had been seen to be doing something.

'I think we've got something,' Connor said, returning to Claire's office two hours later.

'What is it?' John asked.

Connor handed John and Claire a picture taken by a traffic camera. The grainy image showed a black BMW. He handed them three more images of the car from different cameras. In one picture there was an outline of two people, a driver and a passenger, with a shadow behind them. The two passengers' faces were too grainy to make out any kind of distinguishable features. The driver, however ... his face was clearer, and it looked like death. John didn't recognise him.

'These images show the car heading south on the A1. It was picked up originally on a traffic camera on the A1 south of Newcastle. This potentially fits in with the theory that they operate from Northumberland. Now, the cameras don't take pictures of the rear of the car, unless it's a speed camera, but these guys stuck religiously to the speed limits, so we can't see if there's the scratch that John has described, but I'm convinced this is the car.'

'Why's that?' John asked. He took another look at the picture but, sickened by the people who had made an enemy of him and no closer to knowing if he would recognise the driver if he passed him on the street, he dropped the photos onto the desk.

'The number plate on this car is real. It's registered to a Jeremy Carmichael, who lives in Birmingham. I checked Mr Carmichael out. He's a disabled man in his early thirties. He has Down syndrome. What's interesting, though, is his employment history. He used to work for Salinger Autos, a car parts manufacturer based in Newcastle. It's owned by a man called Gary Salinger.'

'Who's Gary Salinger?' John asked.

'He's a 42-year-old, slightly overweight, balding businessman. Divorced twice for adultery on both occasions – he has a history of illicit affairs. He's clean, however, as far as criminal records are concerned. Another department, however, has had dealings with him before. The NCA tried to get a warrant to search his factory compound. They failed.'

'What were they looking for?'

'They believed Salinger used his factories to make bullets for local drug gangs.'

Claire's phone vibrated. She looked at who was calling and excused herself from her office.

'Who's calling?' John asked.

'I don't know. But to leave now, it must be important.'

'Anyway, let's focus on this. So you think he's turned to helping terrorists now?'

'If he has, there's no apparent motive – except money, which might well be the only motive he needs. And he's not on any watch lists, so I doubt he's been radicalised.'

'So he's in it for the money. And he makes the weapons as well – he'll get the deliveries of raw materials. An auto parts maker is suitable cover.'

'Potentially.'

'In which case, we need to get a warrant to search his factory and arrest him. I want to interrogate him first.'

'I'm sure Claire will let you do that. She, like most people here, has a good deal of trust in your abilities, but if you lay a hand on him, then I'm pulling you out, okay?'

'That's not my style, Connor. You know that.'

'I know. But things are different with this one.'

John went to reply, but Claire burst back into the office with a pale face. 'This has just got a lot worse for all of us.'

'What's going on?' John asked.

'Whoever is behind this has threatened to attack again in five days' time.'

'Five days?'

'In their statement they mentioned the 4.2 mm rounds. That's not public knowledge – so it's definitely them. But they haven't named themselves or given a reason for their attacks or what they want or what they're trying to achieve.'

'Are we telling the public?'

'No, we're not.' Claire sat behind her desk.

'We need to get a warrant to search Salinger Autos.'

'We're not getting a warrant in five days with circumstantial evidence. I doubt we'd get one at all, considering we've already tried and failed.' Claire paused for a moment, debating something in her mind. 'John, listen to me. You're the only one here in an advisory capacity. You're officially not one of us. With this deadline hanging over our heads, we need to move this investigation along. I need you to get Salinger and have a look around his factory if you can.'

'That's not exactly legal, Claire,' Connor said.

'I know it's not, but what other option do we have right now?'

John thought about the proposition. Doing it illegally was against what he believed made for effective policing and a sound justice system. Right now, however, he had a gut feeling – and a little boy to get back. If Salinger worked for the terrorists, then he was a gateway to them.

'Do we know about the security at his factory?' John asked.

'We don't. But it's probably a private company, and they won't give us details without a warrant.'

John continued to think, then finally said, 'I'll do it. I'll need his home address, but I'll do it.'

33

John waited outside Gary's house, a large modern home on the outskirts of Newcastle. He watched to see if anyone would come or go through the gate. Until someone did, he wouldn't be able to see into the property – the perimeter wall did a good job of alleviating prying eyes.

He couldn't wait there all night, however – not with five days looming over his head. He checked for security cameras, saw none, then waited for the traffic to pass before getting out of his car and crossing the road.

With a small window of time available to climb over the wall with no witnesses, John jumped up and pulled himself over. He kept tight to the perimeter hedge, staying in its shadow as he advanced towards the house.

How could anyone involved in killing nineteen people live in a place like this? Crime doesn't pay is sometimes the biggest lie ever told. But John was going to crash Gary's party and drag him back to London, cut him off from all the luxuries he enjoyed. John wondered if Gary ever considered the destinations of his bullets. Or did he only think about the money?

Ground lights lit up the house like a monument. The curtains were drawn across the front of the property. Except for the cars outside, there was no sign that anybody was in. And if there were people inside, John didn't know how many. He just needed Salinger. Anyone else was surplus to requirements.

He stopped and reassessed when he saw the security camera looming over the front door. He would be caught going in through there. Even if no one was monitoring the video feed, someone would eventually come across the footage when Gary didn't turn up for work the next morning. So he stuck to the shadows and headed to the back of the property.

Light from the kitchen spewed out onto the stone patio. The hot tub cover was off, steam evaporated into the night sky, and John traced two pairs of wet footprints through the open French doors.

He unholstered his pistol, raised it to his eyeline, and crept into the kitchen. He heard nothing – no voices, no footsteps. He followed the wet prints through to the stairs.

The carpeted stairs had dried their feet and he couldn't tell what direction they had taken at the top of the landing. He stopped and listened. He could hear something. He followed it.

The noise grew louder the closer he got to the door, and light bled out through the gaps in the frame. He pressed his ear and his pistol against it and heard two voices that sounded like they were enjoying their evening.

He took a deep breath, twisted the handle, threw the door open, and burst into the room.

'No one move. Stay exactly where you are,' he ordered, pistol poised at the two people on the bed.

'Don't worry, mate, I intend to,' Salinger said. He was naked, his wrists handcuffed to the pillars of his bed, and a woman with a Mediterranean complexion was sitting on him, her naked body frozen.

'Miss, I need you to get off him – slowly, no sudden moves – and turn and face me.'

The girl did as she was told and put her hands up by her head.

'Where's the key to the cuffs?' John asked, keeping his weapon aimed at Salinger. She pointed at the chest of drawers. 'Get the key, please. Uncuff him. And don't worry, I won't hurt you.'

'It's okay,' Salinger said. 'Do as he says.'

The girl did as she was told and uncuffed the man.

'Gary Salinger, unless you want me to put bullets in both of your knees, you'll do as you're told. Clear?'

'Crystal clear.'

'You can put your clothes back on. Then I need you to leave,' John said to the frightened girl.

'Don't worry. Do as he says, and I'll contact you later. Everything's fine.'

The girl hurried to put her clothes on and ran out of the room.

'What do you want?' Gary said. 'Can *I* at least put some clothes on?'

'Not yet. A few days ago, bullets you manufactured killed nineteen innocent people. You're going to take me to the factory where they're made, and then you're going to tell me everything you know.'

'And if I don't?'

'You don't get a choice. Nineteen people are dead, and you had a part to play in this. Now get your arse out of bed and get dressed.'

'Why should I believe you?'

'You make 4.2 mm bullets.'

'If you're so sure, then why aren't the police here arresting me?'

'Because, unluckily for you, they sent me instead.'

They stared at each other. Whoever blinked first would lose, but John's eyes were fixed on his target.

34

Gary drove to his factory compound with John's pistol pressed into his side. He tried to make nervous small talk, but John cut it off.

They pulled up to the front gates of Salinger Autos. John watched the guard come towards them.

'If I think you've passed the guard a secret message, I'm just going to shoot both of you and make my own way in. So no games, Gary. It's not just your life that's on the line now.'

Gary stopped outside the gate and rolled down his window.

'Evening, Gary,' the guard said. 'What are you doing back so late?'

'Couldn't sleep. Thought doing some work might help relieve the insomnia. Plus it gives me a chance to show my mate around.'

'Hello,' the guard said to John.

'Hello,' John replied.

'I'll let you on your way,' the guard concluded.

Gary rolled the window up and drove past the main factory

buildings. Cars were parked outside, and John assumed the factory ran twenty-four hours a day.

Gary parked up outside a derelict abandoned warehouse hidden in the shadow of the larger buildings at the back of the compound. 'It's in there,' he said.

'Show me, then.'

Gary got out of the car and John followed behind, concealing his pistol underneath his jacket.

'Who's going to be in the factory at this time of night?' John asked.

'In here, no one.'

Gary scanned a card on a keypad. The latch released, and John followed his prisoner inside. It was dark, empty, and their footsteps echoed to the ceiling as Gary used the torch on his phone to guide the way.

'What am I going to get out of this?' Gary asked.

'You get to live, Gary. That's what you get.'

'Look, I know you might not be police, but you're still under orders, right? They'll want you to take me in, won't they?'

John remained silent and nudged his prisoner forward. They continued into a back office.

'What I'm trying to say is, if I tell you things, will I be given immunity?'

'I can't say. It's not up to me. But do as you're told and things might get easier for you.'

Gary pressed a button on the desk and it slid across the room. A dirty orange glow rose and filled the room with light. Down the stairs, John scanned the underground factory.

'Do you want me to show you around?'

'No. I want you to shut up.'

John continued to look, even if he didn't know exactly what he was looking at. He had fired bullets before, but he didn't know how they were made. There was no way of telling, from his perspective, if Gary was leading him down into a trap, but the secretive nature of the facility gave him enough reason to feel comfortable that this was the real thing.

John holstered his weapon to take pictures.

'Don't try anything,' he said to Gary, and Gary put his hands mockingly in the air.

What he needed to see was a box of 4.2mm rounds. Looking around, however, he could not see any. Why would Gary keep bullets here and incriminate himself? Which meant the bullets had been taken elsewhere. And if he wasn't producing any more and the terrorists were planning an attack in five days, the bullets were already out there waiting to be fired.

'The attack in five days' time. Where did you send the bullets to?' John asked, pocketing his phone and unholstering his pistol.

Gary didn't answer. His eyes wandered around the room.

'Gary. Answer the question.'

'We're making them closer to the time.'

John didn't like this answer. He had no way of telling if it was a lie. 'Where are you going to send them?'

'For that sort of information – I could do a deal.'

John wasn't interested in wasting time with deals. That could be sorted out in London.

'What's through there?'

'My office.'

'Show me.'

The office was bare. A desk with a computer and a box of cigars resting on it, two worn leather chairs, and a cabinet in the corner. Gary flicked a switch, turning on the light hanging from a wire.

'Sit in the chair and don't move.' Gary did as he was told, and John went to the cabinet. He flicked through the papers while monitoring his prisoner. He pulled out a blueprint, scanned the document, and concluded that he was looking at technical drawings and instructions for making 4.2 mm bullets.

'Oh, you're going to jail for a long time, Salinger.'

'I know things. Things that might help you. But I want immunity.'

'I'm not interested in deals. We can do that when we get back to London.'

'Then I have nothing more to say to you.'

'Fine by me.'

John folded the blueprint and put it into his pocket. He went through the desk drawers and found three business cards with the name 'Antonia' on them; the numbers on all of them were different and none of them were English.

'Who's Antonia?' John asked.

'She's nobody.'

'You have three business cards from her, all with different numbers. She doesn't look like a nobody.'

Gary said nothing.

'Is she your client?'

Gary said nothing.

'Is she your client, Gary?' John slammed the cards onto the desk.

Gary remained silent.

John looked him in the eye and knew he was hiding something, so he pocketed them.

He went to look in the bottom drawer and had got as far as opening it when the desk slammed into him, knocking him to the floor. Gary jumped out of his seat and onto the desk. He saw John's pistol on the floor and dropped to grab it. John kicked it away before he could, then scrambled to his feet. Gary went for the weapon again, but John wrapped his arm around his neck and pulled him back. He elbowed his captive's stomach until he let go. And when he did, they turned and faced each other. They tiptoed around the office, their eyes locked like wolves waiting to attack. John lunged forward, striking with his fist. Gary parried the punch, then hit back, slamming his fist into John's chin. John tumbled, then charged forward. He tackled Gary over the desk and they landed in a heap on the floor. John punched Gary's face hard several times, busting his nose, and watched as his eyes lost their focus.

John found the strength to stop himself from beating him further. Gary no longer had it in him to fight back. He was, he told himself, still in control.

His mind, his body calmed like the weather after a storm and he found, to his surprise, that he felt nothing when he looked down at Gary.

When Gary coughed, blood spattered out of his mouth, and his breathing was laboured like an old dog. John needed to get back to

London; he had overstayed his welcome here. He grabbed his delirious suspect by the ankles and dragged him through the factory. The occasional smear of blood marked their trail.

The stairs were the toughest. Dragging the overweight body up them one at a time made John sweat, and each step caused Gary's head to jolt back and hit the stairs. John wondered if he felt it but soon realised that he didn't care. It was just another dose of pain he deserved to go through.

John lifted him into the boot of the car and punched him one last time to knock him out. Would it be enough to get him down to London? John didn't know. But he wouldn't hang around long enough for him to regain consciousness.

35

John drove through the night and struggled to keep awake as dawn broke through the cityscape on the horizon.

Guards met him when he returned and grabbed Gary from the boot of his car and dragged him into a holding cell. The night shift took the blueprints and business cards, and he explained to them what he thought they were and what he had seen and what Gary had said. They would investigate during the night and brief him when he came in later. John tried to tell them he was staying to help. Claire, who had suspected this would be the case, had already given orders for him to get some rest.

Reluctantly, he went back to his flat, and when he did, he sat and looked at John the dinosaur, in pride of place on his kitchen table. His stitched-on smile never failed to warm his heart.

It was mid-morning when John woke in a cold sweat. He had relived losing Charlie in his dreams, heard him cry for his mum, for

John, for someone to save him, but no one came. The shooter pointed his makeshift weapon at the boy and grabbed him. A clatter of gunfire burst out, cutting his nightmare short.

He made it into Claire's office slightly out of breath, bags under his eyes.

'Did you sleep at all?' Claire asked.

'I slept enough.'

John crashed into the seat at Claire's desk. He let out a long sigh and rubbed his face with his hands.

'Gary's in good enough shape to be questioned. You wanted to be the first – you can be the first.'

'Would you give him immunity if he told us who was behind all this?'

'What do you mean?'

'Gary's just a middleman. He's providing the bullets and apparently the car. But he's getting orders from somebody.'

Claire thought for a moment.

'I don't know,' she finally answered. 'It depends on what he offers us. If it's a large, well-funded terrorist organisation he knows enough about that leads us to dismantle it, then yeah, maybe. But if it's nothing of merit, then not a chance in hell. What's got you thinking like this?'

'Gary said he would only talk if he was going to be given a deal. I guess he wants some sort of immunity.'

'Is that why you beat him up? To get answers from him?'

'No. I did that because he attacked me.'

'Are you okay?'

John looked at her and hoped she would notice his bruised

face. 'Never ask me that again. He attacked me. You couldn't have thought he'd come quietly?'

'Okay,' she said. 'But just remember, you're after your enemies. Don't lose yourself. Or it will all be for nothing.'

'I won't.'

'Before you go, I've got Connor coming to brief us on your findings.'

John reached into his pocket and retrieved his phone. 'I also took pictures of the place.'

'Send them to me.'

John sent the pictures, then reclined in the chair and thought about Gary, alone in the holding cell. He wondered what he was thinking about. Then he wondered how Olivia was coping, but he forced that out of his mind. He hated to do it, but thinking about her was a distraction. He needed to remain focused. The sooner this was done, the sooner he could be back with her.

Connor walked into the office. 'We analysed the blueprints and they fit with the 4.2mm bullets used in the attacks. So we can definitely link this part of the operation to Gary.'

'Did you see any bullets?' Claire interrupted.

'No. Which to me means they've either made the bullets for the next attack and already sent them to the terrorists or they're going to make them closer to the time. I asked Gary. He said they make them closer to the time. But I wouldn't believe him.'

'I don't think we should follow the bullets,' Connor interrupted. 'We looked at the business cards. Antonia is in Interpol's records. She's suspected of being a small-time arms dealer. Sells rifles and pistols. Nothing major, but it's a perfect fit for our terrorists.'

'Where is she based?' John asked.

'Her last known address is in Venice.'

'Venice? How does she get the weapons to England?'

'We're not sure. She smuggles them all around Europe. Apparently it isn't difficult for her, hence why she is only suspected of the crime, and not convicted.'

John looked at Claire. Another lead, perhaps? Connor handed Interpol's file on Antonia to them, and when John saw her picture on the first page, his fists clenched, crunching the file, and he dropped it onto the desk.

'Shit.'

'What's wrong?' Claire asked.

'Last night, when I detained Gary, he was having sex with some girl. Although that girl turns out to be a small-time arms dealer.'

'What?'

'She was there last night. Which means she's probably delivered more weapons to them. And I could've got them both, but I was so focused on Gary that I was stupid enough to let her go.'

Claire and Connor shared a glance, but neither spoke.

'Look, John,' Claire started, 'don't worry about it. Now we know she came to England, we can start looking through passport records and CCTV at airports. If we can prove she was here—'

'It doesn't prove a thing unless you know she sold them weapons. And more to the point, why was she there? Do you really think she would risk staying in the country just to see Gary? No, she's delivered more weapons. Which means the attack in four days is likely to be more deadly than the last.'

'What do you think we should do about her?' Connor asked.

'We need to detain her, just like Gary. If we cut off the supply of her weapons and Gary's bullets, then the terrorists are going to struggle to carry out more attacks.'

'But they'll just get more bullets,' Connor said.

'Not 4.2mm in that timescale, they won't. We get them both – we'll squeeze them, disrupt their plans, force them to make mistakes.'

'I like your thinking, John, but I think it's best to focus on this attack in four days' time,' Claire said.

'I agree. Of course I want to focus on the attack in four bloody days' time. But when will this stop? We don't even know what these terrorists want. I sat aside and did nothing and now Charlie's gone. I'm not doing that again. Whoever the shooters are, they're my priority.'

'And we'll get them. I can promise you that. We're all working on this. When do you think you're going to get her?'

'Me? Can't we just get the Italians to detain her and bring her here?'

'That's wishful thinking. What are they going to arrest her for? Just like you said, we have nothing that proves a transaction ever happened between them. They won't arrest her without a cause, and the bureaucracy to get her back here ...'

'Guess I might have to go to Italy, then. But I'm questioning Gary first.'

'What makes you think he'll know anything at all?' Connor asked.

'He was with her last night, so he knows something about her – something that might help us get her. And he provided the terrorists with a car. Or at least he coerced an ex-employee into doing it. Why would he do that if he was just meant to be providing the bullets?'

'I don't know. But what does Salinger gain from this except money? Or is he giving the terrorists cars to keep them happy customers?'

'Do you think it might be worth me checking over anyone else in his employment history – see if anything comes up?'

'Yeah. I think it would. Past and present. I'll be as thorough as I can.' When Connor left, a wave of noise crashed into the office.

'Do you want to wait before he comes back with anything before talking to Salinger?' Claire asked.

'No. We haven't got time to waste. He knows things, and I'm going to get them out of him regardless of whether he pleads for immunity.'

36

John thought he looked drained. Gary, however, looked like he had been to hell and back only to be told that he was going again. His bleary eyes weren't focused on John, despite looking in his direction. Life had drained from his face, leaving his complexion as pale as that of a petrified child. He was slouched over the table, hands in cuffs, and a ring of irritation had formed around his wrists.

'How are you holding up, Gary?' John said.

'My nose hurts and my body aches, thanks to you. Now release me, because we both know this isn't legal.'

'Neither is making bullets for terrorists.'

'You have no evidence of that.'

'Yes, we do. Those blueprints I found in your cabinet, we've analysed them and they match the bullets we extracted from the bodies. Is there not a hint of remorse behind those tired eyes of yours?'

'How can there be when it had nothing to do with me?'

'So why was a car, a black BMW registered to a Jeremy Carmichael, an ex-employee of yours, used by the terrorists?'

'Am I getting a lawyer?'

'You can help me get justice for the nineteen people that your bullets killed.'

'You can't give me immunity – you said so yesterday. What about the people watching?' Gary pointed a limp hand at the mirrored glass. 'Can they?'

'The terrorists? Who are they? Did they used to work for you like Jeremy did? Or did they come to you asking for your services? Because we're looking into who you're employing right now and who you have employed in the past. And if we find out something first, then it's going to be a lot worse for you. So tell me, Gary, what is your link to the terrorists? And who are they?'

'Immunity.'

'Fine.' John let out a sigh. 'Let's talk about Antonia, then. I know she was the girl you were with last night and we know what she does, so we know she's involved. We're going to be detaining her soon. We know she's in Italy, but that's not a problem for us. I guess what I'm trying to do, Gary, is paint a picture for you. A picture showing us hunting you lot down. You will all be brought to justice.'

'Immunity.'

'When we talk to her, the gloves will be off. Do you think she'll spill? Do you trust her not to talk to us? Not tell us who the terrorists are? Because if I was in your situation, I wouldn't. If I was in your situation, I'd start talking.'

Gary looked at the two-way glass. His exhausted reflection

stared back at him. Then he looked at his hands, at the irritated skin around his wrists, and breathed out a sigh and sunk further into his chair.

John's eyes were fixed on him, the dishevelled man in front of him who knew he was beat, who knew the law was moving in on him.

Gary looked through John's eyes to the back of his skull and said through gritted teeth, 'Immunity ... you piece of shit.'

John stood up, knocking his chair over, and slammed his hands onto the table. 'You want immunity? Then talk. Tell us who the terrorists are. Tell us what they're planning. And tell us how involved in this you really are. If you do that, then we might, just might, consider immunity. But right now, everything is on our side. You have nowhere to run.'

'Everything except time, it seems. But what about you? Why are you doing this? Detaining me illegally, holding me at gunpoint, forcing me to show you around my facility.'

'Why did you let me? Are you telling me that guns scare you? Or is it the bullets? Because quite frankly that's just ironic.'

'Because I have nothing to hide from you. I'm innocent.'

'You're deluded.'

John thought for a moment, then picked his chair back up and sat down. The redness in his face subsided.

'It's not that you have nothing to hide. It's because the terrorists have promised to protect you. But the reality is they're just using you. You're not the only bullet maker in the country. They'll find someone else when they realise you're in here. They'll panic, make mistakes, and we'll be there to capitalise, while you'll just be here, wasting away before you're put on trial. And when you are, you'll be asking why they didn't come to save you.'

Gary laughed, but his sudden burst of excitement dissolved into a coughing fit.

'You guys really don't know a damn thing about any of this. You can't get to me legally. All the evidence you have was obtained illegally and is inadmissible in court. Whatever idea you have about my connections to the terrorists, you're wrong, and you will come to realise that, and then you're going to have to let me go.'

'I'm going to give you one last chance to answer my questions before we move on to our next lead. Who are the terrorists? Where are they? And what are they planning?'

Gary's laughter returned, along with the coughing fit. 'You guys are desperate. You really know nothing, don't you? I mean, look at you. You can barely keep it together – I can see it behind those eyes of yours. You're not guided by logic, you're guided by anger, and an angry man is easy to manipulate. Sod the people that died. They mean nothing to nobody.'

John stood up again, kicking his chair back, and went to grab Gary by the scruff of his neck and slam his head on the table. A knock on the door, however, stopped him.

'I'll be right back,' John said.

37

Claire and Connor were outside. They shot each other a concerned glance, then Claire said, 'Is everything okay?'

John felt his heart racing in his chest. The adrenaline had locked his eyes open, and he took a long, slow breath.

'Yeah. I'm fine. He's just going to be harder to crack than I originally thought. He's not a stupid man. Were you guys not watching?'

'No,' Claire said. 'Connor came and got me. He's found something important.'

John admitted to himself that he felt more relieved that his outburst had gone unnoticed than he did knowing Connor had found something. If he was going to be a part of this investigation, he was going to have to control his temper, because Claire would get rid of him the moment she suspected him of being a liability. No matter how highly she thought of him.

'What have you got?'

'His current employees are all clean, and I mean there's hardly a parking fine between them. It's the same with his ex-employees, except for one man. Carl Bedford. He worked for Gary two years ago, but before that, he spent twenty years in jail for a double murder – a gang-related killing.'

'He's an outlier, but it means nothing.'

'Well, this might intrigue you, then.' Connor handed him a file, and in the file was a picture of the black BMW from a traffic camera. The face of the driver had been detailed enough to be put through facial recognition, like John had hoped, and it had returned a 52 per cent chance that the person driving the car was Carl Bedford.

'It's only 52 per cent. But it's the best we're going to get, right?'

'We ran the software through the database, all criminals, dead and alive, and those currently on the terrorist watch list. This was the highest match by some 30 per cent.'

'We have him, then. One of them is Carl Bedford.' The beginnings of a smile appeared on John's face but soon disappeared; there was still some way to go to tracking him down and detaining him.

'I'm not sure,' Connor said.

'What?'

'Look at the next page,' Claire said.

John scanned the next page, but the important piece of information sat in the top right-hand corner next to Carl's date of birth. It was his date of death.

'He's been dead for two years? That's wrong. He's alive.'

'You're right – he is,' Claire said. 'We're going to investigate further.'

'He died at Salinger Autos of a heart attack,' Connor said. 'It's a tremendous coincidence. Being dead, however, has its advantages. It makes you much harder to track, for one. But the good news for us is it doesn't look like he's changed his appearance much. We might be able to track him down through facial recognition elsewhere. But it won't be easy.'

'What about the other two in the car? Anything on them?' John asked.

'No. We tried, but their faces are too obscure.'

They were quiet for a moment. Both Claire and Connor waited for John to speak.

'He must live somewhere. Someone must know where he is.'

'They probably do. But look, I'm going to try and find him. Claire and I are convinced he's one of them. And when we have something, we'll come back to you.'

'Okay,' John said. 'Looks like I have something to tell Gary. Hopefully this will make him talk.'

38

'Gary,' John said as he re-entered the interview room. 'Have I got something to tell you!' He sat down and dropped the file on the table, and Gary lifted his head to look at his interrogator. 'Look at that. It's more proof of your involvement in all this. I told you we'd find something, and the more we do, the less the chance you have of getting immunity.'

Gary reached for the file, went to pick it up, but his hand hovered over it. He looked across the table at his interrogator. Gary's face remained expressionless, and John was certain his face didn't give away any emotion either. Gary looked at the file again, his hand still hovering like he was waiting for permission. He looked at John again, and this time he picked it up and flicked through it.

'You guys chasing ghosts now?'

'He looks alive to me. And if he died in your factory, then you must be in on this as well. What made you go from making bullets for drug dealers to becoming a terrorist?'

'I'm not a terrorist.'

'Looks like you are to me. Now, where is he? You tell us that and chances are you can have immunity.'

'You really think I'm going to believe that?'

'I want Carl and the other two more than I want you. You're just a middleman, the hired help, the nobody. I want the actual killers, and it starts with you telling me where Carl is.'

Gary did not reply. He looked down at the file for a moment, then looked up at John. 'Carl died two years ago. I haven't seen him since.'

'Will Antonia know who he is? He must've been in contact with her to order the weapons. Can you really trust her not to tell us? If we offer her immunity, then it will be a race between the two of you. See who talks first.'

'Antonia won't know who he is. He died two years ago.'

'So are you admitting that *you* ordered the weapons from Antonia?'

'I'm not admitting anything.'

'But you know her. She was with you last night, that you can't deny. I was there.'

Gary remained silent.

John took the file from him and reclined in his chair. 'I'll tell you what I think. I think Carl is running the show and he made you help him fake his death two years ago. Being a dead man made it easier to plan this, and he knew you made bullets. All he needed was someone to make weapons. So he got in contact with Antonia.

Now Carl has the means to shoot people in ways that are untraceable. And because he's dead, he's going to be difficult to find. I'll admit that much. But not too difficult for us. And out of this you get a lot of money, I imagine. But what does Carl get out of this? That's the question. What does he want?'

'You don't know a damn thing. And it shows. You're pathetic. Now release me.'

'Like I've told you before, Gary, you're not going anywhere. So, are you going to tell me anything?'

Gary remained silent.

John left the interview room and headed back to Claire's office.

'How did it go?' she asked.

'He's not talking. He's hiding something, though. It's obvious. I think he's been promised protection or something like that. He's riding on that coming through. When he sees there's no way out for him, he'll talk.'

'Let's hope so. Anyway, we've got a bit more on Bedford. We have an address for where he used to live after leaving prison. Might be worth looking at. He's got a brother as well. And I think it'll be worth heading to his old prison – talk to the guards and his supervisors. They might tell us if they thought he had become radicalised or something. From what I've seen, however, there's no suggestion he's ever been suspected of being radicalised. He's never been on a terrorist watch list.'

'If he had, though, they wouldn't have let him out.'

'You're right. They wouldn't have. He might have displayed

some odd behaviour or something, might have spoken to people who had terrorist links, but right now, he's our main guy, and I want you to find out as much as you can about him.'

'Don't worry, I will.'

'Here are the details for the prison. I've contacted them. They're waiting for one of us to arrive.'

39

No one's hospitality needs were going to be met inside a high-
security prison. The uncomfortable chair John sat in was a reminder
of that. He had been waiting for thirty minutes, and his jaded eyes
watched the seconds tick by on the clock on the exposed brick wall.
At least he had been given a glass of water, but a coffee was what
he really needed.

He heard footsteps coming down the corridor and his head
perked up to see if they were heading his way. They were. He stood
up and greeted the supervising officer with a handshake.

'Hi, I'm John.'

'Nice to meet you, John. I'm Rob.' They both took a seat at
the table. 'So, I hear you're asking about Carl Bedford.'

'That's correct. And I hope you understand I can't go into
detail about why I'm asking you these questions.'

'Not to worry. I understand.'

'Good. Right—'

'Do you want a coffee before we start?'

'Yes, definitely.'

'I'll be right back.'

Rob left the room for five minutes. When he returned, he had two plastic cups with steam rising from them. Rob handed one to John. He took a sip. It was disgusting, but it was better than succumbing to his fatigue.

'I want to start by asking you what Carl was like in here. Did he get in any trouble? Who were his friends?'

Rob thought for a moment, trying to recall memories that were years old.

'I was only here for the second half of his sentence, so I can't tell you what he was like when he first got here. But when I was here, he was quiet, kept to himself. He only seemed to talk to others when he needed to.'

'So when he was out of his cell, was he often on his own?'

'Not necessarily. I just think he's unable to form strong bonds with people and because of that, he's not really bothered about friendships or anything like that.'

'Would you say he's a psychopath?'

Rob chuckled, sipped his coffee, then said, 'Look, I'm no psychologist, but you get to know the types we have in here. Psychos can come in all different shapes and sizes and frankly, these people are all murderers. It wouldn't surprise me if they're all psychos.'

'So there were no obvious friends. If I was to ask you who comes to mind, though, when you think of Carl, who would you say are the first two people that come into your head?'

'It's hard to say with Carl. But … if I had to mention anyone, then I'd say … Trent Williams and Wayne Crust.'

John ran the names over and over in his head. He wondered what they looked like. He wondered what they would look like dead.

'And what can you tell me about Trent and Wayne?'

'They were joined at the hip, shared a cell together. Both were in here for murders and arrived at the same time, but Trent got out two years ago. Wayne's still in here – still got three years left.'

'What about Trent? Did he ever cause trouble? Ever say anything of any genuine concern to you, or anything you overheard?'

Rob took a sip of his coffee. 'No. Trent was fine. He had a seventeen-year sentence and got out after thirteen. He showed good behaviour.'

John wondered if they considered that the psychopaths might display good behaviour so that they'd get released earlier. Or did they genuinely think they had been reformed? John went to drink his coffee, but after hearing Trent had been let out four years early, he had to use every bit of control he had in his body not to throw it at the wall.

'So Trent was never a cause for concern, even when he was talking to Carl?'

'No, not that I can recall.'

'What were Carl and Trent's plans after leaving prison?'

'They both wanted to get jobs. They both wanted to just get on in the world and be ordinary citizens, if there is such a term.' Rob chuckled at his own comment, then drank the rest of his coffee.

'Carl liked cars and wanted to go into the car industry. And Trent … Trent just wanted a simple, peaceful life, I guess – he had done his hard time in here and whatever he was up to prior. I think he just wanted to be left alone. Like I said, though, Carl was quiet, and Trent was an exemplary prisoner.'

An oxymoron, John thought, growing more and more frustrated with the lack of progress. He'd wanted to come here and find leads to Carl's turn to terrorism. Instead, all he had gained was one name. And although he wasn't leaving empty-handed, he felt short changed, and after he had dismissed Rob, he still wanted to throw his coffee at the wall.

Outside the prison gates, John called Claire.

'Hi, John.'

'Claire, I've got nothing from the prison. There's nothing here to suggest that Carl became radicalised or anything like that. We still need to keep looking. He could've turned once he got out.'

'Did you get *anything*?'

'Yeah. A Trent Williams. Was in with Carl. Apparently the two got along. He got out two years ago, which fits in perfectly with Carl's death. Get Connor to investigate him. He might well be one of the other two terrorists I'm after.'

'*We're* after, John. We're in this as well. But I'll get Connor to look into him.'

'Okay. I'm going to Carl's old address to see if any of his neighbours have anything to say. Someone's got to know something.'

237

Carl's old house sat on the edge of a council estate; it was all he could afford after being inside for twenty years. John watched the house from his car on the other side of the street and knew he'd stand out the moment he got out. He was neither a kid riding around on a BMX nor an adult riding off a high, wandering aimlessly around the streets.

John got out of the car and felt eyes on the back of his head. He went to Carl's neighbour's house first. The people living in Carl's old house now wouldn't know who he was. His neighbours, however, might.

Loud music was playing inside, and he knocked on the door, thinking that whoever was inside wouldn't hear. After a few moments, however, a middle-aged woman who looked like she had smoked all her life answered the door.

'What do you want?' Her voice was like sandpaper.

'Hi. My name is John. I was wondering if you could tell me

anything about Carl Bedford, your old neighbour.'

'I don't talk to cops,' she said and went to close the door, but John put his hand out.

'I know I probably look like one, but I'm not, I promise. Carl was an old friend of mine. I'm just trying to find him.'

'Well, I know nothing. I ain't seen him in two years.' She went to close the door again, but again John stopped her. 'Listen, you need to get out of here before I call some men around here to make you go.' John smelt the tobacco on her breath.

'Listen, please, it would be a great help for me if you told me what you know about him.'

'I don't know shit about him. I only saw him a few times. Rumours were going round saying he'd been in jail for murder. But I hardly ever saw him, and I had nothing to do with him. No one around here saw him – the house was empty most of the time.'

'What do you mean by that?'

'I mean he was never here, always somewhere else.'

'Did he have any friends around here? People he spoke to, anything like that?'

'What do you think I am, his mum? I don't know. Now get the hell out of here.'

'Please, was there anyone? I need to find him.'

She remained quiet for a moment, staring at the man on her doorstep through her bloodshot eyes. 'Go see Clanky. He might know.' She slammed the door this time. John swore under his breath.

He went to knock on her door again but decided against it – she didn't want to talk to him. Or did she just not want to talk about

Clanky? John wondered, as he returned to his car, if it was even a lead worth pursuing. After all, he was only one man, and if Clanky, whoever they were, was enough to stop a conversation and have a door slammed in his face, then perhaps it was best to leave it. But leave it to who? Who else was going to question a man with a tenuous link to Bedford?

He stopped short of his car and headed towards the group of kids lingering around on their bikes. 'What do you want, old man?' was the welcoming greeting he received from the oldest-looking kid.

'Do you guys know where Clanky is?'

The kids stopped riding and looked at one another. John thought they were going to run. Instead, the oldest kid dropped his bike and walked up to John.

'You want to know where Clanky is?'

'Yeah, I do.'

'What do you think we are, stupid? I don't talk to police.'

'Listen, kid, I'm not police. I'm just looking for my friend. You might know him. Carl Bedford?' His enquiry was answered with an empty look. 'Apparently he knew Clanky.'

'So you're going to ask Clanky about this Carl guy?'

'Yes.'

The oldest kid looked back at his ragged collection of friends, and they all burst out laughing. 'Yeah, good luck with that, old man.'

'Who is Clanky?'

'A man who doesn't talk to cops, that's who. Now you better get lost. This ain't the place you should hang around.' The kid returned to his friends.

'Wait. Just answer me this. Are you scared of Clanky?'

The kid stopped in his tracks, and murmurs from his friends filled the silence between them.

'Nah. I ain't scared of him. I just don't want to be seen talking to cops.'

'Would a cop offer you ten quid to give me his address? If I was a cop, don't you think I'd know that already? And if I was a cop, why would I ask kids for information?'

The kid turned on his heel and eyed up John. 'Ten quid? That kind of information is worth more than that.'

'Fine, twenty.' John pulled his wallet from his pocket, taking his ID out and pocketing it in his jacket, and took out a twenty-pound note.

'You know what? Just chuck us the wallet and we'll tell you. That is, if you really want to find your friend.'

John didn't hesitate. He made to hand the kid the wallet, but when he went to grab it, John pulled it back and said, 'Where does he live?'

The kid looked at John, then he looked down the road and said, 'He lives at 42. But don't tell him we told you where he lives. We know that's your car. We'll burst your tyres if you do.'

John handed the kid his wallet and he dashed back to his bike. The group cycled off down a side street and out of view.

There was fifty pounds in that wallet along with debit and credit cards now needing to be cancelled, John thought. They'd better not have been lying to him.

Number 42 didn't look too dissimilar from Bedford's

neighbour's house, although this one didn't smell of tobacco, it smelt of weed. John knocked and a few moments later, someone answered the door.

'What do you want?' asked the dishevelled-looking man at the door, whose skinny body was almost transparent.

'Are you Clanky?'

'What's it to you?'

'I'm looking for a man called Carl Bedford. Apparently you knew him?'

'Can't help you, mate.'

The man, like the woman before him, went to close the door on John, but he put his hand out and stopped him. John noted it took less strength than it had with the chain-smoking neighbour.

'Unless you got a warrant, you're not coming in here.'

'Fuck's sake. I'm not police. I'm just trying to look for my friend.'

'What the hell's going on over there?' a voice inside the house asked.

'Nothing. Just some loser looking for Bedford.'

'Well, tell him he's two years too late. Then tell him to sod off unless he wants to buy a bag.'

'You're two years—'

'I heard, thank you.'

'So, do you want to buy a bag?'

'Of what? Weed?'

'Do you want a bag, man? It'd be good for you. After coming here and being two years too late.'

'No, thank you.'

John went back into his car and drew a sharp breath – another pointless lead.

If Carl worked for Gary, he wouldn't have lived here – he would have been in Newcastle, John realised, thinking about what his neighbour had mentioned about his sustained absence. This was his only known address, however, meaning he was either homeless when he worked for Gary or Gary had put him up somewhere. Why would Gary go this far to help a terrorist like Carl? John's first thought was money. For whatever reason, Carl had committed acts of terror, and John's current theory saw Carl working for Gary to convince him to make bullets for his cause. But where would Carl have got the money from to fund his own acts of terror?

John rang Claire.

'Have you got anything for us?'

'Nothing from his house or this area. It was pointless coming here. If he was working for Gary, then why would he live here? He would have been up north somewhere and is most likely still up there. And more to the point, where the hell does he get the money from to fund all this?'

'It's a good point. Have you spoken to his brother yet?'

'No, not yet. He's next on my list, but get Connor to check over Carl's finances and Trent Williams's as well. They must've got money from somewhere.'

'Will do. We've got something on Williams.'

'Go ahead.'

'We have a confirmed address for him in Enfield, London, the one he moved into after prison. And we know he's there. He came up on CCTV nearby only yesterday.'

John didn't reply. He wondered why someone who had been involved in a terrorist attack only days ago would stick around his home address. Why wasn't he hiding?

'Are you still there?'

'Yeah, I'm still here. It doesn't make much sense to me. Carl's in hiding and this idiot's walking around like he's not killed anyone. What the hell is that all about?'

'I don't know, but I think it's worth checking out.'

'Yeah, so do I. I'm going to head to his brother's first. See if he knows anything about his terrorist brother, and then I'm going for Trent.'

41

Ben lived ten miles away from his brother's old place. His house — detached, with a front garden and two cars in the drive — was a far cry from the council estate. John walked up the path that cut through the front garden to the house and knocked on the door.

'Hello,' Ben said, answering the door.

'Hi. I was wondering if you could help me. I'm after some information about Carl Bedford, your brother.'

Ben was stunned into silence, like he hadn't heard his brother's name in a long time.

'Carl's dead. He died two years ago of a heart attack. I'm sorry, I can't help you.'

'I'm aware of that. But I'd like to ask you some questions about him anyway.'

'What? Is this some kind of joke?'

'It's not a joke. In fact, it's very serious. I'm with the police, and we believe your brother is alive.'

'Alive? What are you talking about? Can I see some ID?'

John pulled his ID from his jacket pocket. They'd given it to him on his return, and it didn't look like a typical police officer's ID. He hoped Ben wouldn't know the difference and would accept being shown any form of identification.

Ben shuffled his feet. His complexion turned pale, but he composed himself and said, 'What makes you think my brother is alive?'

'How would you describe your relationship with him?' John asked. What he really wanted to know, after seeing the house and the cars, was whether his brother had supported him financially.

'Before or after he went to prison? Do you really think he's alive?'

Convinced the man in front of him was acting a part, John capitalised on this and asked to come in, insisting it would be easier for Ben if he was sitting down.

'Yes, of course.' Ben obliged.

John followed him into the open-plan kitchen, his eyes fixed on the back of Ben's head, wondering what it would look like with two bullet holes in the back of it. He snapped the thought out of his mind – he would not kill a man in cold blood. Frustration, however, was growing inside him – he wasn't getting the straight answers he'd thought he would.

They took a seat at the kitchen table and in Ben's flustered state, which John thought he played well, he didn't offer him a coffee or anything, despite his fatigue crying out for one. When was the last time he had had a good night's sleep? When would the next be?

'What makes you think my brother is alive?' Ben asked.

'Let's talk about your relationship with him first, okay? We'll start before prison.'

'Well, we were close as brothers. We both grew up on a council estate about ten miles from here. Our dad was non-existent, and our mum wasn't present much either – we were like a burden to her. We spent a lot of time causing trouble. No one told us not to, and we felt like we were in control of our lives – like we could do anything.'

Ben stared into the distance and John wondered if he'd practised this performance. It was convincing. But John wasn't in a trusting mood.

'But I saw the path we were taking wasn't good for us. I didn't want to go around causing trouble anymore. I wanted to be more than that. I wanted a better life for myself, but Carl wasn't interested – he always went looking for trouble whenever he could. So we went our separate ways. We didn't speak to each other, and I missed him. Then he shot two people. He got involved with a local gang having a turf war.

'He was sent to prison a year later, and I can't lie to you, I was relieved. Even though I love him, I thought inside he wouldn't cause any trouble and hopefully he'd see the error of his ways.'

'What about while he was in prison? Did you talk to him much then?'

'I went to support him at the trial – paid for the lawyer, in fact. It helped reduce his sentence by a few years.'

John's body clenched like it was bracing for an impact. His jaw locked and he forced himself to remain seated. How could Ben have known that his lawyer getting his brother off by a few years would lead to Charlie being taken from him?

'He always spoke about getting out,' Ben continued. 'Except he wanted to kill again. He spoke about the thrill he got from it. He seemed to enjoy it. Killing people. He actually seemed to enjoy it. I guess I couldn't see that side of him, though. I couldn't see the brother I grew up with as a murderer. Are you okay?'

John snapped back into reality, unclenched his fists, and felt his body relax. His heart pounded in his chest. 'Yes, I'm fine. So what happened then?'

'I decided there was nothing else I could do for him. I didn't even see him get out of prison. It was hard, you know.'

John saw Ben rubbing his ring finger like he was trying to find something that was no longer there. Ben noticed and said, 'I got divorced six months ago. But I got shared custody of the kids, which is better than nothing, I suppose.'

John thought it was, considering what this man might well have funded.

'How do you make a living?'

'I run a carpet business. It's not the most exciting thing in the world, but it pays the bills.'

'It certainly does. Did you help Carl out financially after he got out of prison?'

'I wanted to – you know, help him get back on his feet. They gave him a house on the council estate where we used to grow up. I thought it was a stupid idea, sending him back to where it all began. He mentioned getting a job up north to me once, working for a company called Salinger Autos, I believe. That was the last

248

time we spoke.'

'So after he left, you never saw him again?'

'No. The next I heard, he'd died of a heart attack. You know, I look back at my brother's life and I wonder if he was ever happy. Or was it just a waste of a life?'

John answered the question for him in his own mind. It was unfortunate he was still alive and still wasting it.

'But now you're telling me he's alive?'

'We believe he had something to do with the terrorist incident that happened a couple of days ago. Know anything about it?' John stared into his eyes, searching for the truth. He wanted to catch him lying, he wanted him to confess to funding his brother's terrorism, but the shock behind his eyes was real. There was no way he could be faking the tight inhalation of breath, the sustained cold, pale complexion, and the drain of life from his eyes.

Had he come here for nothing? Wasting time again? The anger inside him burned like a furnace in hell.

'Please tell me you're joking. That's not true. It can't be true. Carl might have murdered people in the past, but terrorism? He'd never do that. Oh God!' Ben got off his chair and wandered aimlessly around the kitchen, rubbing his shaking hands through his hair.

'I know this might be a shock to you, Ben, but he is the prime suspect in this.'

Ben placed his hands on the counter and looked out of the window into his garden and muttered to himself that this was not the truth. He poured himself a glass of water and drank, spilling some out of the corners of his mouth. He returned to the table almost breathless.

'I don't know what to say,' Ben said.

'We are looking into how he funded this.'

'You think I funded it, don't you? You think I would give money to a cause as sick as that?' He pointed a finger at John and said, 'How dare you come to my house and accuse me of funding terrorism! I'd never give money to something like that. But that's what you saw – someone from a council estate who made it in life, and you just assumed he must've done it through criminal means!'

'That's not what I'm saying. Nobody is accusing you of anything. Please, sit down and listen to me. I'm trying to help. I have inquiries to make, and the more cooperation I get, the sooner I can get justice.'

Ben paused. He looked at the haggard, desperate man in his kitchen, then sat down and listened.

'We need access to your accounts just so we can see where the money is going. At the moment it's entirely voluntary, but it might give us some sort of clue.'

'Clue to what? I never gave my brother any money – he didn't want any. But you know what? Fuck you. If you want to accuse me of things like that, then you can damn well have a look, because I have nothing to hide. And then you can be sorry for not only wasting my time but the time of the families who have lost loved ones.'

John took a breath. This man could well be innocent, but his comments riled something in John's blood. He had two leads left, Trent and Antonia. And if they brought up nothing, he didn't know what he was going to do next. But Antonia was out of the equation.

To detain people in this manner in this country was one thing; to do so in another would be next to impossible and would most likely end with John locked up in an Italian jail. He left Ben, who assured John he would contact the number he had been given to hand over his financials.

With a tense mind and body, his fists clenched at his side and his anger only kept at bay with each breath, he left Ben's house and went on to the next lead.

42

John stopped outside Trent's place, a terraced house on a working-class street, and gave the property a thorough once-over. He couldn't see into it because the blinds were closed. Was Trent trying to hide? If he was, he hadn't done a good job of it.

John banged on the front door. His heart raced in his chest. His fists were still tight by his sides, and he was ready for whatever was on the other side of the door.

A man answered.

'Are you Trent Williams?' John asked.

The man said nothing, looked John up and down, then slammed the door and bolted down his hallway.

John barged his way in and chased after his suspect, through the hallway, through the dated kitchen, and out the back door into the garden. The small garden did not give Trent enough room to build up any distance between him and his pursuer, so when he tried to climb the fence into the neighbour's garden, John had made up the ground between them. Just before Trent could drop over to the other side, John grabbed his feet and pulled hard until not only Trent fell back but also the top half of the fence.

Like a panicked snake, Trent twisted and whipped until his feet were free from his pursuer's grasp. But John had let them go, and he waited until his target had started to struggle to his feet before he wrapped his arm around his neck and threw him to the floor. He rested his knee on Trent's chest and still he tried to get free, flailing his arms in the air but never landing a convincing punch. John, on the other hand, could not afford to wait for him to get tired, so when Trent left his face unprotected, John landed two sharp punches in quick succession followed by a third, busting his nose, then just for good measure struck him again and again.

'Struggling's only going to make it worse,' John said.

'Please. I haven't done anything,' Trent said, spitting out droplets of blood.

'Then why did you run?'

'You're police, right? You look like police. I've done nothing wrong.'

'That doesn't answer my question, Trent.'

'I paid for my crimes once. I've never committed another since.'

'We'll see about that. Now get up. You're coming with me. You can plead your innocence during the interrogation.' John pulled up the frightened suspect and, with one hand around the back of his neck and the other gripped around the ends of his sleeves, pushed him back through the house.

'Now, I haven't got any cuffs left on me. But if you try

anything in the car, it may well be the last thing you ever do.'

'I won't do anything; you've got to believe me. I've done nothing wrong.'

'If you're as innocent as you say you are, then you've got nothing to worry about.'

John opened the back door of his car and threw the suspect in. When he'd got in, he locked the doors from the inside and showed Trent his ID card. 'Now just sit there and answer my questions.'

Trent said nothing. He just nodded and sunk into the seat.

'Carl Bedford – do you know him?'

'Why should I talk to you? Why should I tell you anything?'

'Because I will kill you if you don't. Because I know you were in the town that got shot up. So start talking.'

Trent went quiet for a moment, then eventually said, 'Yeah. I know Carl Bedford. But I had nothing to do with the terrorist attack – I promise you I didn't.'

'Did Carl ever mention anything to you about committing acts of terror, shooting innocent civilians?'

'I don't know. I can't remember. I don't think so. Please, listen to me. I might've known Carl inside, but we haven't spoken since we got out.'

'This would be so much easier for you if you didn't lie to me, Trent.'

'Please, I'm begging you – I had nothing to do with any terrorist attack. I might've killed before, but I'm past that now. And I'm definitely not a terrorist.'

'Where is Carl now?'

'I don't know. I haven't seen him since he left prison.'

'You're lying to me. Where is he?'

'I don't know.'

'Do you know Gary Salinger? Does that name ring a bell? How about Antonia? Come on, you pathetic man, answer me!'

'No, no, I don't know any of them.'

John took a sharp breath. Either the guy was playing dumb or he knew nothing. John wondered why he hadn't mentioned Carl's fake death. Did he not know? Had he lost contact with him after prison? Or had his punches muddled his mind, distorted his thoughts so now he didn't know what he was saying? All John believed, however, was that this man could not be trusted. Would putting him in front of Salinger help? Get the two of them in a room together. The first to talk wins.

He looked at the broken skin on his knuckles and then at his tired, bleak face in the rearview mirror. How had his life come to this? This was not the man he thought he was. Yet not a twinge of regret flowed through his body. He hoped it would later. He could understand his mind allowing him to get away with this now – the adrenaline would see to that. Later, however, when it drained out of his system, he would feel it, right? He needed to regain control. He knew Claire wouldn't keep him around if she saw what he'd done to their next lead. But it had been necessary, he told himself.

He put the car into gear and drove off.

43

John told the guard at the gate to get more men and put Trent into a holding cell. They got him out of the back seat and dragged him through the building. John walked behind them, receiving most of the looks that came their way as people wondered if this time he had just beaten a man up. The disparity between their injuries was too much to say they had fought each other.

They dropped Trent in the cell next to Gary and two medics came in to assess his injuries. John didn't stick around. He just wanted to be told when he could sit him and Gary in the same room and play them against each other to get to the truth.

By the time John had left Trent and made his way up to Claire's office, word had got to her that a badly injured suspect had been dragged in.

'What on earth have you done to Trent?' Claire asked the moment John walked into her office.

'I brought him in. I thought it would be a good idea to have him and Gary play off each other – we might get something that way.'

'You know damn well that's not what I meant. Why the hell does he have a broken nose?'

'Well, what do you want me to do? The moment I knocked on his door, he knew I wasn't just an average civilian. He suspected I was police and tried to run, so I went after him, caught him, he fought back, and I won. I wasn't taking chances with him, Claire. He's a convicted killer. And he might well be a terrorist.' John maintained eye contact with his boss.

'Okay, fine. I guess he said nothing to you, then?'

'Correct.'

'So, what's your plan with him now?'

'When he's been cleared by the medics, I'm going to interrogate him and Gary, play them off each other. The person who talks first gets immunity.'

'And if that doesn't work?'

'Then we'd better hope Connor finds Bedford or we get something incriminating on Antonia. We have leads, Claire. It's the lack of time that's the problem.'

'Well, Connor's found nothing so far on Bedford.'

'What about his brother? Anything about the finances?'

'He's clean. He rang up quite distressed,' Claire added.

'Well, what do you expect? I had just told him his brother was a terrorist. He's not exactly going to take that news well.'

'But it means we're no closer to knowing how Bedford funds all this.'

'But what other options have we got? Until one of them

speaks, this is all we have.'

'Except for Antonia. But we can't just go over there and *get* her.'

John sat down and looked at his knuckles. The blood had dried, but they ached, and he was worried they would scar. A permanent reminder to himself of what he had done. The regret he'd thought he would feel still hadn't turned up. But he told himself he was right in what he had done. What other option did he have?

'Do you want the medic to look at them?' Claire asked. 'You should take a nap, maybe; you look like hell.'

'I don't care how I look. Not right now.'

'Fatigue can test a man's judgement. Cloud it over, in fact.'

John looked up. 'What are you trying to say?'

'What's the point of this if you won't be the person you were when you started it all? How are you going to go back to Olivia and Charlie and expect to pick up where you left off if your mind has gone?'

John didn't reply. He rubbed his knuckles and thought about Claire's question. He had only been gone two days. A person's mind, surely, couldn't deteriorate that quickly. It was going to take more than what had happened so far to do that, he thought – he hoped.

An hour later, Connor entered the office and told them Trent had been declared fit to be interviewed.

John marched to the holding cells. A guard had moved Trent into an interview room, and they brought Gary in after him. John had them sat on opposite sides of the table and remained standing, watching over them like an eagle soaring over its prey.

'Trent, do you know who the man in front of you is?' John asked.

Trent remained silent.

'Gary, do you know the man in front of you?'

'If he won't give me immunity, then I don't care.'

'He might help you get it, actually. Or he might not. You see, gentlemen, I'm going to play a game with you. You both know Carl Bedford. And I bet between you, one of you knows where he lives. The first person to give me that information gets the immunity. The person who remains quiet will go to jail for a very long time. Now I'm going to leave the room to give you guys a chance to mull things over. So best of luck.'

Trent looked at the floor, but Gary stared through the man opposite him. John left the room and joined Claire on the other side of the mirrored glass.

'Think this will work?' Claire said, handing John a cup of coffee.

'The way I see it, they either both know each other and know what the other knows and it's a race to see who talks first, or they don't. But they don't know what the other person does and doesn't know. We have one bullet maker and one terrorist in that room, and neither are getting immunity.'

'You can have that conversation with them.'

'Hopefully Carl can feel us closing in on him. It might change his plans for future attacks.'

'He's a man down, and finding another terrorist to replace him can't be easy. He'll make a mistake, and we'll be there to get him when he does.'

John and Claire sipped their coffees and looked at the two detainees on the other side of the glass.

'Do you always look at the floor?' Gary asked.

Trent rubbed his hands together and fidgeted in his chair.

'What the hell did they do to you to make you look like that?' Gary asked.

'I could say the same thing about you.'

'I look better than you, mate.'

They were silent for a moment. Trent continued to look at the floor and Gary continued to eye him up, like a target he was going to shoot.

'You going to rat on Carl, then?' Gary asked.

'I'm not ratting on anyone. I don't know anything.'

'That's the spirit. Neither do I.'

'What? You won't tell them anything?'

'If you're not, then I'm not,' Gary said, leaning back in his chair. He looked towards the mirrored glass and smiled.

'Why aren't you going for immunity? You could be out of here and free. Are you an idiot?'

'Don't call me an idiot. You're the one who's shitting themselves.'

'Aren't you? Carl's a terrorist. If he knows we've been caught, then God knows what he's going to do to us.'

'What are you talking about?' Gary snapped. 'Carl's dead, for Christ's sake.'

'What? When?'

'He died in my factory two years ago. He had a heart attack.'

Trent looked up at Gary. 'Are you serious?'

'Yes, I'm serious. I was there.'

'I didn't know that.'

'Do you know anything about him?'

'I never stayed in touch with him after he left prison. But being a terrorist? I know he mentioned to me a desire to kill again, but this … this is something else.'

Gary slammed his handcuffed hands down onto the table and said, 'Do you not listen to a damn thing that's said to you? Carl's dead.'

'I don't know. I don't know anything; I just want to go home.'

'Well, you're not going home. They detained me illegally and they've kept me here ever since.'

'What did you do?'

'What do you mean, what did I do? I didn't do a damn thing. I'm innocent.'

Trent did not reply and Gary stared him down.

Claire turned to John and said, 'Do you still think this is going to work? Because to me it looks like they don't know each other and still neither are talking.'

John remained silent, his eyes fixed on the two prisoners. They were going to talk, and he was determined to get them to do so. He walked back into the interview room.

'This isn't going to well for you, is it?' Gary said.

John ignored him. 'Trent, listen to me.' Trent's eyes did not move from the floor. John grabbed his face and pulled it up. 'Look at me, Trent. You don't want to go back inside again, do you?'

Trent shook his head.

'If you don't talk, then you will. Because I'm telling you right now, you're one of the prime suspects, along with Bedford. We know there was one other. Even if you give me his name, we'll still give you immunity.'

'But I don't know anything!' Trent sobbed.

'Yes, you do. You know something. You must do.'

'I'm sorry, but I don't.' Tears streamed down his face. 'I did a bad thing once and I'm never doing it again. I just want to go back home and live what life I have left. I would never do anything like this.'

Behind the tears and the bruises, he saw a weakened, distressed man; someone who would never hurt anyone again in his life. The terrified face pleaded for mercy. And it was at that point that John realised he had got it wrong. You couldn't fake that terror, that deep desire to be home and to be left alone, so he took a breath, let go of Trent's face, and looked at Gary. John wanted to strike him hard across the face, beat him until he was unrecognisable, but Claire was behind the glass, watching him.

John exited the interview room and heard Claire call out after him. He ignored her and barged through the door into the toilet. He told the person washing their hands to get out and they did, seeing the rage burning in John's eyes. He looked at himself in the mirror, unsure what he was looking at, then splashed cold water on his face.

Claire walked in. 'Are you sure you're okay?' she asked.

'We're out of leads and Gary won't talk. Even when we hand him immunity on a plate, he's still not going to talk.'

'No, we're not,' Claire said after a pause.

'What?'

'We still have Antonia.'

'We can't get her, Claire; you've said it yourself. That's the bloody problem.'

'*We* can't. You're right. But officially, you're not a part of the *we*. It will be tricky, you're right, but it can be done.'

John looked away from his shattered reflection and at the unemotional face of his boss. He read between the lines. Perhaps that was why she'd forgiven him for his outburst and overlooked the injuries of the detained suspects. John, in his position in this investigation, could be an asset if used correctly. If detaining Gary was dipping a toe into the ocean, however, then this was swimming amongst the sharks.

The answer to her implied question, however, didn't require any second thoughts from John.

44

The Grand Canal shimmered in the moonlight, and the streetlights bathed the narrow, timid streets in an orange glow. Tourists meandered their way through the city, searching for somewhere to eat and drink and take in the romantic backdrop on an evening walk. John was doing neither.

He knew where Antonia lived, a third-floor apartment in a building next to one of Venice's canals, and he had booked a room in the hotel on the opposite side. While he waited for his flight, he had looked on Google Maps at her place and seen, from the street view, that if they put an arm out of their respective windows, they could reach other – he could pull her out of her apartment and drop her into the cold canal below.

He needed answers. He had to extract information from her without backup and without being caught by the local authorities. His job as an adviser could easily be wiped from the records. He was, for all intents and purposes, a rogue operator. At least that was what he'd be officially designated should he get caught.

When he got to his hotel room, he didn't turn on the lights. He didn't want anyone across the canal to know that this room was occupied. He placed his bag on the bed, dragged the chair in the corner over to the window, and sat and watched her apartment, surrounded by the darkness.

Shutters covered her windows, so there was no way he could see in. For all he knew, she might not even be there. This could be another waste of time.

As the hours rolled by, there was still no sign of life. But John was stubborn and stayed up for another hour – an hour in which, to no surprise, nothing happened except his eyes growing heavier. When he woke up in the chair, he went to bed and set an early alarm for himself. He couldn't afford to miss anything.

John's heavy head struggled to lift itself from the pillow after just a few hours of sleep, but he forced himself to turn off his alarm. He threw back the covers, found the chair in the darkness, and looked across the canal. The shutters hadn't moved. He looked at his watch. It was a few minutes after six, so could he really expect her to be up? What time did arms dealers get up in the morning?

After an hour, John got up from the chair, made himself a coffee, and ate the complimentary biscuits. The morning sun shone into Antonia's apartment and the echo of voices filled the streets; still there was no sign of life across the canal.

He started to worry that she wasn't there, that she might be in England selling weapons to Bedford. But John didn't know for sure, and thinking about it made him realise how little he knew about the way they operated. Would Gary's sudden disappearance make her nervous to the point she no longer wanted to be involved? She had escaped the radar of the law for this long, and that cannot be done by accident.

Antonia pushed open one of her shutters. She was awake and John's eyes were locked on her and he noticed that she never looked across the canal; she never felt his eyes staring at her.

John took a breath. He needed to focus while she sat at her breakfast bar and ate her pastries.

Questions fired through his mind, but he couldn't answer them. The woman in the apartment across the canal, however, might be able to. She had moved to her bedroom to get dressed. And when she was dressed, she walked back through her apartment and disappeared. John waited a moment to see if she would reappear. But she didn't, and he guessed she had left out the front door. He jumped out of his seat and left his hotel room. He charged down the corridor and stabbed the button for the lift until one arrived. He pressed the button for the ground floor, and when he burst out of the lobby onto the narrow street, he crossed the bridge onto her side of the canal. He saw her come out of her apartment building and walk away from him down the street. He followed her. The aimless tourists made it easy to conceal himself in the tight Venetian streets, but it also allowed her to disappear from his line of sight for moments at a time.

John had convinced himself she didn't know she had a tail – she walked with purpose and did not, like the tourists, stop every few moments to look in a shop window. But neither did he.

She continued walking. John lost sight of her when she turned a corner, but he jogged to catch up. He didn't want to lose her for longer than he needed to, because in this city, if she disappeared, she would be lost, and he would have no chance of finding her again.

The streets, concealed in shade, eventually opened to a burst of light, and he followed her across the Rialto Bridge over the Grand Canal. Gondolas and boats sailed underneath, watched by tourists taking in the immersive view. John, however, would not get distracted – he could not afford to if he wanted to keep up with his target, whose quick pace over the bridge was alright for her, acclimatised to the heat and humidity. Under the sun, however, John started to sweat.

On the other side of the bridge, Antonia walked through the Rialto market. A strong smell of freshly caught fish hung in the air. The vibrant colours of the fruit and vegetables on display flooded the eyes. And the Italians running the vast collection of stores bellowed their competitive prices with the characteristic Italian passion threaded into their voices. To some, it would have been sensory overload. For John, the back of his target's head remained in the centre of his view.

Finally, free from the bustle of the market, John continued to follow her through the winding streets where the crowds of tourists eventually became sparser until she turned onto a deserted street and stopped outside an anonymous building. She reached into her pocket for a key, and John edged his head around the corner of the street and watched her as she looked around before entering the building. When the door had closed, he hurried up to it, placed his ear against it, and listened. He heard nothing and slowly twisted the handle, edging it open.

John walked into a dark room; could he hear some kind of machinery? The door slammed shut behind him. Someone ran towards him, and pain shot through the backs of his legs. He fell forward, clutching the backs of his thighs. The lights turned on and John tried to get to his feet, but a shot of pain through his back kept him in the dust on the floor.

'First in England, now here. What do you want with me?'

John tried to answer but found himself racked by a coughing fit; his body ached as he turned to look at her. She was holding a metal pole and her dark eyes were fixed on him.

'I know who you are, Antonia. You're the bitch that provided the weapons used to kill nineteen people.'

'I don't know what you're talking about.' She walked up to John and hit him again. He gritted his teeth to suppress the pain. She put the metal pole down and grabbed a pistol from a desk at the side of the room – a make John had never seen before.

'Get on your feet,' she said, pointing the pistol at his chest. John laughed. 'What's so funny? You don't think I'm going to shoot you?'

'It's not that.'

'Then what is it, you English pig? Come on, get up. I haven't got all day.'

John struggled to his feet, his back numb from the bruising. 'We have Salinger in custody. We know you two are working together on this, along with Carl Bedford. Just give it up, Antonia. The game is over, and you've lost.'

'You must've felt stupid, then, letting me go when I was there, completely naked and defenceless.'

'A little. But if Gary talks before you, then you're no use to us and you'll find yourself at the bottom of the canal before the end of the day.'

'It doesn't look that way to me.'

'Now you listen to me. If you tell us where Bedford is and what his plans are for the next attack, which you've provided weapons for, then we'll give you immunity.'

'You have no proof I was in England. You might've seen me, but that won't stand up in court. After that, you have nothing on me.'

John's aching body coupled with his fatigue meant he was not in the mood for a conversation. 'Christ's sake! Do you not care what your weapons have done? Nineteen innocent people are dead because of them. And a child was kidnapped. His name is Charlie. And thanks to you lot, he's gone!'

'I didn't pull the trigger. You want the killers and the people that kidnapped this Charlie kid, then go get them.'

'You mean like Bedford and Salinger? Can't you see, Antonia? We're closing in. You've evaded the police for a long time, but now look. I'm in your pathetic little excuse for a factory, and if I can get to you here, I can get to you anywhere.'

John wanted to kill her; he wanted to rip her in half, but if she knew she had control of his emotions, then he knew he wouldn't get the answers he needed.

Antonia pulled her phone from her pocket and dialled someone.

'Who are you ringing?'

'What have you done with Gary?' She pocketed the phone and held the pistol with both hands. Gary's phone was still on the side table in his bedroom, and John felt a sense of regret for not taking it.

'Does he always the answer the phone to you? Because he won't while we have him in custody.'

'If you have him in custody, then you did so illegally. I know he can't be touched by law enforcement. He told me so. So who's the kidnapper now?'

How dare she call him that?

'I'm not messing around, Antonia. We're closing in. And it's a race to see who talks first.'

Her hands trembled. John judged there to be three feet between them. All he needed was for her to look away for a second and he reckoned he could grab the pistol.

'I know nothing.'

John wanted to shout at her, demand answers from her, but she was pointing the gun at him. Was she going to use it? The noise would be heard on the street. It would attract attention – attention she did not want. She had kept this place a secret, evading the authorities for years, and she couldn't have done that without cunning. She didn't just have to think about the shot, however. There would be a body to dispose of, and in a congested city like Venice, that would not be a straightforward task. Did she, however, think she had any other option? It was a fight for survival in this world, and John was sure she would do whatever she needed to do to keep out of prison.

But he had nothing left to lose. He took a step towards her.

'Stay back!'

John stepped forward again. She took a step back. He stared at her and saw fear, not anger, in her eyes.

'Why don't you put the weapon down and tell me everything you know?'

Her hands trembled. John wondered how she kept hold of the weapon. She wouldn't use it. Not when she was like this. He lunged forward and went to grab it. He pushed her arms to the side. Her fingers clenched and a loud crack echoed around the building. John kicked hard and connected with her knee. She cried out in pain and tried to retaliate, but John dodged her weak attempt and punched her on the chin. Her grip loosened, and he pulled the pistol from her grasp.

She looked him in the eye, then looked towards the pole and made for it. John kicked her again, then grabbed her and threw her to the side.

'You bitch. Charlie's gone. Charlie's gone and your weapons helped.' He felt the veins in his face expand. 'Where is Bedford? How many of your weapons does he have? Tell me, Antonia. I've never killed in cold blood before, but I'll kill you.'

'I don't know where Carl is. Nobody does. But I've delivered five weapons and that's all I know.' Her hands were up, protecting herself from John.

'Who contacted you, Carl or Gary?'

'Gary did. He knew my weapons were untraceable. I 3D print the components. They're all plastic.'

'How do you smuggle them in?'

'I pack them in my suitcase. If anyone asks what they are, I make something up, but they're not metal, so nobody checks.'

'Why would Gary contact you and not Carl?'

'I ... I don't know. I think he's in charge.'

'What are you saying? Gary's behind all this?'

'I don't know. I just dealt more with Gary than Carl. I don't know who's in charge.'

'Why would Gary or Carl want to do this? What are their motivations?'

'I don't know.'

'You don't know? I might never see him again and all you have to say is "I don't know"?'

She tried to speak but could not put a sentence together.

John snatched at the trigger and shot the floor next to her head. Dust spewed up and landed on her face, sticking to her tears.

'Do you know anything now?'

She tried to speak but cried instead. John aimed for her head, felt the first pressure on the trigger. Another little squeeze and it would go off.

The crying fatherless child flashed in his mind as he stood over her. Then Charlie's laughter rang in his ears, and he saw Olivia's smile.

He relaxed his finger and walked up to her, moved her hands from her face, and knocked her out with the butt of the weapon.

45

Carl Bedford was sitting outside a café, enjoying the sun, drinking his coffee, when his phone vibrated. He was trying to calm his mind. The next planned attack was less than two days away and the last thing he needed was distractions.

He looked at the phone and saw that it was a private number. He answered it.

'Hello?'

'This is the client.' He recognised the electronically distorted voice.

'What are you ringing me for? Is everything still going ahead in Cornwall?'

'For now, it is. But we're having issues getting to Gary. And Antonia is compromised. Police found her unconscious this morning.'

Carl thought about what this all meant. Not being able to get hold of Gary? There could be many reasons. But police finding

Antonia unconscious? That might change things.

'What are you saying?' Carl asked.

'I'm saying that I don't think it's a coincidence that this is happening. I think Gary is compromised and the same people tried to leave Antonia for dead.'

'I've not been compromised. No one knows who or where I am.'

'I know that. But I must think about the bigger picture and take precautions. I have a Plan B and I'm going to execute it alongside what you're doing. I think it's the best and safest thing to do to protect our overall mission.'

'Precautions? I'm getting the job done in Cornwall and you will have what you asked for.'

'Maybe. But I don't want to take chances. I'm coming up with another plan that won't involve you. Don't take it personally. You've been perfect throughout. The others, however, have let you down, and I can't risk anything.'

'Do you think I'm going to get caught?' Carl sipped his coffee; he was confident he would not get caught. He felt no one over his shoulder.

'Nothing is guaranteed. But if you can tell me where Gary is, then that might change things.'

'I'm focused on Cornwall, not Gary. If he's compromised, then neither of us should attempt to talk to him until he can prove otherwise.'

'How will he know we've cut him off?'

'When he doesn't hear from us, he'll get the message.'

The distorted voice went quiet. Carl kept the phone to his ear.

He wanted to know what the client had planned that he couldn't be involved with. He was annoyed that they didn't trust him to finish the job. Had he given them reason to think so? He knew he hadn't. But maybe the client saw these as desperate times, and with it, desperate measures were needed.

'Go to Cornwall and stick with the plan. My contingency plan may well come into play. Stick to the timings. I'll call you when it's done.'

'Understood,' Carl said, but the line was already dead.

46

John checked outside; there was no one there. He looked back at the unconscious body, wiped the gun and pole clean of prints, then searched Antonia and pocketed her phone.

He admired her ingenuity. 3D printing untraceable weapons wasn't something he had heard of before. Some parts of the weapons had to be metal, of course, but if Gary could make bullets, then he could make the metal parts for weapons.

He could not leave any trace of evidence that he had been there. Would the metal pole have his DNA on it? He wasn't sure and decided not to take any chances. So when he left, he took the pole and pistol with him and when the street was quiet, he threw them into the canal.

When he got into his room, he chucked his things into his bag and went downstairs to check out. It was nearly lunchtime and the streets were filled with tourists. John was grateful he wasn't following Antonia through this. He got onto a boat that would take him straight to the airport, and he did not look back as the boat sailed out to the Mediterranean.

He thought it would hit him later. The feeling he still waited for after beating up Trent and Antonia. In the airport ready for his flight, he continued to think about it. And the more he thought about it, the more comfortable he was with what he had done. There were no regrets, just a comforting feeling of satisfaction, and he despised it. Would Olivia and Charlie still want him in their lives if they knew what he had done?

When John landed in London in the early evening, he called Claire. 'How did it go?' she asked.

'Antonia was basically a dead end. Although she said she delivered five weapons to Gary.'

'To Gary? Not Carl?'

'That wasn't exactly clear. But five weapons? Five people? We're talking about a larger second attack here. And she said she had more to do with Gary than Carl. It sounded to me like Carl wasn't in the picture, but she knew of him, so they must have met.'

'They must have done. But a larger attack … that sounds shit.'

'It is. I'm trying not to think of it like that. But get the Italian authorities to go to her makeshift factory – I'll tell you the details when I get back. She 3D prints the plastic components of her weapons. They're easy to smuggle in small quantities. And I'm guessing Salinger makes the metal parts in his rudimentary factory. They make quite a team, those two. But how Carl fits into all this, if what Antonia is saying is true, is not clear to me. Other than his killing and kidnapping.'

'I guess maybe Carl wants to keep contact to a minimum – some kind of air gap between the two to plead ignorance or something like that. But who knows?'

John heard the haste in Claire's voice. 'What's going on?' He heard some rushed voices in the background.

'Connor's had something come through. The black BMW has been picked up by traffic cameras heading south.'

'This could be it. They're moving to the next location and preparing to attack.'

'You'd better get back here, then.'

John cut the call. He didn't bother waiting for his bag and rushed out of the terminal.

47

'What have you got?' John asked Claire as he arrived in the operations room. He noticed the silence – the quietest it had been since before the first attack. All the personnel were standing around the wall of screens. They showed footage from multiple traffic cameras, with software searching each car to locate their target vehicle.

'Connor got an alert from the system. Their vehicle was south of Leicester. They must've taken a route down from Newcastle on roads they knew didn't have traffic cameras.'

'They're worried someone might be watching them. But what are we standing around here for? Let's get after them. We can intercept them on the M1 and finish this.'

'That alert came through thirty minutes ago. We haven't had a hit on them since.'

'So they could be anywhere.'

'We're running with the theory they're continuing south.'

'South? They're heading for London. We need to deploy.'

'You honestly think that? Think about their previous targets. They don't hit urban areas. They stick to rural.'

'So they could be over halfway to Northampton by now. *If* they're still heading south.'

'Yeah, they could be.'

And that was the problem, John mused. Without so much as a sign of what part of the country they were targeting, it was anyone's guess where they were going. Deploying a team in one direction could be an embarrassment if the targets were heading in the opposite direction.

'What if they make it to the target without the car coming up on CCTV? What are the chances of that?'

'Quite high. We've only selected to have feeds from motorways and dual carriageways fed into our systems, because they won't be able to take any more data than this. They've used those routes before, so we thought they'd do so again.'

'Except now they're disproving that theory.'

'I know you're frustrated, John, but what else do you want me to do? And don't say get a team out there. We don't know where they're going.'

'So you're just going to wait? Wait for them to attack and react? Christ's sake, Claire, we might not react quickly enough, or worse, we might lose them again.'

Any murmuring conversations died out, and everyone in the room avoided looking at John and Claire. The situation was uncomfortable enough without having someone come in and play devil's advocate.

'Unfortunately, that's a risk we might have to take. And I don't like it any more than you do. But we have a job to do, and the least I expect from you is some kind of focus.' The assertive reply reminded John who was in charge here, and, to avoid a loud public argument that would not help his cause, he reluctantly took a seat at an empty desk at the back of the room.

Connor manipulated the feeds to keep the most relevant footage on the screens. Even though they never stayed on one for too long, constantly cycling through them, nothing came up. It was like they had disappeared from the face of the Earth.

John glared at the screens with a face like thunder. His targets were out there. They could be a couple of hours away from him; in a couple of hours, he could have them in his sights, ready to take them down or detain them. That depended on how foolishly they wanted to act when he got to them.

An alert shot around the operations room. John stood up and walked through the crowd to Connor. 'What have you got?' he asked.

'They're just south of Birmingham now, on the M40.'

John looked back at Claire, who hadn't moved. He wanted to see a look in her eyes that gave him permission to go, but he never found it.

'It's going to be interesting to see how long they stay on there. They have the entire south of England in their grasp,' Connor said.

All eyes zoomed in on the middle screen, showing the footage of the next junction.

'How long until we should see them again?' John asked.

'About ten minutes. The traffic is light. They won't have any hold-up.'

Ten minutes. A period of time that would normally go unnoticed when you weren't trying to get a hit on a target. At this moment, however, each minute dragged by, and it could very well be for nothing.

Five stagnant minutes passed. John looked back at Claire, but her expressionless face had not changed. In fact, no one's facial expression had changed. All eyes were on the screen. The longer they waited, the longer they sat back and did nothing, the higher chance there was that they were waiting for nothing and the target had got away again.

At what point would Claire give the order to move? Regardless of where the targets were in the country, they themselves needed to get there. A decision would need to be made; a bet placed that might well gamble with people's lives. But anything was better than sitting there doing nothing.

Ten seconds until the ten minutes were up. John's gaze flicked between the second hand on his watch and the screen. The seconds ticked down. Ten minutes was up. Where were they?

'Just give it another thirty seconds,' Connor said. 'Their speed might not be perfectly consistent.'

A fair point, John conceded, and his eyes continued to flick between his watch and the screen. Time slipped through his fingers like sand. It was running out. But after thirty seconds, there was still no alert.

'Another thirty,' Connor said.'

'Another thirty?' John said and turned to look at Claire.

'Another thirty,' she ordered. 'It's only 10 per cent.'

It might have only been 10 percent, but a lot of bullets can be fired in sixty seconds.

John didn't bother looking at his watch anymore. What did the seconds matter? It was the footage on the screen that told the story, and after another thirty seconds, it had told them nothing.

'Where the hell are they?'

'Connor, get a road map up. We need to make sure they haven't given us the slip on a side road,' Claire said.

Connor pulled up a road map on a different screen, zoomed right in between the two junctions of interest, and quickly concluded there was no other road they could have disappeared down.

'Wait a minute,' John said. 'There aren't side roads, but there's a layby. That P symbol means layby, right?'

'Right,' Claire said.

'They could have parked in there ...' John trailed off, his thoughts not yet fully materialised.

'Why would they park up unless they were going for a piss or something?' Connor suggested.

'It's been three minutes now,' Claire said. 'They wouldn't have stopped for that long.'

'They've swapped vehicles,' John said. 'They've swapped vehicles. What better way to get someone off your back than something as simple as misdirection? Connor, can you set this thing up to make a note of all the cars that passed between the last junction and this one from the time our target vehicle was picked up by the camera?'

'I can. It'll take a little bit of time – a few minutes, maybe.'

'What are you thinking, John?' Claire asked.

'If we know what vehicles drove between the previous junction and this one, knowing that there is nowhere to exit the motorway on that stretch, then there should be no new vehicles coming up on the camera at the next junction. Do you follow me?'

'I think I do,' Claire said. 'If they changed vehicles, then the cars going past the cameras at the next junction should only be different by a single vehicle.'

'Exactly.'

'What if they travelled in tandem with the secondary vehicle?' Connor asked.

'They wouldn't,' John said. 'Why risk travelling together?'

Connor accepted the answer and went about reprogramming the software. John and Claire looked at each other with a glimmer of hope in their eyes.

A few minutes later, a list of registration numbers filled the next two screens. All the numbers matched except one.

'This is our outlier,' Connor said. He rewound the footage and they saw an anonymous-looking white van in the left-hand lane.

'Track it,' Claire said. 'I want another hit on it before we even think about moving. There are still too many options available to them.'

'Claire, we need to go now.'

'Go where, John?'

They looked at each other and it became clear to both that neither knew, with enough confidence to say it out loud, what was going on and where they were heading.

'The M40 will take it to London. In about 25 minutes,

however, it will pass junction 15. If it gets off there, we can track its exit from the roundabout, but once it's on one of those A-roads, we'll lose it. And that's the same with every other junction they might get off,' Connor said.

'Then who knows when we'll find them again?' John said.

'And who knows if we won't?' Claire questioned. 'Listen to me, John. We're waiting it out until we can be surer of where they're going than we are now. I'm not sending you guys in the wrong direction. Think of the bigger picture here. If you want to get Charlie back, you need to actually get to these guys first.'

John did not reply. He took a breath and forced his racing mind to accept her answer, whether he liked it or not. He couldn't sit in the operations room, however. It felt to him like he was waiting his life away, so he went to Claire's office, and she followed him in.

The wait only got more tedious, and John never settled in one place for more than a few minutes at a time, much to the annoyance of Claire. She, however, never mentioned it. John wondered if she knew what he was going through. He knew she had once been an operator, and therefore must know that for him, not acting and waiting to react, was like keeping him in a cage – he only longed to escape. The only part he knew she wouldn't understand, however, was how he felt about Charlie's kidnapping. He'd seen the car and his instincts had told him something was wrong, but he'd done nothing. He'd ignored them and now he was paying the price with guilt.

'It's getting off at junction 15,' Connor shouted through to the office.

John and Claire raced out to the operations room. 'What exit has it taken on the roundabout?' John asked.

'We're tracking it … it's taken the exit onto the A429.'

'It's heading southwest. We need to go now.'

'No, not yet. It could easily take a turn east,' Claire said.

John wanted to argue but knew he couldn't. Claire was in charge, and despite his frustrations about her decision making, he had no choice but to respect her orders.

'Connor, what cameras are on that road?' Claire asked.

'There's nothing. I've only got the motorway and dual carriageway cameras. This is a single-track road.'

'I want one more hit on this vehicle – something that can give us a clearer picture of where it's going before we move.'

'What if it doesn't head onto another motorway or dual carriageway?' John said.

Claire thought for a moment, then said, 'We need to wait it out, because even if we go now and don't get another hit, where are you going to go?'

With this, John retreated into Claire's office and tried to calm his racing mind.

It was three and a half hours later when the van was caught on camera again. John shot out of his chair like a bullet and saw the van on screen, south of Bristol, on the M5. He looked at Claire. She must decide to go now. They were heading southwest towards Devon and Cornwall – the attack had to be there. 'John, Connor, get two teams together and start heading west. Look to intercept them on the M5 if you can.'

'I'm not sure about intercepting them on the motorway. I think we wait until they get to their destination. Wait until they're stationary, then take them,' John said.

'Okay, if you think that's best, then go for it. But you're going to have to drive like hell to catch up with them.'

'Why now? They could just as easily head north again, or east, or anything,' Connor said.

'I'm aware of that, Connor, but now the targets aren't in the middle of the country. It seems a more reasonable risk to take.' Claire looked at John and she gave him a nod before he left.

48

With John at the wheel of the lead vehicle, they sped down the M3 and were soon on the A303. The updates from Connor suggested this was the most appropriate route to take. The target vehicle had continued southbound on the M5 towards Exeter. Why they chose now to remain on the motorway, no one knew. In John's mind, the terrorists probably thought that their change in vehicle would be enough to stop anyone finding them.

When they joined the M5, they were twenty miles behind the target vehicle. John's foot remained firm on the floor, and the light traffic was a gift that allowed them to catch up.

'I see it,' John said over the radio. He cut the lights and the sirens and slowed down. The van was two hundred yards in front of him. Two hundred yards was all that separated him from the people responsible for kidnapping Charlie. He had to remain composed, he could not let himself be guided by his feelings, but his hands were wrapped around the steering wheel like they were gripping Bedford's neck.

The white van peeled off the M5 at the next junction. It drove through the town of Cullompton, and John dropped back, fearing that two large black vehicles on their tail might spook them. And it would be anyone's guess what they would do next.

'What other towns are down this road?' John asked the man in the passenger seat. Henry scrolled through the maps on his phone.

'The next town is a place called Bradninch.'

'What do we know about Bradninch?'

'Only what I can find on here. It's a small town in the middle of nowhere.'

'Sounds like the kind of place they'd be looking to shoot up.'

They continued through Bradninch, the white van just in sight. The white van, however, did not stop and drove through the town.

'What's beyond this town?' John asked.

'The next town is Silverton. It's a similar size to Bradninch.'

'Then that could where they're probably going to attack. There are likely to be five of them in that van. So whatever part of it they're going for, they're going to be looking to achieve a higher body count than their previous attack.'

John held his rifle close to his body. His heart raced faster the closer they got to Silverton. John thought about why they had chosen this location. Did it have any connection to the previous places? He couldn't think of any immediate links. This place was not a tourist town. It was too far inland, so it would be frequented by locals, and what had the locals of Silverton ever done to deserve to be shot like game animals?

The white van parked up in the centre of the small, quaint town in a parking space outside the local shop.

Their two vehicles stopped further up the street, almost out of the van's line of sight.

John eyed the target. He wished he could see them in there, waiting to strike, see the joy on their faces that was soon going to be wiped away.

A crack of thunder ripped through the sky and rain started to pour down.

'When are we going to strike?' Henry asked, over the sound of rain hitting the windscreen.

John turned to him and said, 'Tell the other team to be ready to move. We're going in sixty seconds.'

Henry passed the message on, and Connor replied to say that his team was ready. John counted down from sixty. When he hit zero, he got out of the car, his rifle pointed at the van. Henry and the other two operatives followed his lead.

A few locals who had been lingering around bolted from the scene.

The rain bounced off the road; they wouldn't hear them coming. John, however, hadn't noticed the weather. It was irrelevant to him now that Bedford was in his sights. The man was enjoying his last moments of freedom.

They moved on the van from the side, so no one inside it would see them coming. The element of surprise was going to give them their victory. John's fingers were wrapped around the trigger. His rifle was pushed into his shoulder. The moment was now.

He gave the nod to Connor to proceed. Connor grabbed the handle, took a breath, then ripped the door open.

'Don't move! Nobody move!' John ordered as he scanned the surprised faces inside. Someone reached across for a rifle and John dispatched them with a single bullet to the head. No one moved after that.

John locked eyes with Bedford, who returned the stare, his face as thunderous as the weather. John wanted to shoot him dead, to end this right now, but surrounded by the rest of the team, he knew it would be an unwise move.

'Get out of the van,' John ordered. He fought to keep in control of his emotions and his trigger finger. One by one, the four remaining terrorists got out of the van and were pushed down onto their knees with their hands behind their heads.

John inspected their weapons. He thought it would be ironic if he killed the terrorists with them. But he pushed those thoughts out of his mind. He had to keep control.

'John,' Connor called to him, and John got out of the back of the van. 'I'm going to call this in to Claire and get the police to cordon off the area. That way, we can keep prying eyes out.'

John thought for a moment. He wanted to agree with Connor. It was the right thing to do, but the moment he did, his chance to be alone with Carl was over, lost like a drop of rain in the ocean.

'Call in the uniformed police. But not Claire. Not yet. I want a moment with these bastards before we call anything in.'

'What do you mean?'

'Just trust me, okay?'

Connor paused, then said, 'Okay. But don't do anything stupid.'

'Don't rat on me if I do.'

291

'I'm not making promises.'

John walked down the line of detainees, looking at each of them, trying to get a glimpse of their faces, but they all looked at the ground. And as the rain continued to pour down, another crack of thunder echoed in the distance.

John stood in front of Carl and said, 'If you want to live, Carl, tell me who took the little boy.'

Carl remained silent.

'Listen to me, Carl. I will put a bullet in your head if you don't tell me who took the little boy.'

'You listen to me, you coward. What did you do to Gary – to Antonia? Answer me that and I won't kill you.' Carl looked up at John, saw the guilt in his eyes, and laughed.

'Why are you doing this, Carl? Where the hell is Charlie?'

'It couldn't have been easy to detain Gary legally in such a short space of time. Is everything you do illegal? Because if it is, then I'm going to be let go and remain a free man.'

'You're never going to be a free man. You're going to jail until you die for real this time.'

Carl continued to laugh.

'You won't be laughing much longer,' John said.

'It's funny,' Carl started, 'because the way you're stood there after telling your friend not to call Claire, who I presume is your boss, after leaving Antonia for dead, after detaining Gary illegally, one would think you have a personal connection to this. Who the hell is this Charlie kid, then? Your son?' Carl's laughter grew louder than the thunder.

'Why are you doing this? What are you planning, Carl?' John

gripped his icy fingers around Carl's throat and forced him to look into his eyes.

'What makes you think I have a plan, you desperate little man? Do you want to know how Charlie cried for someone to save him?'

John punched Carl in the face.

'You're going to need to do worse than that to get me to talk.'

'You want more? Then you're going to get it.'

John jumped back into the van, dragged the dead body out, and threw out their makeshift weapons.

'What the hell are doing?' Connor asked.

John pushed him away. 'Stay out of this. You know what he took from me.'

'This isn't right, John. You can't do this.'

'Neither is kidnapping Charlie.'

'I'm not sure about this.'

'You're not sure because you've never lost someone the way I have. Now give me this one chance to settle the score.'

They stared at each other for a moment. John would never concede, not now when he finally had his target right in front of him.

'You have half an hour,' Connor said. 'Then I'm calling it in. Any pushback is on you.'

John frisked Carl for the keys and found them. He picked his prisoner up and threw him into the van. He got into the driver's seat, turned the engine on, and sped away.

49

John tore through the revs as he drove down the winding country roads. Carl was thrown from one side to the other. His cable tied hands were never in the right position to stop himself from falling, and his head bled from where he'd hit the side of the van.

John didn't have a destination in mind. He knew he should turn back and return Carl. But this thought was drowned out by the lust for pain, for violence, for revenge.

He saw a barn on a hill. It looked empty, derelict. The perfect place for privacy – a place to deliver his own warped version of justice. The result of his own distorted grief had caught up with him, and despite his mind trying to stop him, trying to flood his thoughts with images of the times when the three of them were together and happy, these thoughts only fuelled his anger further on his trip to oblivion.

He stopped outside the barn. The rain had turned the ground to mud. He got out and locked the doors as he assessed his chosen location.

It was empty except for a few bales of hay, and in his rage, he never noticed the horrid stench. Why would he allow Carl any sort of luxury?

He dragged his prisoner from the van. Carl struggled to put his feet down and walk in the mud. John sat him down on a bale of hay and a sharp wind cut through the barn, spraying their faces with rain.

'I can't wait to hear you explain this one to Claire,' Carl said.

'I can't wait to see you buried in the ground.' John charged at him, punched him hard, and saw a tooth fly out.

Carl fell to the ground, tried to pick himself back up, but only got as far as his hands and knees.

'Charlie, then, eh? Must have been a good kid to make you do this,' Carl spat out between bloodied teeth.

John kicked him in the chest and he tumbled backwards to the floor. John stood over his prey.

'I bet you're enjoying this.' Carl tried to laugh.

'You're damn right I am. But I want to enjoy it a bit more.' John grabbed Carl's muddy hand. He pushed his fingers back until they snapped, and Carl's cries echoed around the barn. John punched him in the eye again and again until it closed. He wanted to hit him more, but his prisoner lost consciousness.

John took a step back and admired his work. He took several deep breaths and tried to piece it all together. But there was nothing to piece together. He felt nothing for the unconscious man in the mud.

It was close to being over. Carl would talk. There was nothing left for him to bargain with. And all they had to do was wait for him to do so. John had done the hard part. Charlie, if he was still alive, would soon come home and he could go back to Olivia. He hoped she would sleep better at night knowing Charlie was in touching distance of being returned to her.

He went and stood out in the rain and was enjoying the sensation of each drop hitting his face when a jolt from behind sent him into the mud. He tried to pick himself back up, but a kick to his stomach rolled him onto his back. From there he saw the battered, bloodied face of Carl Bedford looking down at him. He had freed himself from the cable ties, and he raised his boot and went to stamp on John's head. John rolled to the side, then pushed himself back up.

Carl made for him and tackled him to the ground. They rolled around in the mud, swinging punches that never connected. John kneed his prisoner in the stomach, then finally executed an accurate punch to the face. He pushed Carl away and got to his feet. Carl did the same and the two men stared each other down.

John punched first. Carl ducked and parried, knocking John back a couple of steps. Carl went for John's torso, but John blocked and kicked out, hitting Carl's knee, and he buckled awkwardly. It gave John an opportunity to swing a hard punch. He took it, but Carl saw it coming and blocked it with a forearm. But John struck again, catching him in the side of the head. He kicked out at his prisoner, hitting him in the chest. The impact left Carl breathless, and he staggered backwards towards the van. One hand clutched his torso, the other was held out towards his attacker.

John swung more punches and did not stop until Carl collapsed against the van, then he grabbed his head between his hands and smashed it into the vehicle repeatedly, leaving a sizeable dent. John looked at his weakened prisoner and almost felt sorry for him. His life was only going to get worse. He knew, however, that he deserved every ounce of pain that was to come his way. Prison wouldn't be a nice place for someone like him. When they learned he had kidnapped a child, they wouldn't take too kindly to him.

John dragged Carl back and lifted him into the van. As he drove away, back to the town, the rain stopped, but the sky remained overcast. He wondered how he was going to explain the mud to Claire but decided not to worry about it yet. An excuse would come to his mind in good time.

He was just glad he could return home and hold Olivia in his arms again, kiss her beautiful red lips and tell her that everything would be fine, that they would get Charlie back soon.

50

John returned to the town caked in mud. He got out of the van and joined Connor and the other operatives. The police had put up cordons and crowds grew around them.

'What happened?' Connor asked.

John ignored him and spoke to a police officer instead. They went to the van and put Carl in cuffs.

'I wanted to talk. He wanted to fight.'

'And what about the mud? As you can see, there's no mud here.' Connor waved his arms out.

'It rained, didn't it? Tell her we had it out on the grass or something.'

'I'm not telling her anything. You can. If she believes you, good for you. If she doesn't, then I've got to tell her the truth.'

'No, you don't. If you lie as well, she won't ask any more questions.'

'Jesus Christ, John. This isn't you.'

'The job's done and these bastards are getting the justice they deserve. And with Carl in custody, we can get Charlie back.'

'What makes you think that?'

'He'll tell us where he is. What other options does he have?'

After a pause, Connor changed the subject. 'What are you going to do now?'

'I'm going back to Olivia. My job here is done for now. There's no need for me to stick around while these guys are processed and put in holding cells.'

Connor's phone rang. He answered and put it on speakerphone.

'Claire, we've got them—'

Claire cut in and said, 'You lot need to get back here now.' Judging by the noise in the background, Claire was in the operations room. Phones were ringing and people were shouting across the room.

'What's going on?' Connor asked.

'There have been four more attacks across the country. I don't know the full details; we're getting more information coming through every minute. But they've hit the entire country. Villages and towns everywhere.'

'Shit,' was all Connor could say. 'Do you know how many people have died?'

'I haven't got a clue. But I guess it's over a hundred. Finish up in Cornwall and get your arses back here now.' The line cut off.

'What the hell has happened?' John asked.

Connor looked at the ground, then up at John. 'There's been four more attacks across the entire country. We need to go back to London. This isn't even close to being over.'

51

John, along with everyone else, was silent throughout the journey. He could think about nothing else, and while no one displayed any emotions superficially, his had boiled over and the anger and guilt were branded on his face.

Was it his fault that more innocent people had died? Could he have done more to stop the terrorists? How would he get over this? He questioned himself, trying to search for answers, and none of them were pleasant. But he was beyond morals and ethics now. The gloves were off, and punches were going to be thrown at anyone connected with the attacks.

John and Connor raced up to Claire's office. The entire building was alive; John had never seen it like this before.

'Over here, gentlemen. I'll tell you everything we know so far.'

John and Connor stood in front of a large map of the UK pinned to the wall. On it were six red dots, each representing the location of a successful attack. But John struggled to avert his eyes from the dot that represented the reason he was there.

'As of this moment, 147 people have died. The terrorists attacked four locations simultaneously in the midlands, northwest, the south, and the southeast. Along with their two other attacks, they've covered the entire country.'

John and Connor were too stunned to speak, too caught up in disbelief.

'We, at the moment, believe the attacks are related and the work of the same terrorist organisation. Early forensic reports suggest the weapons used are untraceable, but the bullets are not 4.2 mm. It's the first thing we got them to check. They're a more commercial size. Easy to buy on the black market.'

'That implies they don't need to rely on Gary or Antonia. These bastards had a Plan B,' John said.

'Correct. But it might show that this wasn't part of the original plan. If it was, then surely they'd have had the weapons and bullets there already,' Claire said.

'What else do we know?' John asked.

'We believe one of the dead was, in fact, one of the terrorists. A local farmer had the good sense to shoot him with a shotgun, according to an initial report.'

'Can they ID the body?' John asked.

'We're hoping they can. And then we can see what we have on him.'

'Is there CCTV footage of vehicles or anything?' John asked.

'As of now, we have nothing. That's the problem with rural areas. They seldom have cameras. And to that extent, the PM is in a COBRA meeting now. But I'm hearing rumours the military is going to be mobilised and police from the cities are going to be redeployed to rural villages and towns. Quite frankly, gentlemen, this is a shit show, and we don't know yet if there's going to be an encore.'

'There probably will be if we take police out of the cities.'

'Nothing has been confirmed yet, John.'

'And what about us?' Connor asked. 'What do we do?'

'Nothing has changed with us. We're still in charge of this investigation. There's no one else. But don't be surprised if you see a few fresh faces round here. The entire world is looking at us – either in solidarity or pointing at us and wondering where it all went so bloody wrong.'

They remained silent for a moment. But this was not a time for silence; it was time for action.

'When are we likely to get any sort of reports come through?' Connor asked. 'If it's all over the country, that's a lot of different constabularies, a lot of moving parts. Some things are going to get missed.'

'I'm not exactly sure. I've made it clear to all of them that any reports come here first. Any leads come here and nowhere else. We're judge, jury, and executioner on this.'

'Sounds good to me,' Connor said. 'Hopefully the four guys we brought back might talk.'

'Four? I thought there were five of them.'

'One made a move for his rifle, so we put him down,' Connor said. 'We also ran into a problem with Carl. Well, John did.' John shot Connor a look but said nothing else.

'What happened?' Claire asked.

'He tried to run away,' John said. 'I chased after him and we had a fight over it.'

'In the mud?' Claire looked John up and down.

'Yeah. But I got him. He's battered and bruised, but he'll be fine.'

Claire looked at John and John looked back. Then she looked at Connor, who opened his mouth to speak, but Claire spoke first. 'The police will bring them here in about an hour. When they get here, I want us all interrogating them. We can't waste any more time.'

Time, John thought. Why would the terrorists move their plan forward? Did they not think they had the time? Or did they have a deadline they didn't yet know about?

'Let's go back to this,' John said, pointing to the map. 'The terrorists used different bullets, therefore different weapons, and attacked all these places at once. Assuming they are the same group, this seems out of sync. Like they've played all their cards at once and gone all in.'

'What are you thinking?' Claire asked.

'Why have they sped everything up? Why the sudden need to do everything at once? Something drastic must have changed to make them do this.'

'Can you give us a second, please, Connor?'

'Yeah, sure,' Connor said, giving John a look of innocence.

'I need to talk to you about something, John,' Claire said once Connor was out of the room.

52

'Take a seat.' They'd moved over to Claire's desk.

'What's going on? I'm pretty sure if you can share information with me, you can share it with Connor as well.'

'This isn't about Connor, John. It's about you.'

John didn't know where to look, so he kept his eyes on Claire. He still felt no regret for his actions.

Claire twisted her monitor around so John could see it. It was an article from an Italian newspaper.

'Do you want me to translate it for you? Seeing as it appears to make no sense to you.'

'Yes, please. You know I don't speak Italian.'

'It says, "Arms dealer arrested". Anything you want to tell me, John?'

'The Italian authorities did their job. And did it quickly.'

'Cut the shit, John! She was found unconscious. Blunt trauma to the head and now she's in intensive care. And you returned without a scratch.'

John wanted to intervene, to tell her about the metal pole and show her the bruises on his back. 'It's not like that,' he started, but that was all he got to say.

'It bloody looks like it is to me. I kept a close eye on the Venetian news while you were out there. Your previous with Salinger and Trent gave me cause for concern.' John tried to defend himself, but this was a one-way conversation. 'And I was worried you'd pull something like this in Venice where there were absolutely no prying eyes on us. But what other choice did I have?

'The police were notified by a terrified neighbour who thought they heard a gunshot. So at least you didn't shoot her. I guess that really is something, isn't it, John?' Her sarcasm bit like a hungry animal.

'It's not like that. She tried to beat me with a pole—'

'Oh yes. The usual excuse of "there was a fight and I fought back". The same excuse for Gary, the same for Trent, and now for Carl. Is there someone in this investigation who you haven't beaten the shit out of?'

John went to speak, but Claire put out her hand. 'You're in over your head, John. This is too personal for you, and you're falling apart at the seams. You're not the same man that walked into my office at the start of this.'

John stood up, throwing the chair back. 'Those bastards took him from me. I was starting a new life and then they took him from me. What am I meant to do? Sit back and not try to get him back? I did nothing and now he's gone.'

'That doesn't matter right now. It doesn't change the fact that your irrational actions likely sped the terrorists' plans up. You were too hot-headed to see the big picture.'

'Are you blaming these attacks on me?'

Claire took a breath. 'In some respects, yes, I am. Your irrational actions have caused the terrorists to speed up their plan and over 140 people are dead.'

'Don't you dare blame this on me. I'm the only reason you have four terrorists in custody. I'm the only reason you're not looking at seven successful attacks.'

Claire went quiet for a moment and John knew in that respect that he was right. But he knew Claire well enough to know that she wasn't going to drop this now.

'That may be the case. But there's a terrible pattern forming here. And it gives me no other option but to label you as unstable and take you off this case. With how this has changed in the last couple of hours, I can't have you getting in the way.'

'Take me off the case? If I wasn't on the case, you wouldn't have any answers.'

'You think you can get me answers?'

'You're damn right I can.' And with that, John stormed out of her office. He pushed his way through the densely populated operations room and down the corridor to the holding cells. He still had a pistol tucked into the back of his trousers, concealed underneath his top.

His body was tense, his nostrils flared.

'Open this door,' John ordered the guards. The guards looked at each other and John noticed their discomfort with his request. His stern eyes and bellowed order, however, helped to make them comply.

'Now back off,' John ordered, and again the guards did as they were told. He entered the cell, pulled his pistol out, and pointed it at Gary. 'Stand up, you piece of shit.'

Gary put his hands in the air and stepped off his bed.

'Who are the terrorists, Gary? Who are the terrorists that have just attacked four more villages?'

'I don't know. I don't know anything.'

'Stop fucking lying! Give me the fucking answers, Gary! Who the fuck is behind all this?'

'I don't—'

Gary didn't get to finish his sentence because the bellow of the pistol erupted around the cell. John fired it twice, one bullet for each knee, and Gary collapsed on the ground, screaming in pain. Blood poured between his fingers as his hands tried to keep his knees together.

'Tell me, Gary. Tell me everything, because I've lost my fucking patience with you.'

Gary didn't speak, he didn't even move.

'Put the gun down,' Claire said.

'Not yet. I haven't got the answers.'

'I have a gun aimed at your head and believe me, I will use it if you don't put that gun down.'

John looked down at Gary. The chances of him ever walking again were slim. But the chances of him seeing Charlie again were similar.

'I haven't got the answers. Just give me more time. Please, Claire, I need more time.'

'You've had time, John. Now put the bloody gun down. Don't make me shoot you.'

'Seriously, put the gun down,' Connor said, out of breath.

John looked at the pistol in his hands, then at Gary's knees. How much more suffering was he going to cause to get to the truth? He dropped the weapon. It clattered against the floor and the two guards grabbed John and pulled him away.

'You're off the case, John, effective immediately. I can't have you around here in this state.'

'You're making a mistake. You need me.'

'Not right now I don't. Go back to your flat. Calm yourself down and I'll speak to you when I have the time and capacity to do so. We're not finished with this.'

John didn't reply. There was nothing more he could say. He looked back at Gary, who was sobbing to himself, his hands, with blood still leaking between his fingers, wrapped around his knees. Then he looked at the crowd that had gathered. He met each person's gaze, but they all looked away from him. Gary's muffled cries were all that stopped the corridor from being blanketed in silence.

He walked out of the building and did not look back.

53

His flat was cold and empty. And even though he had lived there for years, none of it felt like it belonged to him. Except for the dinosaur on the kitchen table.

It did not judge him with its stitched-on smile. Its eyes looked at him like he had done nothing wrong. He joined the toy at the table and stroked his fingers through its soft fur.

To go back to Olivia and tell her the people who had taken everything from them had paid for their actions, tell her they could never hurt them again, was something he had hoped for all this time. And now that chance had gone in the snatch of a trigger.

The dinosaur. It was the only thing he had left that made him feel close to Charlie. Tonight, however, he struggled to feel any connection.

Had he lost himself in all this? Had he changed forever? He should just go to the other side of the world where no one knew him, but what would he do if he fell for someone over there only for the cycle to repeat itself? How could he think of being so selfish? The people in his life never seem to come out of it well. Knowing him was a hindrance, a curse, yet people still found their way to him. Was there any of the old him left inside, or had it been dissolved by his grief, his desire for revenge?

He wanted to see Charlie's smile one last time, to hear his laugh and listen to the wondrous things his five-year-old mind could conjure up. It was supposed to have been a new start for him. A new lease of life. Now it was gone, all gone.

He tried not to cry, to suppress his emotions, but tears ran down his cheeks. This was not the life he had wanted, but it was the one he found himself in. He was not the person he had wanted to be, but he was the monster his actions had turned him into.

Could he go back and change anything? It was impossible. The right people had paid for what they had done, but now he was reeling from it. The person being punished was him. He was reaping the inevitable consequences of what he had sown, and he had never felt so far removed from Charlie and Olivia.

He sat back, letting go of the dinosaur, feeling unworthy to touch it, to look at it. He slammed his fist on the table and knocked the dinosaur over. His heart rattled, and he sat the soft toy back up and cursed himself.

Couldn't he get anything right?

His mind danced from question to question, but he never found the rhythm to answer any of them. He couldn't think through the fog that had taken over his mind. Lost inside his own head, he got up and went to his drinks cabinet, where he found an expensive bottle of whiskey to be opened on special occasions. But when was he ever going to have anything like that? The only people he would want a special occasion with were gone, incapable of looking him in the eye.

The potent whiskey burned the back of his throat. For the first time in days, however, he finally felt something different. With each chug of booze, the burn in the back of his throat subsided bit by bit and John the dinosaur no longer sat still. It swayed across the table, trying to avoid the hand of the drunken man.

John got out of the chair and stumbled into the lounge. He went for the TV remote and tried to turn the TV on. But no matter which button he pressed, the screen only showed his horrid reflection, and, sick of the view, he threw the remote at the screen – his reflection shattered into a thousand pieces.

The burning sensation that came from chugging more whiskey faded, and he staggered through his flat. He knocked his knee on a side table and went to kick it, but in his drunken state he missed it and tumbled to the floor. The bottle of whiskey smashed, cutting his hand.

He cried out and swore at the empty room. Tears joined the mixture of blood and whiskey on the floor. It took three attempts before he was able to push himself to his feet and walk to the kitchen. He got a towel to clear up the mess, but tears blurred his path and he hit the chair he hadn't tucked underneath the table. He picked it up and threw it aside.

He grabbed the kitchen roll and noticed it was covered in red stains. He looked at his hand covered in blood and swore at himself, swore at his flat for hurting him, and tried to wrap sections of the kitchen towel around his bleeding hand. It was to no avail. Only a few sections stuck to the blood and the rest fell in a pile on the floor.

John looked down at the pile, perplexed by the mess. He bent over to clean it up, but he fell and kept falling … falling … falling.

54

The orchestra in his head started its symphony with a clash of cymbals and played off key while his eyes opened and his head registered the strain behind his eyes. He groaned. His body felt like it was floating in the ocean, and he remained on the floor for a few minutes, hoping the pain and swaying would subside. After a few minutes, however, it had only got worse as his mind got over its sleep inertia.

A simple roll onto his back caused his body to panic, and he rolled himself back over. After he had heaved up all that was left inside him, he felt no better. Instead he felt worse, as his waking mind registered the pain in his hand. He tried to focus his drunken eyes and saw it was covered in dried blood. He attempted to lift it off the floor to get a closer look.

How had this happened? But he soon remembered the broken bottle of whiskey.

He inspected his hand, picked himself up off the floor, and

decided to clean the wound and see what damage had been done. It took him a few moments before he felt steady on his feet. His headache got worse when he stood up, like two orchestras were battling to be the loudest.

He staggered over to the sink, ran the cold tap, and put his hand under it. The dried blood needed scrubbing, and he was careful not to scrap the blood that had clotted over the wound. It wasn't a deep cut. It would heal by itself – a relief.

He splashed water over his face and drunk as much as he could. Then, when he thought his day couldn't have got off to a worse start, he turned and saw what he had done to his flat.

Like an overcast sky above a still, empty ocean, without a hint of wind in the air, not a single noise could be heard. Reality had ceased to exist. The last time he had felt real was in the moment just before Charlie had been kidnapped.

The place had been turned upside down. It wasn't just a smashed TV, an overturned side table, and a broken bottle. Every bit of furniture had been tipped over and marked with a bloodied handprint. He went through his flat, his shoes crunching on the glass, and stepped over the clutter of broken furniture.

His bedroom told the same story – a dumping ground for his emotions – along with the spare room and bathroom. The mirror over the sink had been smashed, and he looked at his hands again, wondering if there were more cuts he did not know about. After a quick inspection, however, he didn't find any.

He waded back to the kitchen, suddenly aware of what he might have done to Charlie's dinosaur. In amongst the mess, however, the toy was still sitting on the table. Its stitched-on smile was still smiling and its open eyes still looked at him without judgement. It was a relief to him that he had not touched it. It was still intact, not stained with his blood. He picked it up and kissed it, then placed it back down and turned its eyes away from the mess.

If Charlie could see him now, the state he had got himself into, what would he think? Would he know what was going on? Would he be disappointed? John didn't want to think about it. His immediate answers made him feel awful, because he knew he had betrayed Charlie's and Olivia's trust in him and lost himself in his vengeance. Was this how his father had felt waking up each morning, hungover and walking around his house to see what damage he had caused, to see how little he cared? John thought he still had the upper hand on his father, however. While drunk, he hadn't beaten anyone. Sober, however, he had done a lot worse, and seeing Gary holding his knees ... where was the regret, the guilt? Was it being kept at bay by the alcohol? How could anyone become like this?

A shower, even in a ruined bathroom, made a slight improvement in his mood. The superficial mess that covered his skin had gone. He didn't bother to shave – who was he going to see? Who would want to see him?

He got dressed, looked at his flat again, and wondered what point there was in cleaning it. What was the point of anything when he felt nothing inside? He thought about calling Olivia. Maybe that would make him feel better. But he couldn't bring himself to hear her voice just yet. He didn't want to hear her cry when he told her the truth.

His phone, however, vibrated. At first he thought it was Claire, but he saw Olivia's name and, against his better judgement, answered it.

'Hey, John,' she said.

'Hey.'

'Are you okay? You sound a little rough this morning.'

'Long day yesterday. I've just woken up.'

'That's why I'm ringing. Are you okay? I've seen the news; it doesn't look good.'

'It isn't good. But I'm fine, I promise. I won't let anything happen to me.'

'I'm so glad to hear it. But the people that …' She didn't finish her sentence. Her voice choked up, and John's body tensed as he thought about how she had coped without him for the past week. Alone with no one to hold her, no one to tell her it would all be okay.

'We've got them,' he said, breaking the silence. 'The ones who took Charlie, we got all of them. I promise you, Olivia, we will get them to talk – they will tell us where he is. I'll get him back for you, for us.' Was it an empty promise? His words, to him, felt like they no longer carried meaning and he was speaking to keep the peace instead of telling the hurtful truth.

'It makes me feel safe knowing you're out there, John. I assume you're involved with it all.'

'I am. I'm more involved than anyone else. I won't stop, you know, until I know we can live the rest of our lives with this behind us. I won't stop.'

'When do you think you'll be back?'

He paused for a moment, knowing he could never go back to

her – not when he was like this.

'I hope every day that I'll see you tomorrow. But at the moment it's not looking that way.'

'Please come back as soon as you can. I miss you. This is harder than I thought it would be, and even with you out there, it's no substitute for you being here.'

John suppressed the tears. He had met the most wonderful, beautiful woman. Now a void was open between them, and he was the only one who could see it.

'I miss you too, Olivia. I'll be back soon, I promise.' He ended the call and put the phone down on the table. Had he just spoken to her for the last time?

55

Connor stood behind the mirrored glass, looking at the terrorist sitting in the interview room with a lawyer at his side. Claire joined him and handed him a tasteless cup of coffee.

'They've got lawyers now?' Connor asked.

'I felt we detained them legally enough to allow it,' Claire said, sipping her coffee. 'Carl's stable this morning, the hospital has said. It's only taken three days. Christ, what a mess.'

'He won't be getting a lawyer, then.'

'No. Thanks to John.'

'Why did you let him—'

Claire interrupted. 'Because I thought he was going to be the best person for the job. Highly motivated and he knew something that we didn't – he had a lead. Instead, revenge turned him into a monster.'

'Why not ask him over the phone to tell us what he knew?'

'I thought I could use him.'

'You let him detain Gary illegally.'

'We had nothing at that point and the entire country was looking at us. The government was begging for answers, and I saw it as a quick win.'

'And then you decided quick wins were the way to go.'

'We're not falling out over this, Connor. We had five days. We couldn't exactly play the long game.'

A silence fell between them. Both knew the mess they were in, but neither could see a way out.

'The last thing I want is for this to come between us,' Claire said. 'We need to keep it together. Because we really will be up the creek if we don't.'

'I agree. But where does this leave us in terms of convictions? We can't get Gary or Carl; our case will be thrown out.'

'Gary's, maybe. But Carl's, maybe not. If you guys stick to the story that John made up, then hopefully our word will go against theirs.'

'And if one of my guys grows a conscience?'

'Then we're fucked.'

'Any news from the PM?'

'The rumours are true. The Army are going to be patrolling the countryside and police from the major cities are going to be pushed out to bolster the numbers in rural areas.'

'Let's hope crime statistics in cities don't spike, then.'

'Are you going in now?'

'Yeah.' Connor sighed. He left the room behind the mirrored glass and sat opposite the detained suspect. He dropped a file onto the table and pressed the record button on the machine.

'Suspect C, or should I call you James Threston? At least that's the name that's connected to your fingerprints. You've been in jail before for drug-related incidents, involved with gangs in Birmingham since before you were a teenager. You've been out for two years and now you're suspected of committing acts of terror on UK soil. Anything you'd like to say?'

'No comment,' James replied after a nudge from his lawyer.

'In fact, all three of my clients are going to respond with no comment,' the lawyer said.

'All three?'

'Yes. I'm going to be representing all three. After all, it's the same case. It makes sense to me.'

Connor looked over at the mirrored glass. 'Okay,' he replied, not wanting to give the impression this interview had already not gone to plan. He took a breath, opened the file, and continued. 'James is being shown picture A. Picture A is a photo of Carl Bedford, the suspected leader of this terrorist organisation. How did you meet Carl?'

'No comment.'

'Why were you in Cornwall yesterday with five workshop rifles and ten magazines of workshop ammunition?'

'No comment.' James didn't bother looking up from the table to speak.

'Why do you want to commit acts of terrorism in the UK?'

'No comment.'

Connor flicked through his file and pulled out another picture. 'I'm showing James picture B, which is a photograph of Gary Salinger. Do you know Gary, James?'

'No comment.'

'You're not even going to deny it. We caught you red-handed and there are other terrorists out there. Help us and we can help you.'

James turned to his lawyer and whispered into his ear.

'My client only wishes to answer questions with "no comment" and is not interested in a deal.'

'Are you not interested in a deal for him? You work for his best interests, right?'

'If he doesn't want a deal, then we will not negotiate one.'

'But you know full well it could take years off his sentence. You won't try to persuade him?'

'My client does not wish to make a deal, and neither will my other clients.'

Connor sat back and looked at the helpless young man in front of him. 'Listen to me, James. If you help us, then you will get years of your life back. You can start a new life under a witness protection programme. You'll be free from all of this.'

'No comment.'

'What about the people who undertook the attacks yesterday? Do you know them?'

'No comment.'

Connor pushed the button to stop the recording. 'I'm not sitting here and listening to you answer "no comment" to all my questions. You're wasting my time.'

56

'Don't bother interviewing the others. Tell the lawyer he can get lost,' Claire said as she returned to her office deflated and worried about where the next lead would come from.

'You don't think it's worth trying?'

'No. They're too scared to speak or stupid enough to think that whoever is behind all this will come and save them. Either way, we're getting nothing out of them.'

'But maybe if we—'

'Connor, just do what I've asked. Go down and speak to the lawyer, then ask your team what they've got on these four attacks. Then come back and debrief me.'

With the lawyer having been sent away and with no desire to question them if they were only going to respond with 'no comment', Claire wondered whether blowing their knees out would get them to talk. They were just four people involved in a wider terrorist organisation. Stopping them from killing again was the primary aim. Conviction would come later. The methods to achieve this, however, were what she had to question. She had helped to create a monster. And that same monster could not be tamed to work for her.

After an hour, Connor returned to Claire's office. 'What have you got for me?' she asked.

'We're corroborating witness reports from all the locations that were attacked. But witnesses are scarce. The body count is 202 now.'

'Any chance it's going to go higher?'

Connor nodded and said, 'Yeah, it might.'

Claire rubbed her face with her hands and asked herself how much worse it could get.

'Forensics have confirmed the weapons are workshop jobs with commercially available bullets. But who supplied them is still unknown. We're working with every agency we have on this. If we follow the bullets, we should get a lead. But I must admit I have a feeling that Bedford isn't the man behind all this.'

'I agree with you,' Claire said. 'There has to be a bigger player involved in all of this. How about the one the farmer killed? Have we got anything on him yet?'

'The coroner hasn't released their report. But we should get an ID before the end of the day.'

'Well, I guess we'll just have to wait for that. The three guys we have detained downstairs, they're not killers. They used to be in gangs and might have stabbed someone, but that's gangs fighting over turf. This is gunning down innocent civilians. It's a different thing entirely. Whoever is behind this must have paid them a lot of money or messed with their heads. None of them have been on any terrorist watch list. Have you looked at their bank accounts yet?'

'Not yet. I'll ask the financial investigators to get on and have a look. But they've covered their tracks so far – I wouldn't hold out much hope.'

'Do we have any known addresses for any of the three?'

'No to all of them. None of them has had a known address for two years. But we could try to get search warrants for their previous addresses. I don't feel like we should shut off any avenues.'

'I agree. But getting the warrants is going to be tough.'

'I'll add it to my list.'

'So where do you think we should go from here?'

'The finances might be a good start while we wait for the ID on the dead body. But chances are they've paid them cash, or the money is offshore, so very hard to find. Interviewing the three downstairs is pointless. The bullets might give us something. But for now, I think we need to identify anyone else involved with the attacks. Keep searching on CCTV and gathering up whatever witnesses we can. Even if we get the type of car they used like last time, that's got to be better than nothing, right?'

Claire sighed, then said, 'This won't be easy, will it?'

'No. But we'll find something.'

'I really hope you do.'

After Connor had left her office, Claire brought up a live news feed on her monitor. The reporter was walking around a cordoned-off area where bodies still lay under white sheets and the streets were still littered with blood spatter. Yet this hadn't been enough to deter people from turning up with flowers and notes of condolence.

The reporter walked away from the scene and went to

interview a couple standing close by who were probably wondering what to do next in their lives. They had been witnesses to the atrocities, and their white eyes and pale faces told Claire their minds had been branded with what they had seen. Their words, a collection of distress and tears, only brought home further the substantial cost of these attacks.

And it was then that an initial report from the coroner was emailed to her.

57

John, unshaven, unwashed, and unchanged for four days, hadn't left his apartment. He kept the blinds and curtains down, cutting himself off from the world. He had spent his time sitting on the sofa watching the news, which currently only had one story running.

His phone rang – the last thing he wanted to do was talk to someone. He went to cancel the call. Instead, his finger hovered over the end call button. He saw it was Claire calling him.

He answered.

'Claire. What are you calling for?'

'How are you holding up?' she asked with undertones of haste in her voice.

'I'm doing just fine. How's the investigation going?'

'Oh, you know, same old. Information taking its time to come through to us, suspects not talking …'

'Not talking? Are you asking them the right questions?'

'They have lawyers who have told them to answer with "no

comment".'

'Sounds like a tough crowd you're dealing with. Immunity?'

'They don't want deals either.'

Their conversation took a pause while John tried to read between the lines. But it was obvious what Claire was asking. She wanted him to come back and deal with the witnesses using the same method his vengeful self had done with Salinger.

'How do you plan on tackling this, then? If they have lawyers, I guess you have to stick to the law.'

'I told the lawyers we wouldn't be questioning their clients anymore if they were only going to answer "no comment". Frankly, it's a waste of everyone's time.'

John didn't reply. He waited for Claire to make an offer first.

'Look, John. I know this might sound … look, we need you to come in.'

'What's this about? I thought you didn't like my methods.'

'I don't. But something has come up and we need you to see it. You might be able to help us.'

'*Might* be able to help?'

'I'm not explaining this over the phone. You're going to need to come in so we can show you some things.'

What else was he going to do? He knew there was no going back to Olivia, so this was second best, and it wasn't all that bad, because maybe this was a final redemption, his ultimate chance to get Charlie back, and perhaps then he might be able to return to them. But at least if he got him back, he wouldn't be leaving her empty-handed. She deserved so much better than that, and John knew it more than anyone else.

'I'll be there in an hour.'

58

For the first time in over a week, the operations room was silent – silent because it was empty. John wondered where everyone had gone. Was Claire keeping everyone away from him for their own safety? What were these things she wanted him to see? The large screens lining the back wall were all turned off except the middle one. It displayed the profile of a deceased man.

'What is this?' John asked.

'Take a seat.' He did as he was told, and Claire joined Connor in front of the screens.

'So,' Connor started, 'this man is the terrorist killed by a farmer. His name is Luis Alonso. They ran fingerprints and, with the help of Interpol, we found him in a criminal database in Columbia. He had been arrested previously for drug smuggling. He did seven years inside and he was let out two years ago. Bedford *died* two years ago and the guys you detained in Silverton were all released from prison two years ago. I thought these can't be coincidences.'

'Are they all linked, then?' John asked.

Connor stepped forward and the screen behind him switched to Columbian news reports.

'Over two years ago, Columbia had a large successful crackdown on some of their biggest cartels. Why does this matter? Because this man used to work for a cartel. Although they weren't caught up in the crackdown.'

'What's this got to do with anything? This is about terrorism, not drugs. This man moved from drug trafficking to terrorism. He couldn't hack it and now he's dead,' John said.

'Not exactly. You see, this drug lord' – Connor switched to a picture of a different man – 'known as Caballo, a Spanish word for heroin, had been trying to make it on the scene in America using heroin, not cocaine – unusual for a Columbian drug cartel. Hence why he wasn't caught up in the crackdown. Unfortunately for him, heroin isn't as popular as cocaine in the States.'

'I'm still not seeing the link,' John said.

'The link,' Connor said, 'lies in the fact that he has links with Gary Salinger. Salinger Autos makes parts for cars that are shipped around the world, including Columbia – just Columbia, mind, nowhere else in South America. And part of the reason the NCA wanted to search his facility in the first place was his potential link with cartels, not just in the UK but also in Columbia. We think he smuggles bullets to them in these shipments. There isn't definitive evidence to support this yet, but we've contacted the Columbian authorities for more information. With heroin not being big in America, we have theorised that Caballo is using his links with

328

Salinger to smuggle heroin into the UK.'

'So what? I don't see the link between the terrorist attacks and this Caballo's cartel. How does committing acts of terror help him ...?' John trailed off, because he had answered his own question. 'Oh shit. He's trying to drive police out of the cities to make it easier to distribute drugs. Only he's already achieved that. You need to stop the redeployment of police.'

'With what evidence? This is all circumstantial, plus the main threat right now is terrorism. Public perception means we have no choice, no matter what we might suspect.'

'What do you mean, it's all circumstantial? Do we not have anything concrete on this guy yet?'

'Narcotics don't. So we can't prove he has drugs in this country, and we can't link him with the terrorist attacks just because he has links with Salinger.'

'I need to go and get answers from Caballo. And I think a few bullets in his knees will help.'

'No, John. They won't. He won't have any answers.'

'What are you talking about? He's the central pivot of this entire operation.'

'Caballo is dead. He was found dead in his home in Columbia six months ago.'

Connor switched the screen to a Columbian news article reporting on his death. Next to it was the profile Narcotics had on Caballo.

'Caballo's real name is David Rojas. And these pictures are of people the Columbian authorities believe are linked to him but who they haven't yet positively identified. Do you recognise anyone in these pictures?'

John's heart stopped beating. The air was sucked out of the room. He was standing in the vacuum that remained, staring at a picture of the woman he had grown so fond of. It was definitely her. There was no mistaking her dark eyes, her tanned skin, and, of course, those scarlet lips.

Time stopped.

John thought he was going to be sick, but his body had ceased to function, frozen by the shock. He felt the life drain from his skin, drip out of his fingers, and drop to the floor. His eyes glazed over, his head felt light, and he stumbled out of the chair. He staggered into Claire's office, pressing his hands against anything to stop him from falling over. When he got to the bin next to Claire's desk, he collapsed on the floor and heaved into it. But nothing came out.

He'd thought he had betrayed her. He'd thought she would never take him back. Yet it was she who had kept a secret from him. She was the monster kidnapping her own child to plead her innocence – or to get him out of the country.

He wanted to hate her, but mixed with the anger were his feelings for her and Charlie that just would not go away; he could not shake them from his soul.

'I'm sorry, John,' Claire said, placing a hand on his shoulder.

The two of them sat in silence.

'I guess you want to bring her in?' John asked.

'Yeah, I do.'

'Let me do it. I'll get her to come in quietly.'

'That's why I called you back.'

59

'You still want to do this?' Claire asked.

'I don't think I have any other choice,' John said as he started his solitary walk down the road towards Olivia's house.

His time there replayed itself in his mind; the first time he'd seen her through the frosted glass of the front door; the time he'd heard Charlie's feet scamper across the landing and race down the stairs; when he'd smelt the coffee she'd made for him. The time they'd made a fruit cake; Charlie's happiness beaming out when they went to the museum. He remembered being out in the garden with him, making bug houses and playing tag. He remembered the first time Olivia had cooked for him, the first time they had kissed. He remembered the first time he'd stroked his fingers through her hair, when he'd woken up next to her.

It had been a dream. And now he had woken up to reality, left to question if any of it had been real. It must have been real, though, surely? She couldn't have gone through all that with him and not felt a thing. Although he would never be able to believe it with enough confidence to stop it being a question in his mind.

She'd had her child kidnapped; she had played him. Used him as she bided her time, playing with him like a puppet, and he'd gone along without resistance to every string she'd pulled. And now he was standing outside her house waiting to go in, to see her for the first time since learning the truth.

How would he feel when he saw her again? He was unsure as he unlatched the gate and walked towards the front door. He knocked and waited for her with a rush of adrenaline shooting through his veins, the same rush he had whenever he anticipated seeing her. But she never came, and the house looked at him like he was a stranger. The silence should have been the first giveaway. His mind, however, was too full of noise to hear it, and the solemn property waited for this stranger to leave. There would be no returning to pick up things left behind.

It could not end here. She could not have already left the country. He pushed the door open, surprised she hadn't locked it. He walked into the living room, and it felt small, empty, with nobody here. She had left everything behind, but the picture of the villa was gone. She had hardly added any personal touches to the house – a deliberate act all set up so she could make a clean getaway when the terrorist attacks achieved their desired effect. And he had been there, lived with her, slept with her, looked her in the eyes, and he had never suspected a thing.

She had left without him, left him there alone to pick up the pieces of her plan and revel in the simplicity and effectiveness of it. In some respects, he admired her for what she had planned; it was a testament to her. But why did she have to leave him behind?

He continued into the kitchen, saw where she used to stand in front of the window, looking out and watching him in the garden. Next to the kettle he found an envelope with his name on it. A letter of apology? An explanation? Inside there was an address, a photograph of the villa from her picture, and the picture she had taken of the three of them that one sunny day in the park. John sucked in a sharp breath and tensed his body to keep his emotions from firing up.

On the back of it, she had written a note expressing her desire to see him soon and kissed it with her red lipstick. He stared at it for a moment, feeling the weight of it in his hands. It was not the apology he had been expecting – it was an invitation. A chance to be with her again. He turned it back over and admired the picture. He drew his finger over her beautiful face and could feel her tender skin through the polaroid. Seeing Charlie's smile made him well up. This was a moment in time reserved for the three of them.

And now he had to hand it over to Claire.

But why leave it lying there for him to find? Did she always expect him to come back to her, no matter what he learned about her? He had done exactly that. Where else did he have to go? And he looked around one last time. Except now, the house wasn't empty or small. It was a large paradise filled with the three of them – all smiling, all laughing, all in their own perfect world. This was what he wanted. A few days ago he was certain that he had lost all of this, but now, was there a chance to get it all back? They were waiting for him.

When he left the house, he realised there was nowhere else for

333

him to go.

As he walked back up the road towards Claire and the collection of vehicles and men with guns, he kept his hand in his pocket, keeping the photograph firmly in his grasp.

Claire saw her rogue operative return alone and swore under her breath.

'I'm sorry, Claire, but the house is empty. She's moved on.'

'Any idea where she's gone?'

John paused before he answered. He had to tell Claire the truth, to finish this. But what if he didn't ...?

'No, sorry.' His finger stroked her face in the photograph.

She swore under her breath again, then turned towards her team and said, 'Right, everyone, get in your vehicles. We're heading back to London.'

'You don't want to search the place?' John asked.

'You just said it was empty. She wouldn't have left a damn thing, would she? The plan has been too detailed to overlook something like this. And what are we going to find except proof that she lived here? We can't prosecute her for living in a house.'

John got into the car and during the return journey wondered if she had boarded a commercial aircraft to leave the country. He doubted it. If she was in the drug smuggling business, she could smuggle herself out of the country or use a fake passport. He felt a sense of relief dissolve the adrenaline. He would be reunited with them soon. He just needed an excuse to get out of Claire's way for a few hours to make his getaway.

'Until we find her, John, there isn't much for you to do. Go home, get some proper rest, and come back in the morning. I can't begin to think about what you're going through.'

'Thank you,' John said, grateful for the opportunity being handed to him.

He was dropped off at his flat. He immediately packed and booked himself on the next flight.

The taxi dropped him off at Terminal 4 at Heathrow and John did not look back. He checked in. He went through security with no issues, then sat and waited at his gate. When the gate opened, he was the first to board the British Airways flight to Larnaca International Airport, Cyprus.

Part 3

Part 3

60

Even though it was close to midnight when John landed in Cyprus, a wall of heat hit him as he got off the plane. He collected his bag from the conveyor belt and hailed the next taxi outside the terminal. The driver spoke English and John showed him the address. The driver told him it would be an expensive trip up the mountains. John, however, did not care.

Larnaca's city lights were soon an orange haze in the rearview mirror, and the taxi's headlights pierced the darkness of the Cypriot countryside. The mountains, illuminated by the half moon, looked down on John, awaiting his arrival.

The road twisted up the mountain, climbing higher and higher. John saw a speck of light in the distance and assumed that was where he was heading. The road, he had only just come to notice, was deserted, and it felt like he had the entire mountain range to himself.

The taxi stopped outside a metal gate and John paid the driver, who didn't hang around once John had retrieved his luggage from the boot. As John approached the gate, it opened slowly and he walked down the meandering driveway that crossed over the stream trickling down the mountainside.

He stopped and admired the villa when it came into view. The speck of light turned out to be a large estate sitting proudly on the side of the mountain, just like in the picture. The darkness made it impossible to see what the view was like, but tomorrow he would see it. Tonight was about him and Olivia and Charlie, and he couldn't wait to hold them in his arms again.

As he headed towards the front door, he didn't feel any guilt for the choice he had made – not even a single sliver of regret. He had crossed the moral line with no consequences and felt like a new man because of it, and this was the last path of his journey. He had done the hard work, and now it was time to be rewarded.

He knocked on the door. A tanned Cypriot guard opened it, a pistol holstered at his waist and a tight black shirt on his broad frame.

'Good evening, John,' he said. 'Let me take your bag.' John was distracted by the extravagant open-plan villa with its faint echo and didn't listen to what was said to him. The guard took John's bag himself and led him inside. 'Ms Santiago would like you to join her. Just follow the roses.'

The guard pointed at the tiled floor and John saw the trail of petals leading into the villa. He followed them up the stairs. He had sweated on his walk down the driveway, but the villa was cool inside. The petals led him up to the second floor and down the landing to the door at the end. It was ajar, and he could smell her sweet scent.

He pressed his hand against the door and took a breath to calm his racing mind. What would she look like? He pushed it open and noticed first the mountain breeze flowing into the room from the open doors that led out onto the balcony.

She appeared in a veil of white in the corner of his eye, her dark eyes fixed on him as she sauntered towards him. Her striking beauty numbed him into muteness. This silence allowed him to think, and, for the first time, a pinch of doubt echoed in the back of his mind, but it disappeared when she was right in front of him and he felt the ecstasy running through his blood. They didn't need to say anything. She took his nervous hand in hers, rested it on her waist, and wrapped her arms around his neck. They never broke eye contact.

John looked at her lips and longed to kiss them, but he said, 'I have so many questions.'

She drew her lips closer to his neck and kissed it once before saying, 'And I will answer all of them.' She continued to kiss his neck, and John drew a sharp breath and brushed his hands through her hair before pulling her in and kissing her. And despite their bodies already being pressed together, John pulled her in tighter and her hands dug into his back and pulled him closer still. Their lips, pressed hard together, continued to dance, and their hands explored each other's bodies like uncharted territory. They only released each other to take a breath, but even then, their lips still touched.

And when they were under the covers, their clothes a pile on the floor, their bodies wrapped around each other, they paused for a moment and looked into each other's eyes. The desire to hold each other came from knowing they were embroiled in a secret life that neither felt they could escape from. They had crossed boundaries together, and together they would do so again and again. The thrill of living on the other side of the law drew them closer, and when the final symphony played in perfect harmony, hitting each note with rigour and passion, they fell onto the bed like it was the entrance to their new life together.

61

It was the column of light reaching through the balcony doors that woke him the next morning, and he had to check with himself to make sure last night hadn't been a dream.

A warm breeze drifted across them, and her head, resting on his chest, raised and lowered with each breath. He hoped his beating heart wouldn't wake her; it would disrupt the still of the morning. He felt her heart beating against his torso; he glided the tips of his fingers through her hair and he knew he had everything here. The faint echo of doubt from the previous night had not returned. Of course it hadn't, because what could be more perfect than this?

He could feel Charlie's absence, however. Yet the excitement of seeing him again, handing him his dinosaur and playing with him in the garden, blew away any doubts. He had questions, of course, but they would be answered in good time, and if they weren't, what did it matter? He was here with them, and the money that was sure to be made from this would pay for the best life for the three of them. At least, that was what he had gathered from the stories he had heard during his time in the police.

He got out of bed, careful not to wake her, and stood on the balcony, where the Mediterranean sun beamed down on him, and looked over the airy mountains like a lion surveying his kingdom. He admired the view for a moment, adjusting to his new surroundings and falling for them instantly – they were a far cry from the glass and steel of London. But it was the serene silence that stood out to him. The view stretched for miles, but he could not see any other sign of life, and with only Olivia and Charlie here, it felt like they were the only people on Earth.

Olivia wrapped her arms around his waist and said good morning. If there was one thing that could improve the view, it was having her standing in front of it. He spun her around, pressed her back against the balcony and kissed her.

'It's not a bad view, is it?' she said.

'It's better with you in it.'

A faint engine noise drifted between the mountains, and a small aircraft rose from the valley into the sky.

'That's one of mine,' she said. 'I have an airstrip in the valley. Let's have breakfast first and I'll answer your questions.'

John kissed her instead of saying anything, and she took his hand and led him downstairs to the dining room. The patio doors were open, and the pool glistened in the sun. The long dining table had been set for two people, and John struggled to take his eyes off the woman next to him.

Two waiters served them breakfast and poured coffee. Olivia held her mug in both hands and looked at John, waiting for him to drink first, and when he did, he relished its taste as memories of the coffee she used to make him flashed through his mind.

'It's good coffee,' he said.

'I know. And just wait till you try the food. I picked out the best chef I could find.'

'I'm sure you did.'

'I missed you.'

'I missed you too.' He reached out and held her hand. 'How did you know that I'd … you know …?'

'Follow me out here? When things weren't going quite as I planned, I knew it was you causing the trouble. I knew Salinger was untouchable after failed warrants from the NCA, and when I couldn't get hold of him, I knew someone had detained him illegally. I guessed you weren't properly employed by them, or at least you would've been the most motivated, so I knew it would've been you. And when I saw Antonia had been put into the hospital, I guessed again that it was you. Frustrated, I can imagine, by not getting any answers. But to me it was the most amazing, romantic thing I'd ever seen. You really wanted him back, didn't you? And I couldn't help but fall more for you. You went through all of that just for us. And when I planned the extra attacks after I suspected you were going to stop the others, I knew you'd come back to me, because you'd need a break eventually.'

Although what she had said was not the whole truth, John chose not to correct her. She had created a narrative in her mind that had worked out perfectly for him. So who was he to correct that?

'But why leave this address out? What made you so sure I'd

344

come and not tell anyone?'

'Because I knew there was nothing left for you in England. My only concern was you not being okay with the way I make my living. But after seeing the way you handled everything, I was sure you'd warm to it.'

John said nothing and instead smiled at her. They ate their breakfast and drank their coffee and when they were done, the waiters reappeared to clear up.

'You're right about one thing,' John said. 'There was nothing left for me in England. But I only have half of what I once had here.'

'I know what you mean. Charlie is here. And you will get to see him. But when I think the time is right.'

'When will the time be right?'

'I hope for us it will be soon. I'm convinced it will be. Now come on – if I'm going to tell you what's going on, then I want you to see something that I think you're going to love. For the time to be right, you need to see and understand everything.'

She held his hand and led him through the patio doors, the light breeze dampening the effects of the harsh heat of the sun, and they walked down a path tunnelled in vines, their silence broken only by the crunch of their shoes on the gravel. Eventually they stopped outside a gate.

'This is all for us,' she said. 'The moment I knew we'd be together, I had this place built.' She opened the gate and led him through.

The walled garden, cut off from the rest of the world, left John without a word in his mouth or a breath in his body. The flowers flared with colour, the trees provided shade in all the right places, and the paths were straight and clean. The garden, a replica of the one he had once worked on, had been crafted to perfection.

'You like it?' she asked. 'I thought this could be ours. You can do what you want with it, but I wanted to make it perfect for you first.'

'It's quite something.' His gaze travelled around the garden, trying to soak in all its beauty, but the faint echo of doubt returned. A spark of disdain for the fake, manicured green grass, perhaps? Or the flowers that had no place on the side of a mountain? It was missing something; he could sense it. He brushed these lapses of reason to the side, judging himself to still be overcome by the shock of being here.

They wandered down one of the paths and sat on the bench at the end – a new addition compared to the garden in England.

'You're still in shock, I can tell,' she said.

'I am a bit. But it's not just the garden. It's all of it.'

'I know how you must be feeling, but you'll get over it. This is your life now – our life. We're in this together, and I couldn't be happier.'

John looked at her, kissed her, then said, 'How did you get involved in all of this?'

'It all started with an ex-lover of mine, this ex-husband I told you about, who, make no mistake, was a bad man. Seeing that cartels had been brought down by the police, he started making heroin instead of cocaine. But he couldn't see that heroin wasn't selling in the US. People there wanted cocaine, and Mexico has the monopoly on that now. We needed to come to the UK, the drugs capital of Europe. But he wasn't interested – he said the market was already well established and there was no gap for heroin. If we were going to make it in the UK, we were going to need to do something drastic, but he wasn't up to the task. So I came up with this plan, with the help of my dad, as a way to escape from him while he tried to hold on to his American dream. Behind his back, I worked all of this out and put it all into place. They all thought my idea had great potential. So I promised them a share of the money. Then, when the time was right, I killed my ex-husband and a few months later moved with Charlie to start the plan.'

'I bet they were happy to take that offer. Did you know Salinger asked for immunity?'

'Did he?' She sounded shocked.

'He did. But he knew nothing, or appeared to know nothing, so we didn't give it to him.'

'He was probably just wasting your time.'

'I think he was. But I wouldn't use him again. I don't think he'd be up to it.'

'Why is that?'

'Because I shot him in the knees. I lost patience with him. I'm not into playing games.'

She held his cheek in her hand. 'I won't play any games with you, I promise. We're in this together now. There's no backing out.'

'No, there isn't.' He kissed her and when he pulled away, she continued.

'Once we told him about the money, Salinger got more and more involved. He recommended Bedford as the guy to oversee the shootings. So he faked his death.'

'That was two years ago.'

'I've been planning this for a long time. We only had one chance to get it right, and I'm not just talking about the plan to get the police out of the cities. We needed to make sure our supply lines into the UK were all ready as well.'

'What are your supply lines?'

'I'll show them to you tomorrow. I'm going to show you the whole thing because I know you'll like it. Anyway, Carl recruited others involved with drugs and gangs and told them about the money, and of course they were soon on board. The next phase was executing the plan. And with no known terrorist links with anybody involved, we knew it was going to be hard for the authorities to get to us with this decentralised model. There are no obvious links back to me and what I'm really doing.'

'You can say that again.' John chuckled to himself.

'But of course it wasn't as smooth as we thought it was going to be. You got in the way.' She smiled at him and nudged his shoulder. 'You're quite the warrior, John. And I'm glad I have someone like you here with me. It makes me feel safe. But you getting in the way meant I had to speed things along a bit. I got worried you'd get to the bottom of it and stop us. But I had a Plan B in place anyway, in case anybody got close to stopping us. So I ordered four more attacks using my people. It was a risk, but one that paid off.'

'But with the police out of the cities, what was going to make your drugs more appealing than any others? After all, it's a crowded market, like you said.'

'Tomorrow, I'll show you. We're going on a trip to Afghanistan to see the people who grow my poppies.'

With Olivia in the shower, John unpacked his suitcase, and when he opened it, the same stitched-on smile and open eyes were looking at him. Holding the toy in his hands, he couldn't contain his smile. He kissed it and laid it between the two pillows at the head of the bed. Charlie should have been here now. It would have made everything perfect, but all in good time, he reassured himself.

Olivia walked out of the en suite with wet hair, leaving footprints on the carpet. She saw the stuffed toy and sat down next to John. 'You'll see him soon.'

He kissed her on the shoulder and said, 'I know. A part of me feels lost without him.'

'After I've told you everything, you will get to see him. There'll be no secrets between us. We have the entire world to take on.'

He wrapped his arm around her warm, damp shoulders and said, 'Right now, I'm not going anywhere unless it's with you.'

62

They suspected something when John didn't show up the next day, and they spent half the morning waiting for him until Claire decided that he had gone, another agenda on his mind, and they started the search for him. Initially they feared the worst until someone checked whether his passport had gone through security and saw he had taken a flight to Cyprus. Claire and Connor both agreed he had gone there for a reason, and both decided that the reason was Olivia and Charlie. Claire gave the order to find him.

Connor contacted the Cypriot authorities, explaining they were after one of Britain's most dangerous terrorists and they had good reason to believe she was based there. The Cypriot authorities declared they would support Connor however they could, and he asked for access to the CCTV at Larnaca International Airport. He saw on the grainy feed his former colleague walking through arrivals, taking his bag from the conveyor belt, and hailing a taxi. He watched as the taxi left the airport, its destination, however, unknown.

Claire told Connor they were getting on the next flight out there. Although they had their own ideas about why John had gone, they didn't voice them, because despite what he had done, painting him with the same brush they painted their targets with did not sit right with them. Maybe he had gone there to get Charlie back after finding something in Olivia's house. Maybe he had completely lost his mind only to find it amongst the people he used to bring to justice.

In the early hours of the morning, they took the next flight, arriving in Cyprus in the late morning, over a day behind John. The chief of police met them outside the airport and told them that his resources and men would support them. Claire thanked him, but Connor did not wait until the small talk was over to hand the chief a screenshot of the taxi John had got into with a request they find the driver. The chief obliged and said they would get on with the task straight away.

They stayed in a hotel near the police headquarters and undertook the painful wait for information – nothing came the first day. The chief debriefed them on progress. They had started an extensive search for the taxi driver. They knew who was working around the time John had landed and were getting in contact with each driver, and the chief cursed the grainy photos, embarrassed that they could not get a number plate from them. He had started a search for Olivia too, but so far nothing had come up – their records showed she had never been in the country. The chief bid them all goodnight and said he would return first thing in the morning to inform them of any overnight developments.

Claire and Connor remained behind in the hotel conference room. They were silent for a moment until Connor said, 'I'm beginning to understand how John felt, because despite what he's done, this still feels slightly personal to me.'

Claire remained quiet. She looked out of the window at the dark sky and noticed not a single star.

'We'll find him,' she eventually said.

'But in what state?'

Claire turned, looked at Connor, and again chose not to answer straight away. 'I'm trying not to think about it. This really could go either way.'

'But I think there's more of a chance he'll stick to our side, right?'

Again, Claire's reply was delayed by her thoughts. 'I hope so.' She rubbed her eyes, sighed, then continued, 'If he hadn't got in contact with us about the car, would we have found it?'

'What does that matter?'

'Would we have found it?'

'I like to think we would have done somehow, but … if it had been in the witness statement …'

'That's too bad. But he must have seen it as a way back in, and we all – well, I certainly did – thought that there was a benefit to that, having someone on the team who would bend over backwards to get results. And when they came forward and said they'd attack in five days' time, I thought I'd got it perfectly right. But I chose to cut corners.'

'None of us really stopped you. We all knew what needed to be done. The question you should ask is whether we could have done it without John, and the answer is no.'

'And yet here we are, tracking him down like any other target.'

They remained quiet for a moment.

'I think you had no option in all of this,' Connor said.

'Really?'

'Seriously. We've had nothing like this before. No one this well organised, well planned – it's stretched us all.'

'But at what cost?'

'We might well be on the verge of getting them, but hundreds have died.'

'It would have been more if it wasn't for John giving us the information about the car.'

Claire took a seat at the long table, and Connor sat opposite her.

'I should have gripped it sooner,' Claire said.

'Gripped what?'

'I could forgive what he did to Salinger, because he came back with a few bruises. The injuries and his story married up. But then it happened again to Trent – but John had no new injuries. He'd just beaten him up. I could see it in his eyes. It was there, right in front of me. But I let it go because I thought that was the only way.'

'I haven't thought of another way. Like I said, we let you. No one challenged your decision to let him carry on, because the situation required it.'

'It required John to operate illegally without it being obvious that it was us. It didn't require him to beat the shit out of people – one of whom is innocent.'

'He didn't know that at the time.'

'He also didn't know if he was guilty.'

The silence remained. This time, however, it was weighed down with the accumulation of events and reflections on the investigation.

'What are you thinking?' Connor asked.

'If I had put a stop to it, he wouldn't have beaten up Bedford and Antonia. That was the kicker, you see. It's easy to keep this quiet in your own country, but in someone else's it's a damn sight harder, and I knew then that I needed to rein him in. It was getting out of hand and didn't just put me at risk of losing my job and this investigation, but it put you guys in the firing line as well. But it was too late – the damage had been done. But if I had got to him sooner, he wouldn't have shot Salinger in the knees. I wouldn't have needed to get him off the case. And he wouldn't be out here.'

'You're only thinking like that because you fear the worst – that he's come out here to be with Olivia and Charlie and move to the criminals' side. But he could be out here to get him back from her and put a stop to it all.'

'I guess we'll only know when we track him down.'

63

The cars were lined up outside the villa to take them to the airstrip in the valley. They travelled in convoy down the mountainside, and a small jet waited for them on the runway, its engines idling.

They landed on a desert strip in Afghanistan. The aircraft's wheels kicked up a wave of dust and the heat was more intense here. They got off the plane and were greeted by a man with open arms.

'Olivia, it's good to see you again.'

'Hamed, it's good to see you too. I'd like you to meet John, my partner.'

'It's a pleasure to meet you, John.'

'It's nice to meet you too,' John said, shaking Hamed's hand.

Hamed led them to the line of vehicles. The journey was brief, but over this rugged terrain, John was glad they had not walked it. He had only heard of and seen Afghanistan through the eyes of the media and the harrowing stories of soldiers who had fought there.

But the place he found was a different world than he had thought it would be. It was not just ugly blown-up cities; it was vast open landscapes with mountains towering over them in the background. He held Olivia's hand, thinking it was the only thing on this trip he would find stability in, but there was nobody around, and Hamed had greeted them with such warmth, he felt he could trust him already. So he let go, worried she would think he was scared. She, however, took his hand straight back.

He saw it in her eyes, the attachment, the dependency she had on him. If he had stayed in England, this other world would have been closed off to him; if he had stayed within those confines, then this, all this between them, would never have existed.

'I must tell you, Ms Santiago, that we did have a slight issue,' Hamed said from the front seat. 'But let me reassure you I saw to it personally.'

'What was the problem?' she asked.

'Two of my farmers were caught smuggling heroin out. It was only a small amount; it would've been negligible to us. But principles are principles.'

'How did you catch them?'

'My guards searched them after they saw them acting suspiciously. I tell you, Ms Santiago, nothing gets past me. I am in complete control of all this.'

'What did you do with the farmers?'

'I thought maybe you would like to oversee their punishment.'

Olivia glanced at John, smiled at him, then said, 'I would like that very much. Thank you, Hamed.'

The farm, as Hamed called it, turned the lifeless desert into a sea of green. The poppy fields stretched to the horizon, bleeding into the mountains. How much money came from this single field? How many lives could be destroyed by it?

Hamed called out to two of his workers. They ran off and returned with the two farmers. Their hands were bound and their faces hooded. They were dragged towards them and thrown in the dust. Hamed pulled a pistol from his trousers and handed it to Olivia. He snapped his fingers and one of his workers handed one to John.

'Deal with them as you wish, Ms Santiago. And don't worry about the mess. We'll sort it all out for you.' Hamed smiled at them both like he had delivered a valuable service.

The two farmers wept underneath their hoods; the cloth clung to their faces and John could make out their features. The one in front of him had a round face and a large nose. Did he think about the consequences when he stole heroin? Did he have a family to provide for? Their bodies trembled like the ground before an earthquake. They knew their fate, and the longer it was drawn out, the more agitated they became, the more they cried, the more they sweated. Olivia smirked at their suffering and John watched as her pupils dilated. Her knuckles faded to white around the pistol's grip, and she breathed in slow motion when she raised the weapon. John could tell that she wanted to enjoy this. She was only going to get to do it once.

The crack echoed over the poppy fields. The farmer fell back and landed in his own blood spatter, and John's thief stopped trembling, stopped weeping. A dark patch grew around his crotch.

'This is how we deal with people who look to wrong us, John,' she said to him.

John took a breath. He looked at her, then back at the hooded farmer. He raised his pistol – it felt heavy in his hand – and, aiming at the thief's head, he struggled to keep the barrel steady. He tightened his grip, then held the tip of his index finger against the cold metal trigger. He took another breath, then snatched it. John watched the limp body fall to the ground.

'Very good, both of you. It looks like you're made for each other,' Hamed said.

'Thank you, Hamed. We really are.' Olivia handed the pistol back to Hamed, and John, distracted by the thief's body, did not see the outstretched hand of the worker claiming his weapon back.

'John,' Olivia said, 'you don't need to keep it. It's safe here, I promise you.'

John jerked back to reality, smiled at her, and returned the pistol. Hamed led them into the poppy field and Olivia ran her hand through her crop.

'Hamed, tell John about the modifications you made to the poppies,' Olivia said.

'Oh yes. When Olivia told me her plan, I was so impressed by it, I had to get on board. But of course there's plenty of heroin in the UK. How can we make ours the best? Can we make it work faster? Not really; it works fast enough already. Can we make it more addictive? Not really; it's already an addictive substance. But what about withdrawal symptoms and aftereffects? If we strengthen them, the user will have no choice but to come back for more – not out of addiction but out of desperation. And as they build a tolerance to it, eventually their old dose will only make them feel normal, and they'll have to take more and more to get the same high.'

'And with reduced police numbers in the cities, getting more and more heroin sold has become a lot easier. Remember that plane you saw yesterday taking off?' John nodded. 'That was full of heroin. Soon we're going to need to double our fleet,' Olivia said.

Olivia and Hamed laughed with each other, and John managed a nervous chuckle. This was all so real.

'How do you increase the withdrawal symptoms?' John asked.

'By genetically modifying the drug. My Cambridge education had to come in handy eventually.

'Essentially, your body likes to maintain a state of balance, and taking heroin changes that balance and acts on the brain's reward system, triggering the release of chemicals. If you stop taking it, your body is thrown off balance. The more chemicals your body releases, the more you'll feel the withdrawal symptoms. So our poppies are genetically modified to be more potent, releasing more chemicals, so the withdrawal symptoms are stronger.'

'It's impressive stuff,' John said. 'So you're going to hook them on a drug they'll have little chance of ever getting off.'

'Yes, unless they realise the error of their ways.' Hamed laughed. 'But it's going to be hard – impossible, even – for anyone to get free of our heroin. People who take drugs soon find that all they have to live for in life is taking more drugs. Everything they do becomes a part of their habit – starving themselves, even, so they have more money for drugs. Soon their lives won't have a purpose at all except to be high.'

John thought about this. Was it worth going through all that just for a high?

Hamed said, 'Anyway, let's have some coffee.'

John and Olivia followed Hamed into his office inside the warehouse, where the poppy resin was refined to make morphine and further refined to make heroin.

'Now, Ms Santiago. The next shipment will leave us in about half an hour, just like you ordered. So, as you can see, with my management, everything is under control.'

'It certainly is, Hamed. I'm happy with your work here. Now please tell John how it works. I need him to know.'

'It's quite simple. We send our aircraft, a small twin prop, to Cyprus. They refuel there before heading to Italy, where they refuel again – Antonia had some useful contacts there. From Italy, they head over to the UK, flight planned for small airfields near London. We change the airfield each time to avoid creating a pattern. With this, there is no suspicion when they enter UK airspace, but they fly low in Class G airspace, where they don't need to talk to anyone in air traffic control. This means they can fly low and drop off their cargo before landing. Then they make the return journey with the money.'

'You really have everything figured out, don't you?' John said, sipping his coffee.

'And now I get to share it all with you,' Olivia said, taking John's hand.

John looked into her eyes and said, 'I'm glad you left your address for me. I'd never have a life like this if it wasn't for you.' He leant over and kissed her.

'I can see you two are going to be very happy together,'

Hamed said.

When they landed in Cyprus, it was dark, and the journey up the mountain was nothing like the one John had experienced two days before. His mind was calm, settled. He was not returning to Olivia's villa; he was returning to his home. He had found a new life here and he intended to stay, despite the occasional echo of doubt. Whenever that appeared, one look at Olivia, one thought of Charlie, soon made it disappear.

64

John woke the next morning hoping to find Olivia asleep on his chest. The bed, however, was empty. He walked out onto the balcony, the overcast sky and drop in temperature a disappointment.

'It's a shame it's not sunny this morning,' Olivia said, joining him outside, carrying two cups of coffee and handing one to him. He took it and kissed her.

'We'll just have to get into bed, then,' he said.

They sat with the sheets draped over their legs and watched the mountains through the windows; they saw a plane fly down into the valley.

'Come on, drink up and get dressed – I've got something else to show you,' she said.

Down in the lobby, guards were carrying in boxes from the vehicles. Olivia went to the kitchen and returned with a knife. She opened one of the boxes and pulled out a handful of notes. A burst of elation shone in her eyes. Her plan was working.

'Look at all this. It's all for us.'

John stepped forward and grabbed a handful of notes. 'That's a lot of money.'

'It should be about two million.'

'We'll count it once we get all the boxes in, Ms Santiago,' said the guard.

'You don't look too enthusiastic about two million pounds, John.'

'This isn't about the money for me. It's about being with you. But I am wondering how you're going to change two million pounds into euros.'

'Don't worry about that. I already have a plan in place. And this isn't about the money, is it?'

'No. I'm just glad I'm finally back with you. You know it's feeling normal now, all of this. I think I've been in a state of shock, and waking up this morning to you not being there made me know for sure that it's real, because I miss you when you're not near me.'

'I know the feeling,' she said, taking his hand and leading him into the dining room. Breakfast was the same affair as the previous day, and John was grateful for that; routine was taking effect, and if he was required to make the occasional trip to the Middle East, then who was he to complain if that was the price to pay for the comforts of home? Even though the weather wasn't perfect beams of sunlight today, he still felt warm here. And it wasn't until he'd finished his breakfast that, despite knowing how the money was earned, he realised there were no more echoes of doubt in the back of his mind. It might not have been about the money, but knowing it was there – a lot of it was there – filled him with the sense of calm that comes from never having to worry about paying the mortgage or not having money for food.

He spent the afternoon in the garden, and although there was not much to be done, he kept himself occupied by tidying the vegetable patches and picking up the apples that had fallen in the orchard. Every six hours, sprinklers grew out of the ground and watered the plants, and when they did, he took a seat on the garden furniture next to John the Dinosaur. It must be soon now – what else did she have to show him?

He wondered if one day they would have children of their own when they retired from this world. Considering how much money had arrived that morning, retirement could realistically only be a few years away. Where would they go? They could travel the world together, create a new life wherever they wanted to.

The only thing John missed from the replica of the garden was the kitchen window where he used to catch Olivia looking at him while he worked. He missed the jolt of adrenaline that came with each passing glance and the nervousness that grew across her face whenever he caught her looking. But what was a window? He had views of the mountains whenever he left the garden and returned to the villa.

Olivia appeared with a mug of coffee in hand, which, on a cooler, overcast day like this, was welcome.

'Thank you,' he said.

'They've finally counted all the money. Two point two million pounds.'

'Any idea what you're going to spend it on?'

'I need nothing else. I have everything I need right here.'

'So do I,' he said and kissed her.

'Have you finished here?' she asked.

'Yeah. I was only tidying a few things up, keeping it looking as perfect as it can be.'

'Good,' she said, reaching out to take his hand, 'because there is one last thing I want to show you.'

'You've shown me plenty of things already,' John commented.

'I know, but this is the most important thing. When I told you I'd tell you everything, I wasn't lying to you. And now I know for sure you're not going anywhere, I feel like I can finally show you this.'

She led him out of the walled garden and back up to the house. They walked up to the first floor, a floor John had seen nothing of except when he passed through to get to the second floor. They walked down the landing to the door at the end. Olivia opened it, and when he saw what was on the other side, John's heart burst out of his chest.

'John!' the small voice called out. The child dropped his toys and raced towards him.

He wrapped his arms around John's legs.

'The time is right,' Olivia said to him.

John was too relieved, to overcome to speak, and he crouched down and hugged the boy, who was too young to understand what this meant to him.

'John, will you play with me? John, please play with me.' John looked up at Olivia, her face was a picture of joy. Charlie had two people here who loved him more than anything in the world, and John was determined they would see he was brought up to live an honest life, a prosperous life away from this nasty business of narcotics. They would only ever do what was best for him, and his life would be perfect because of it.

He played with Charlie. The hours rolled by like minutes. They went out into the garden and John united Charlie with his dinosaur. He held it tightly and promised never to let him out of his sight again. They ran around the garden together, playing tag, and made their first bug house out there. For Charlie, this unknown country was home. The two people who made up his little world were finally reunited with him, and he didn't know what it had taken to get them both there. He couldn't understand that he was the pinnacle of all that John and Olivia had done; he was the centre of their world, and they would make sure he knew it.

They were still out in the garden as the sun set below the horizon. The clouds provided a canvas for the vibrant scarlet sunset that stretched across the sky. John carried Charlie back up to the villa after he said he was too tired to walk, and when they got back, he had fallen asleep in his arms, so John carried him up to bed and tucked him in. As he walked out of the room, he looked back, grateful that tomorrow he could spend another day with him.

'John,' Charlie's tired voice called out. 'Can you read me a story?'

'Of course I can, Charlie. Which one would you like?'

Charlie told John what his favourite story was, and John got it off the shelf. He did the voices perfectly first time, and Charlie clapped the achievement. He was reading it a third time when the boy fell asleep.

65

The next morning, as promised, the chief of police returned to deliver the news that nothing had been discovered overnight, except that they now knew the taxi driver who had driven John. One of them had confessed that his colleague had complained about having to drive one man to a large villa up in the mountains. When asked to come in for a voluntary interview to look at the pictures, he obliged and identified his colleague.

The chief of police was confident they would get in contact with the man in the next few hours and they did. The taxi driver told the police where he had driven that night and Claire received a phone call moments later, picking it up in her hotel room after the first ring.

'Do you have something?' she said.

'Yes. He was driven to a villa in the mountains. It's a large place owned by an offshore company. My guess is that this terrorist of yours is definitely there.'

'What are you guys going to do now?'

'We're going to try to get the plans of the house so we can work on a raid. We're also going to do some reconnaissance. '

'Connor and I will join you.'

Halfway up a mountain opposite the villa, they could look down and watch the rear of the property. A police officer handed Claire a pair of binoculars. She scanned the villa and saw nothing of any interest, then followed the vine-covered path that led to a secluded garden, where she could see two adults and a child. They were relaxing like any other family, happy, enjoying each other's company. She lowered the binoculars, letting them rest by her side for a moment as she continued to look at the garden.

'Can I have a look?' Connor asked, and Claire handed him the binoculars.

Connor saw what Claire had seen, then said, 'It means nothing. Of course he's happy to be with them. But it could be nothing. He could be playing, going along with it all, waiting for the right time.'

'Let's hope so,' Claire said.

The police officer pointed at an airfield down in the valley and said, 'We've tracked a plane coming in to land. And when it took off a few hours later, we saw its tail number and have, thanks to online sources, been able to find out that it has flown to England via Italy. We've made the calls and it's always flown with a flight plan and always remained in communications with air traffic. We're not sure if it's related, but we're still going to investigate further.'

'Thank you,' Claire said. 'Do you know when you're planning

on raiding the property?'

'We've had no luck with getting floor plans, but we've made extensive notes from here. We'll be raiding it once it gets dark. We usually go in the early hours of the morning, but with what's been going on in your country, the sooner we get them, the better, right?'

'Right,' Claire said. 'And once again, thank you for your cooperation.'

66

When John came into their room, he lay down next to Olivia and she rolled over to lie on his torso.

'It's great, isn't it? Everything is finally perfect,' she said.

'It is. But I just don't get how ...'

'That afternoon, after we picked Charlie up from school, I was always going to drop my phone and hope the screen cracked. It was a good excuse to head into town. Salinger had been briefed on what I needed him to do. They were going to take Charlie, but they wouldn't hurt him or anything like that except for picking him up and taking him back to their car. He would never be treated poorly.

'Then, after the attack, they drove to the nearest airfield, where one of my aircraft waited to pick him up and bring him out here. The guards out here are superb with him, so I knew he'd be okay.'

John thought on this for a moment, then said, 'What point did you leave?'

'It was after the second wave of attacks. I put the picture of the three of us and a photo of this villa and the address on the side for when you came back. You know, you were the only part of the plan that I overlooked. I didn't expect someone like you to come into my life. But I'm so glad you did.' She kissed him.

'Why did you ask for a gardener, though, if you were never going to stay?'

'It helped with the cover. Showed my intent to stay, along with getting a job and everything else. Plus Charlie liked the garden in Columbia, so I knew doing it up would make him happy there, even if it was only going to be for a short time.

'Look, I'm sorry I had to put you through all that. I hated what I was doing to you, but it was necessary for me, because no one would've suspected me after having my child kidnapped. They would only see me as the victim – it was the perfect cover.'

She kissed him on the cheek, and he looked at her and smiled. It hadn't been an easy ride, but it was worth it now – everything was as it should be.

John wondered if he should mention to her how he had come to find out the truth. Would it be a problem later? Would they ever find him up here? He doubted it. And even if they thought to come looking, they could sneak themselves out of the country and go somewhere else. Or would they even bother? Going after someone who in the eyes of the public was a victim – a single mother of a kidnapped child, hunted down by England's finest – to John, it seemed unlikely.

For now, however, he kept the truth to himself. Why let it ruin the moment?

'It certainly was,' John said. 'Even if you had to put me

through all that.' He had come around to seeing the lighter side of it. How could he be angry now that he was here with both of them?

'I never intended to harm my son.'

'I know. Of course you didn't. But with the money we have, we can give him a life away from all this. He'll never need to worry about looking over his shoulder or wondering if he has a target on his back. He can go to school, make friends, have fun, be a kid. We can make sure he gets the best childhood possible.'

She lifted her head from his chest and shot him a confused look and got one in return. She sat up and shuffled herself away from him towards the side of the bed.

'John, I don't think you understand.'

'What don't I understand?'

'They'll eventually declare him dead. Why would terrorists take a hostage and ask for nothing in return? They'll declare him dead when they can't find him. It's the only thing that makes sense. He has to die on paper at least. They'll never look for him then.'

John thought this over for a moment. 'Well, I guess you're right. Any enemies we might make along the way won't try to hurt him if they don't know he exists.'

'Exactly,' she said. The smile returned, and she lay back on his chest.

'We can always make a new identity for him. Surely that won't be difficult for us. He can still have his normal childhood; he'll just have a different name. I'm sure he'll understand.'

She sat up again and edged away from him. He looked at her, bemused by her inability to remain still.

'What?' he questioned, sensing a sudden tension between

them.

'He won't have a normal childhood. We need him dead for a reason. One day, with our guidance, he'll run this cartel and we can retire. He'll oversee all this, and it'll be nearly impossible to catch him. This is what this is all about. This is what I wanted to keep from you until I knew you were on board with all this. I need you to understand that Charlie won't have a normal childhood. He won't go to school in the traditional sense and all the other traditional things that come with growing up.'

'What are you talking about? You want to make him a drug lord?'

'That's exactly what I want to do. And we can retire in thirteen years' time with all the money in the world, knowing we raised not just a perfect son but a perfect businessman who can provide for us. Between the two of us, we'll give him everything he needs to succeed. We can go anywhere in the world. This is all for us, John. For the two of us to live a perfect life together.'

'But what about Charlie?'

'Like I said, with our guidance, he'll conquer this world and he'll be happy. He'll have all the money and power a man could want, thanks to us.'

John remained silent, waiting for the punchline, waiting for Olivia to tell him that this was all a joke.

'This was going to be the hardest thing for you to come to terms with. Ever since you told me about your childhood and how you felt about Charlie, I knew you'd want to stop him being exposed to any sort of violence, but think about it. Think about the life we could have; think about the life he could have – he'll have all of this.'

Still John remained silent. His breathing was methodical, controlled. He looked straight ahead. He wasn't sure what he'd do if he looked into her serious, unmoving eyes.

'John, please say something. Say that you think this is the greatest thing you've ever heard. We can go anywhere, be anyone we want to be. John, please say something. Say you're on board, please. Just say yes.'

The echo in his mind returned – the tune of a fatherless child crying in the corridor outside the flat he had once called home. And the little boy he had once been sitting with a pillow wrapped around his head to block out his father's shouting, his mother's cries. The cowardice he had felt, and the hatred that it had bred in him. The aroma of baking cakes with his mum now filled his mind, and the happy afternoons he had spent with her to relieve her of some of the pain of living with his father. Then he was back in the garden, the actual garden, with Charlie making bug houses, playing tag and the hours drifting by with endless laughter and smiles. The trips to the museum and the boy's happy face. How could he forget each time he'd put his dinosaur's nose into the cream and laughed? He always laughed, always smiled. And he knew now what duty he had to fulfil. And this one did not come from a place of hate. It came from a place much greater than that. How could he sit aside and let this happen to the little boy who had inadvertently showed him what matters most in life?

He looked at her, and she flinched when she saw the fire in his eyes.

'No.' This single word cut through her like a knife. 'No.

You're not doing that to him. I won't let you.'

She reached towards the bedside cabinet and opened the top drawer. 'I hoped it would never come to this. But I had to have a plan in case it did.' She pulled out a gun. John went to grab it, but she pulled the trigger and a surge of electricity shot through his side.

'I can't bear to kill you, but I must do what I have to do,' she said. She looked at him one last time, then ran out of the room, shouting down the corridor for her guards.

John sucked in gulps of air as he tried to calm his shuddering body. He crawled off the bed and landed on his back. He had to get up. He had to be ready to fight. He struggled to his feet, grabbed the lamp off the bedside table, and pulled it hard, ripping the plug from the wall. He rolled the cable around his hand, staggered to the en suite, and hid himself behind the door. He left it open just enough to keep one eye on the room.

A stampede of footsteps charged up the stairs, then along the landing. They kicked the bedroom door in; it crashed against the wall. A set of footsteps entered the room.

'Come out. Make this easy on yourself.'

John watched the guard tiptoe across the room. The guard looked under the bed before moving out onto the balcony, and with his back to John, John opened the door a fraction more and scanned the rest of the room. No one else had entered. With the guard on the balcony, John seized his chance. He dashed across the room. His legs still wobbled, but they had enough life in them to carry him. The guard heard him running. He turned to shoot but got a faceful of glass and collapsed to the ground, dropping his pistol. John picked up the weapon and shot the guard in the chest. The shot echoed over the mountains. Would she think they had killed him? The clatter of gunfire from the landing would have been enough to tell her they hadn't, not yet.

John took cover behind the wall. He fired blindly in the direction of the landing. They were accurate enough shots to force the guards to take cover, and the lull in the battle gave him time to reach out, pull the dead guard towards him, and take his spare ammunition. He had nowhere to store it except the pockets of his trousers, but he had no other choice and pocketed all he could, then fired off the rest of his magazine.

While he reloaded, the guards shot back and advanced on him. John guessed there were three of them. Had the other guards taken Olivia and Charlie to safety? But where else could they have gone that he didn't know about?

With the pistol loaded, he stuck his head around the corner and fired towards the landing. The guards took cover. He took the chance to advance. He emptied another magazine as he shot across the room and took cover against the en suite wall.

'There are more of us than you, John. Make it easy for yourself.'

Ignoring the threat, he reloaded his pistol. He took a deep breath, then edged his way to the end of the wall. He stepped an arm's length back, enough of a distance to see his targets while having enough cover not to get shot. He saw one guard and that same guard saw him. John, however, got his shot out first and ducked back as a hail of bullets answered his second kill. He breathed, told himself he was going to get through this. He may have only got two of them. There were still many more to kill. But he would get through this, he told himself, for Charlie.

John fired a burst of three rounds. There was no reply. He poked his head out – there was no one there. He walked down the landing with his eye trained on his pistol's sights. If anyone appeared in his crosshairs, he would not hesitate to fire.

The stairs wound around the supporting pillar, and John took them one at a time. Rushing would get him killed. And he could not, for Charlie's sake, afford to die. Would it be worth checking to see if he was still in his room? Olivia must have already taken him somewhere else unless she hadn't thought John would make it this far.

A guard grabbed his pistol from around the pillar and pulled him down the stairs. He fell and landed in a heap, dropping his weapon. The guard went to kick his face. John jerked his head to the side and the boot hit the floor. He kicked out at his attacker's shins, and they backed off enough to give him time to get to his feet. They exchanged punches. Most of them swung through the air. This was no time for technique – they weren't fighting in a ring with rules. The guard landed a hard punch to John's nose, and he felt warm blood trickle into his mouth. The guard threw another. John ducked, parried, then charged at him. He took him by the waist and tackled him to the floor. John had the reach against his opponent and landed several hard blows to his face, knocking him unconscious. Then bullets flew over his head. He rolled the unconscious body over and tucked himself behind it. The body jerked as it soaked up the bullets, and John saw his pistol on the floor. He reached out, grabbed it, and returned fire over his makeshift cover.

When the gunfire ceased, John got to his feet and sprinted across the landing, and when he was close to the stairs, he dropped and slid across the floor, shooting the guard when he exposed himself from behind his cover. John collided with the wall at the top of the stairs. Another guard made their way up. John cut his progress short by putting a bullet through his head. Then he continued down the stairs.

Shouting from the ground floor alerted John to more men coming his way. He went to fire a warning shot, but nothing happened. His magazine was empty. He reached into his pocket for another one – his last one – and quickly reloaded in time to shoot the first guard coming into view.

A bullet sped past his head. John crouched, returned fire, and took out another guard. Did he have enough bullets left?

But the ground floor was empty except for a collection of bodies on the floor. Could that have been all of them? Or were they waiting to ambush him? He moved tentatively through the house, entering the kitchen first. He stopped shy of the door, took a breath, and went in. He scanned the room – it was empty. Were they all dead? They couldn't be. There must be more. Unless they had all left.

John raced to the front door and saw the cars parked outside. She was still here. But where? And where was Charlie?

He looked around. The patio door was open. Had she made her way to the garden? The outside lights gave enough light to illuminate the path. Of course she would have wanted it to end where it had all begun.

John walked down the path, past the pool. He had just dropped his guard, thinking it was now only between him and Olivia, when, out of the shadows, the last guard fired a shot that ripped through his upper back. He fell face down into the water.

The lone guard appeared out of the shadows and walked to the pool's edge. John's body had drifted to the centre, and he got in to retrieve it. He waded through the lukewarm water, grabbed both of his feet, and pulled him out. His foot was on the first step when he realised what he had missed. The pool was carpeted in darkness; it was easy to miss, and now at the edge, closer to the light, he had seen it. If John was dead, then why was he still holding his weapon? He dropped his legs. His wet fingers struggled to unholster his pistol, but he got enough grip to pull it out. When he looked up, John was already there, floating on his back, waiting to see his face before he took the shot.

John got out of the pool and saw the blood from the exit wound tangled in the hairs on his chest. He had been shot in his left side, and his left arm could not move without significant pain. He examined the wound. The bullet hadn't hit any major organs. But that didn't mean he wasn't in danger. How much blood would he lose? He took a seat on a sunbed and monitored his breathing. But it was fine. He didn't need to worry about a sucking chest wound collapsing his lung. He got up and continued.

The blood continued to flow down his chest. But he kept going. He had to keep going. It was cooler on the vine-covered path, or was that the blood loss? A haze of light rested above the walled garden, and he was certain he could hear Charlie's voice. Or was that the blood loss too? He opened the gate, leaving a smear of blood on the handle.

Olivia was standing in the middle of the garden. Waiting for him.

'It had to end here, didn't it? Unless you've changed your mind.'

'Where is he?'

'He's safe, I promise.'

John staggered forward, his grip on the pistol loosening.

'What did they do to you?' she said, seeing the blood on his torso as he came into the light.

'Stay back.' His shaking hand raised the pistol. 'There's no chance I'm letting you ruin Charlie's life.'

'Ruin it?' She laughed. 'Look at all I can give him! This place is perfect.'

'No, it isn't. It's fake. Even this garden is fake. I can't let you do this to him.'

'But it's real between us. We love each other, right? Tell me you love me. Tell me you love me and we can go back inside, I promise.'

John went to reply but fell to his knees. Blood dripped from the tips of his fingers into the fake grass.

'What have they done to you?' She ran forward and held him. She tried to look into his bleary eyes. 'I should never have left you with them.'

'But you did. Now where is he?'

'Tell me you love me; tell me you're with me, with us, and we can go back to the house and forget that this happened. We can start all over again and live this perfect life.'

'Not at the expense of Charlie's.' It was a struggle to talk; he was out of breath after a few words and the pistol felt like it was nailed to the ground.

'Then you're a fool not to see what we can have. I fell for you, John, when I had no business falling for anyone. I fell for you more than anything in this world. But now I feel stupid.'

John fell forward against her chest; she caught him and wrapped her arms around him.

'You could've had it all.'

John went to speak, but words failed him.

'What's that?'

'And ... I ... I ...' The words were stuck inside his mouth; his weak body struggled to push them out. 'And I ... fell ... for you too.'

He looked into her eyes and caught the exact moment when she felt the cold metal against her chest. He pulled the trigger with all the energy left in him. Her blood sprayed up into the night sky and she fell back onto the grass. He dropped his pistol. Then he collapsed on the ground and darkness descended on his world.

67

When the order was given to raid the house, Connor and Claire insisted they join the party. The chief of police had no objections. He armed them with pistols and told them to remain behind his men.

The front gate was closed, but they pulled no punches and drove straight through it. They had lost the element of surprise, but in their vehicles, the police officers maintained their stoic expressions – their plans would not be ruined by sudden panic.

The cars pulled up outside the front of the villa in a haze of dust kicked up from the gravel. The men burst out of their vehicles, and Claire and Connor remained close behind. Whatever resistance they had thought they would meet, however, was not there to greet them. The villa was silent. One team inspected the vehicles parked out front but turned up nothing.

When they looked through the windows next to the front door, they saw bodies strewn across the floor. The point man ordered the door to be kicked down.

After a few swings, the door caved in and the men flowed into the house, each covering their respective area and their colleagues' backs. They crept through the property, careful not to tread on the bodies or the blood.

The team leader ordered a team upstairs and told Claire and Connor to stay with him, so they followed him through the rest of the ground floor and found nothing. Claire hoped John was not among the dead. She inspected each body but didn't recognise any of them. Did that mean he'd escaped with Charlie?

Outside, red veins rippled across the pool's surface, emanating from the floating body. The team leader found spatters of blood on the gravel path leading to the garden and ordered his team to follow them. They grew larger and larger the further they went, and when he walked through the gate, the torch on the end of his rifle illuminated two bodies: one woman and one shirtless man.

Connor and Claire recognised John and moved past the line of men, ignoring their protests.

They got to his body. It was still except for his laboured breathing and the blood seeping from the wound in his back. Claire immediately applied pressure; blood wept through her hands.

'It's going to be okay, John. It's all going to be fine.'

John tried to turn his head in the direction of her voice, but he didn't have the strength, and his glazed-over eyes struggled to focus on anything. He saw the blurry outline of someone standing next to him, then he registered the weight on his back – it hurt, that was for sure. But they weren't here to kill him – they would have done that by now.

Connor shouted back up to the Cypriot police, ordering them to get medical assistance. Two of the officers acknowledged the order and ran off.

'Come on, John,' Claire said. She saw his eyes rolling backwards and forwards; they were losing their last pinch of focus. She wasn't going to let him die here, but how long ago had he been shot? Had too much time already passed? She refused to think about these questions, not while she was here and he was still alive. For now, that would do, but how much longer could she keep him like this?

Noises came from his mouth, but nothing that resembled words.

'Don't talk. Don't talk. Save your energy. I'm going to get you out of here, I promise.'

Still his eyes continued to dip in and out of focus, his mind in and out of consciousness. She applied more pressure, hoping to get a response, but all it achieved was his eyes opening for a second before he drifted back into unconsciousness.

'Where the fuck are the medics?' she asked.

'All I know is that they're on their way.'

'Fuck.' She pressed down with all her weight; more of John's blood flowed between her fingers.

Connor checked for a pulse on Olivia's body and didn't find one. She had a patch of blood on her chest, a bullet hole through her top, and there was a pistol lying between her and John.

'She's dead,' Connor said.

'Good. What the hell happened here?'

Neither of them attempted to answer the question. It was not a question that they really wanted an answer to right now, not when their colleague was in this state. It wasn't the what that mattered. It was the why. Why had John come out here and not told them? Why had he been motivated to do this? But he had killed her. Along with everyone else. Why had he waited until now to do so? Why not get it done during his first night here? Claire mused that he must know something. He must have investigated what was really going on.

'Come on, John. Stay with me.' Her voice cracked; she fought back tears. Now was not the time for emotion. She could not reflect on the events that had led them to this point. She had to keep him alive.

John groaned like a whisper. His eyes were struggling to open for longer than a second now.

'Connor, go and find out where the medics are. And where the hell is Charlie?'

'I'm on it.' Connor ran back up to the house.

Did it matter his reasons for coming here in the first place? After all, he had killed her, killed all of them, and no sign of Charlie's dead body must be an indicator that he was still alive, that John had saved him. Or was this wishful thinking? Nothing was known until it was seen. But this job was done. Olivia was dead, and she did have John to thank for that. Did it really matter what his motivations were for coming here? He might well have come here for love, she thought, but in the end, he had killed her. She didn't know if this had been his plan all along. It didn't matter to her right now.

Claire heard the medics coming. They were running down the gravel path. She looked up and saw them. They hurried over just as John's eyes closed.

68

The first thing he registered when he came to was the beeping. A consistent, slow, steady rhythm, and he wondered if it would stop. His eyes squinted at the light shining in his eyes. There was something warm lying next to him. He tried to find out what it was by reaching his hand out and touching it. His fingers stroked what felt like soft hair and he heard a giggle alongside the beeping. A small hand grabbed his outstretched arm and his blurred vision saw something rise and fall on his chest.

'Charlie. Charlie,' a voice called out – a voice he recognised. 'Come with me. The doctors need to look after him.'

'Okay,' a small voice said. Why were they taking him away? He reached out again, hoping to grab him, stop him from leaving, but he was already gone.

He didn't know how much more time had passed when he next opened his eyes. But his vision was static, and his body was as heavy as a sinking ship.

'John, can you hear me, John? My name is Dr Marcou. You've been shot and you're waking up post successful surgery in hospital. Can you hear me?'

'Yes.' His voice laboured over the word.

'The bullet missed your vital organs, but it caused some internal damage and a lot of blood loss. That's why you lost consciousness. But it's nothing too serious, and you don't have life-changing injuries. You just need time to rest. Lucky for you your friends brought you in. Or else you would have been in a morgue.'

John raised his head like he was pulling an anchor from the ocean floor. Claire was sitting in the corner, and she managed a smile. Dr Marcou went about taking the readings he needed and judged his patient to be okay and, for the time being, on the road to recovery. Then he left the two of them alone.

'Well, I'm glad you're okay, John. You and Charlie were the only two people we found in that house alive.'

'Charlie?'

'He's with Connor. We found him in the boot of one of the vehicles. We guess once she was done with you, she was going to take him away.' Claire stood up and walked over. 'I need to debrief you with a few details, though. Do you want me to sit your bed up?'

'Please.'

Claire pressed the button on the remote and raised John up.

'You're lucky, you know that? And so am I,' she added more for her own ears than John's.

John managed a laugh, then a coughing fit, then said, 'Yeah.'

'You'll be fine in a couple of days. Want some water?'

'Please.'

Claire poured water into a cup and handed it to him. John took a few sips and handed it back.

'How did you know?' his first full sentence felt like a marathon.

Claire told him the story of how they had come to find him. When she was done, she paused to see if he had any questions. But he remained quiet, whether because he didn't know what to say or it was still too painful to speak, she didn't know. Instead she said, 'He was a little frightened, you know, when we first found him. It took a bit of effort to get him to come out. We didn't want to grab him and scare him even more, especially when we didn't need to. But when I said he'd get to see you, he brightened up and was no trouble at all.'

'It's great ... having him back.'

'I'm sure it is. You know, I would ask you what you were doing out there, but I think we managed to figure it all out.'

'What?' John tried to sit himself up, but he didn't have the energy or the strength.

'It's okay. It's quite clever, really, going over there by yourself and infiltrating her little cartel. Of course it was clever of you not to involve us, and I can forgive you for that, because, well, we got her in the end.'

John went to speak, but his weak body struggled to talk over her.

'It's okay, John. You don't need to give us any more.'

Should he tell them the truth about his motivations for going over there? Or should he stick to the narrative that Claire had already made up?

'Do you know about Afghanistan?' he asked.

'Yeah, we do. We found flight plans in the house, and when we had a look at the airfield in the valley, the pilots all decided to make a run for it. They didn't get very far, though. Although we aren't going to be able to do much about her poppy fields in Afghanistan. But at least we've stopped her getting the stuff into the UK.'

'Is she …?'

'She's dead, John. You killed her.'

To kill her … a feeling he hadn't even considered during his time with her. He wasn't going to lie to himself and say that he only felt relief, because at the same time, she had been Charlie's mother. She had been someone who, for whatever deluded reason, he had wanted a future with. And now she was dead, courtesy of his pull of a trigger. He wasn't sure what to feel. But he knew he wasn't overcome with sadness or regret. Still, he waited for the regret to sink in. But what was there to regret? He had Charlie, and the woman behind all this was dead. Regret, then, was hard to find, and he concluded that it hadn't hit him yet, because he knew for sure, and had no reason to doubt, what he needed to do. And with his mum looking down on him, he knew that she would be proud of him for finally realising this. He knew she would be smiling, a tear in her eye, no doubt.

'You know, they found two million pounds in that house,' Claire said.

'Two?'

'Yep. Two million.'

'I thought … it was two … point two.'

Claire shrugged. 'You know, you've left me with quite a mess to clean up. But it isn't really all your fault. I let you do those things that I'd never have let slide if you'd been a full operative. And for that, I must take my share of responsibility. I'll probably be suspended pending an investigation, and chances are you'll be investigated as well, but I'll take care of you. I'm close to retiring anyway, so don't feel bad about it. I know for you, the chances of ever getting back into counterterrorism no longer exist.'

John smiled. It seemed to him that it was all fitting together nicely, like it was always going to be this way.

'You're not bothered, then, about never being able to come back?' she asked.

'I've found … what I need … to do.'

'I thought that was the case. After all, it takes a lot to shoot the woman you love. I'm sure that 200,000 will pop up somewhere convenient.' She smiled at John and John smiled back, and that was the last they would ever speak about that.

'What will … happen … next?'

'Well, the police won't be moving out to rural areas now. And we're still working with the Cypriot police out here, but as for the mess back home … well, we're going to struggle to prosecute Gary and Carl, considering what happened to them. We'll probably have to let them go. But measures will be put in place to keep a close eye on them. The other terrorists you caught, we can get them behind bars for sure. Other than that, it's all going to be handed over to the NCA, as it's drugs related. But with your information, prosecutions will come, and no more innocent people will need to die or be hooked on heroin.'

'So it's all … worked out, then?'

Claire laughed and said, 'Just about, John, just about. But thanks, I guess, anyway, for your help. I honestly don't think we could have done it without you. And I don't think we could have done it any other way. But like I said before, that's on me.'

'It's not … all on … you. I wasn't honest.'

'You were in a difficult situation, John. No one is going to question that.'

'But I—'

'I won't hear any more of it. We both did what we had to do, and now we have to do what we need to do again. Except this time, it will be completely different.'

'Yes … it will.

'Take care,' Claire said.

A moment later, Charlie thundered into the room and jumped onto his bed with John the Dinosaur in hand and hugged him. Despite the pain it caused, he hugged him back, because above all else, it was worth it. And he would go through it all again if that was what it took to keep him safe. He made a promise to Charlie that he would never be involved in a life where danger lurked. Charlie, however, wasn't sure what this meant. He was just glad to be back with John, and John hugged him tightly. Eventually he would have to tell him about his mother, and John wondered what he understood of the situation currently. But it didn't seem right at this point in time to bother him. They had been gifted with a precious moment; all of that was for another day. It would not be a straightforward conversation; Charlie did not know her as the evil person she was. So for him, coming to terms with it, John thought, would be a struggle. But he would be there for him every step of the way. This was his duty now, and he would make sure he did everything to fulfil it.

'John,' Charlie said, placing a book in John's lap. 'Can you read me a story?'

Charlie lay back against John's chest, thankfully on the side where he hadn't been shot.

'Of course I can, Charlie. Of course I can.'

About S. C. Rozée

S. C. Rozée was a commissioned officer in the Royal Air Force serving for five years before deciding that the pen was mightier than the fighter jet. Published in 2023, The Reluctant Gardener, is his first novel. He currently resides in a small village in the Cotswolds with his family.

CPSIA information can be obtained
at www.ICGtesting.com
Printed in the USA
BVHW031012280323
661284BV00009B/617